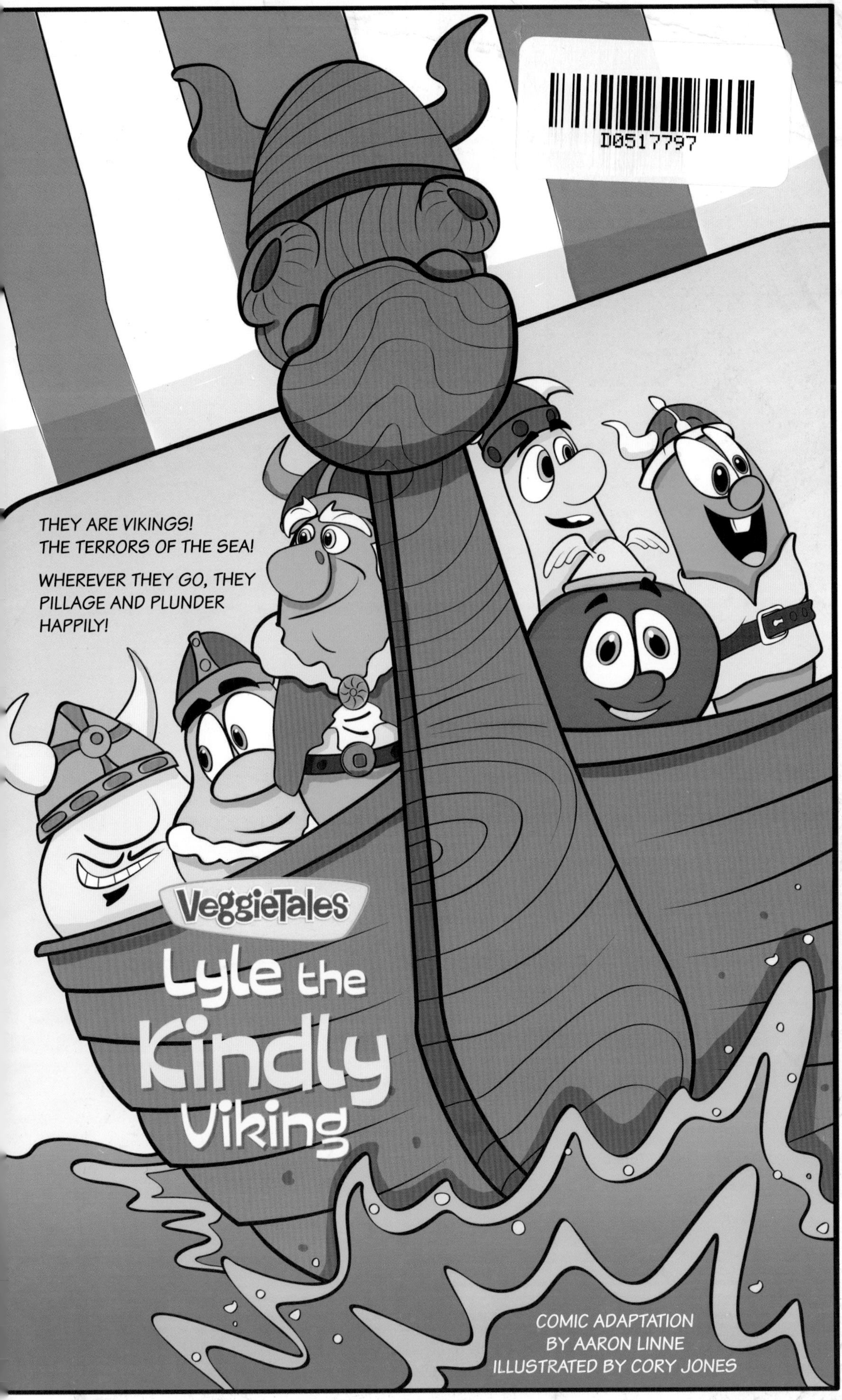
THEY ARE VIKINGS!
THE TERRORS OF THE SEA!
WHEREVER THEY GO, THEY PILLAGE AND PLUNDER HAPPILY!
VeggieTales
Lyle the Kindly Viking
COMIC ADAPTATION
BY AARON LINNE
ILLUSTRATED BY CORY JONES

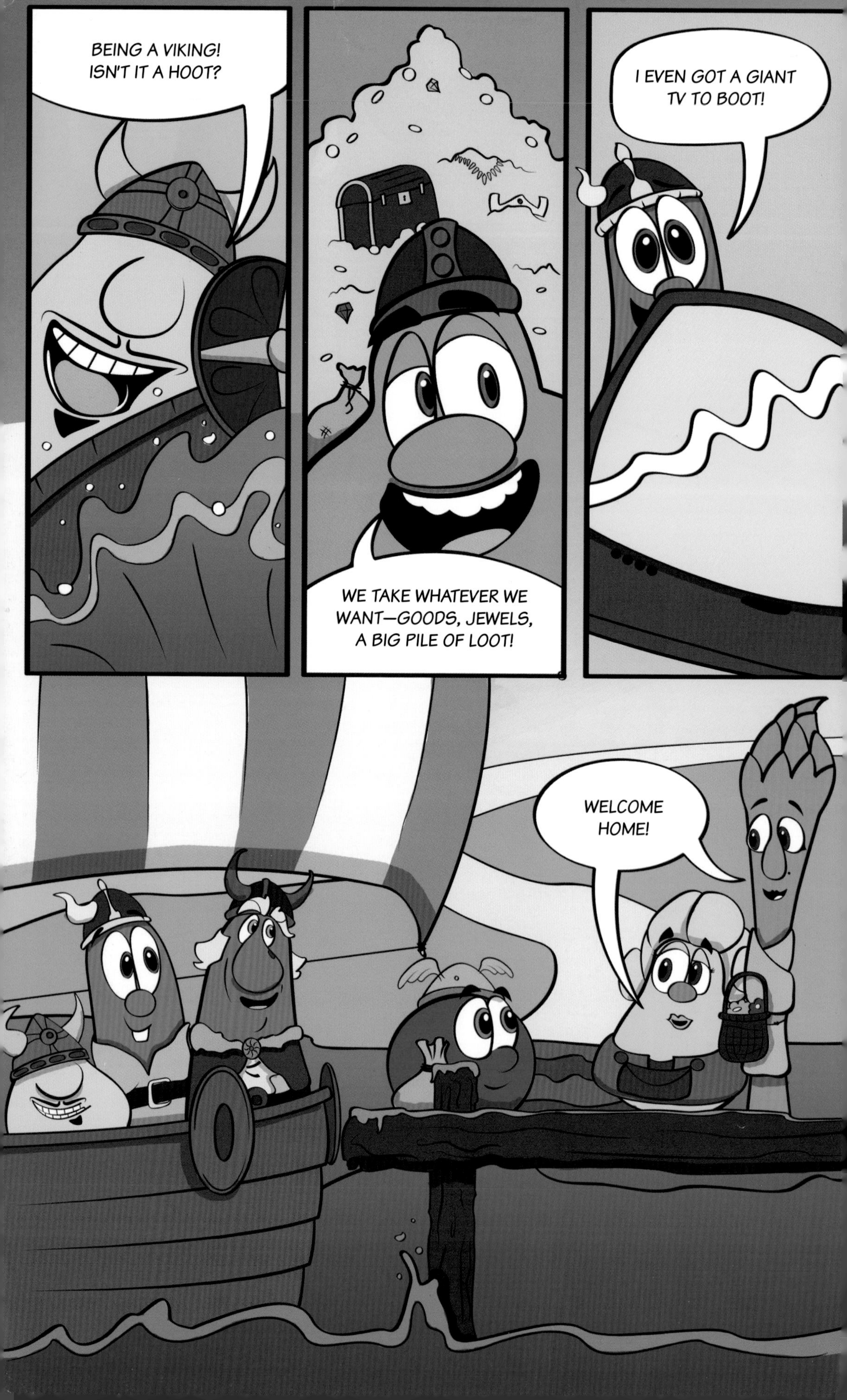
BEING A VIKING! ISN'T IT A HOOT?
WE TAKE WHATEVER WE WANT—GOODS, JEWELS, A BIG PILE OF LOOT!
I EVEN GOT A GIANT TV TO BOOT!
WELCOME HOME!

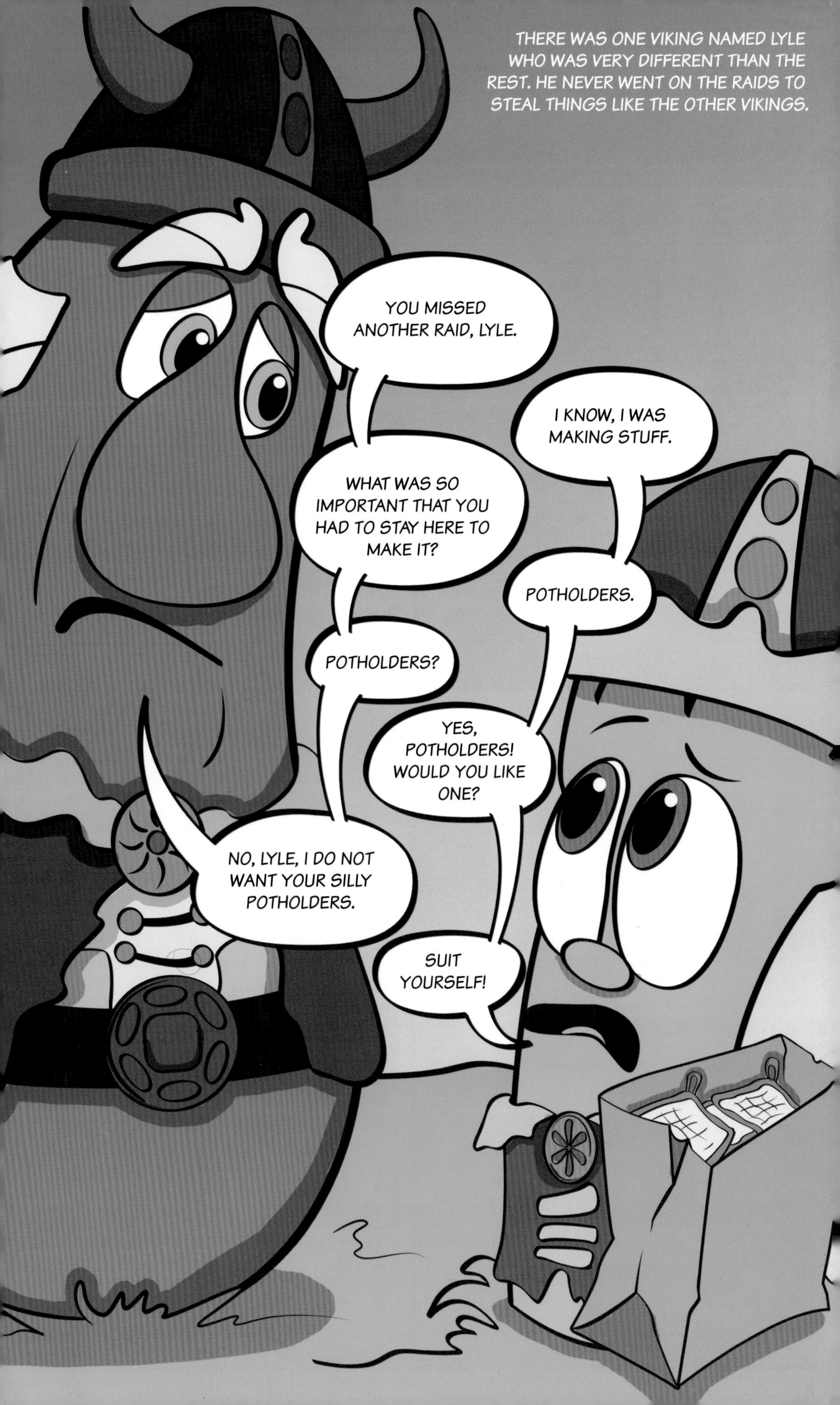
THERE WAS ONE VIKING NAMED LYLE WHO WAS VERY DIFFERENT THAN THE REST. HE NEVER WENT ON THE RAIDS TO STEAL THINGS LIKE THE OTHER VIKINGS.
YOU MISSED ANOTHER RAID, LYLE.
I KNOW, I WAS MAKING STUFF.
WHAT WAS SO IMPORTANT THAT YOU HAD TO STAY HERE TO MAKE IT?
POTHOLDERS.
POTHOLDERS?
YES, POTHOLDERS! WOULD YOU LIKE ONE?
NO, LYLE, I DO NOT WANT YOUR SILLY POTHOLDERS.
SUIT YOURSELF!

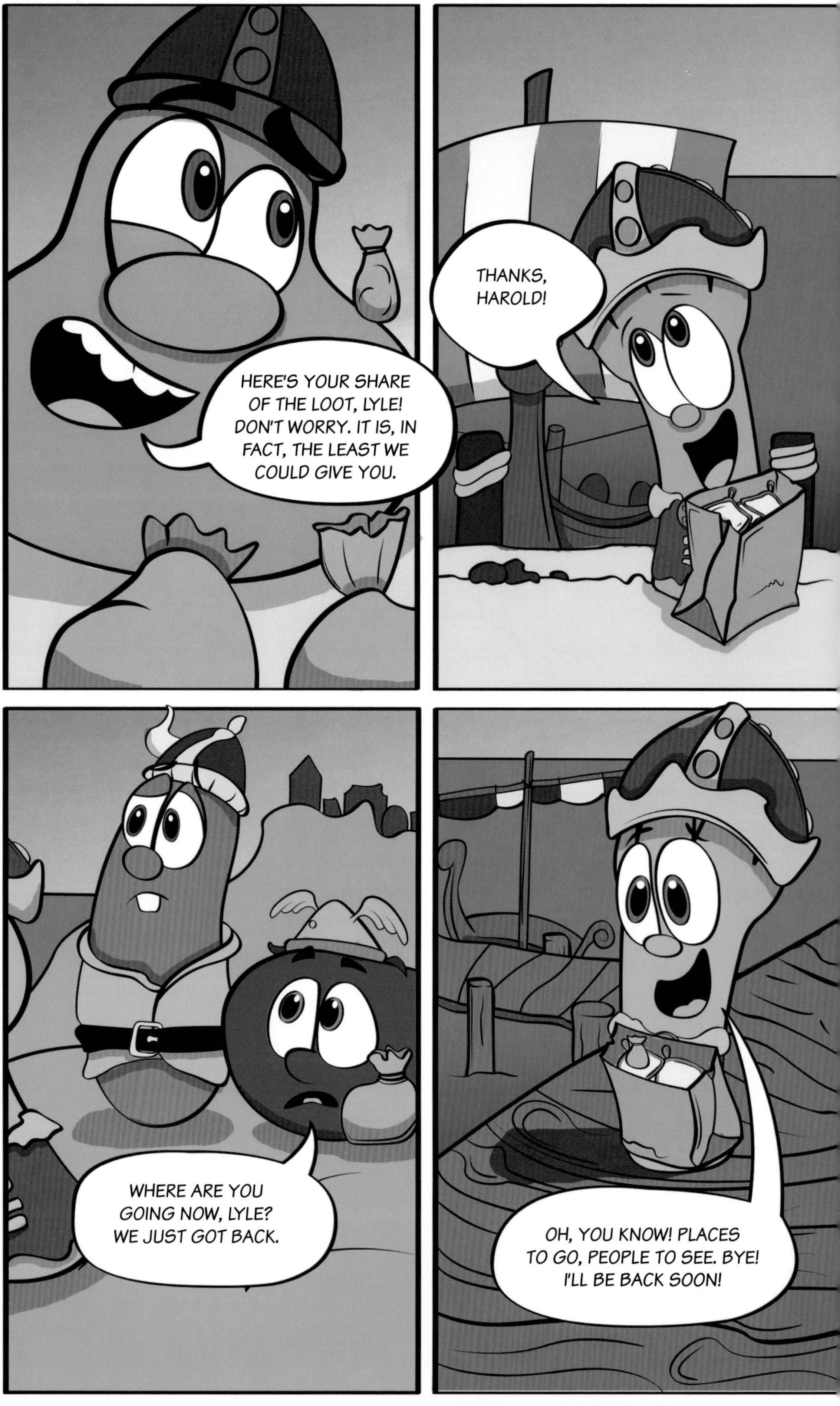
HERE'S YOUR SHARE OF THE LOOT, LYLE! DON'T WORRY. IT IS, IN FACT, THE LEAST WE COULD GIVE YOU.
THANKS, HAROLD!
WHERE ARE YOU GOING NOW, LYLE? WE JUST GOT BACK.
OH, YOU KNOW! PLACES TO GO, PEOPLE TO SEE. BYE! I'LL BE BACK SOON!

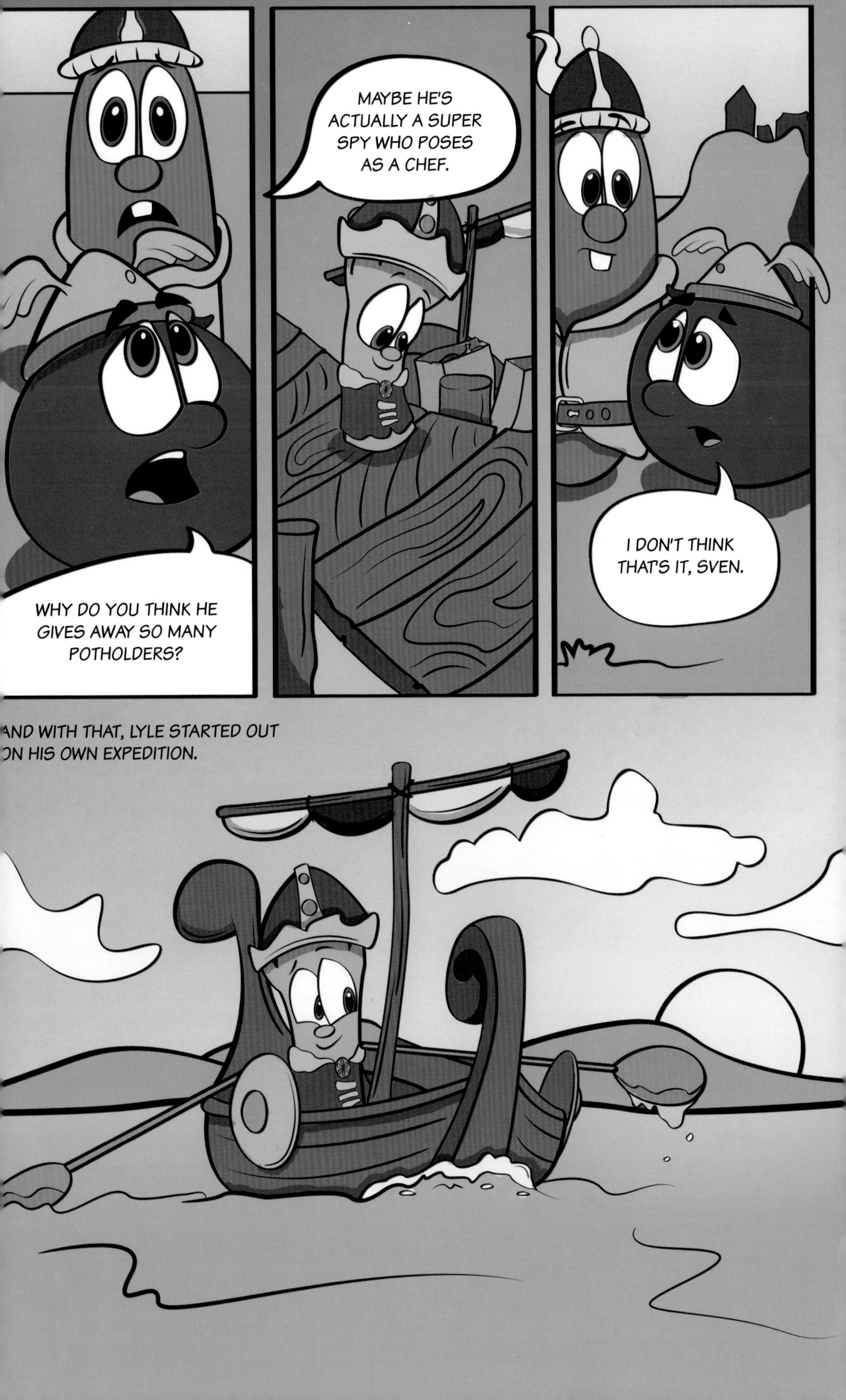
WHY DO YOU THINK HE GIVES AWAY SO MANY POTHOLDERS?
MAYBE HE'S ACTUALLY A SUPER SPY WHO POSES AS A CHEF.
I DON'T THINK THAT'S IT, SVEN.
AND WITH THAT, LYLE STARTED OUT ON HIS OWN EXPEDITION.

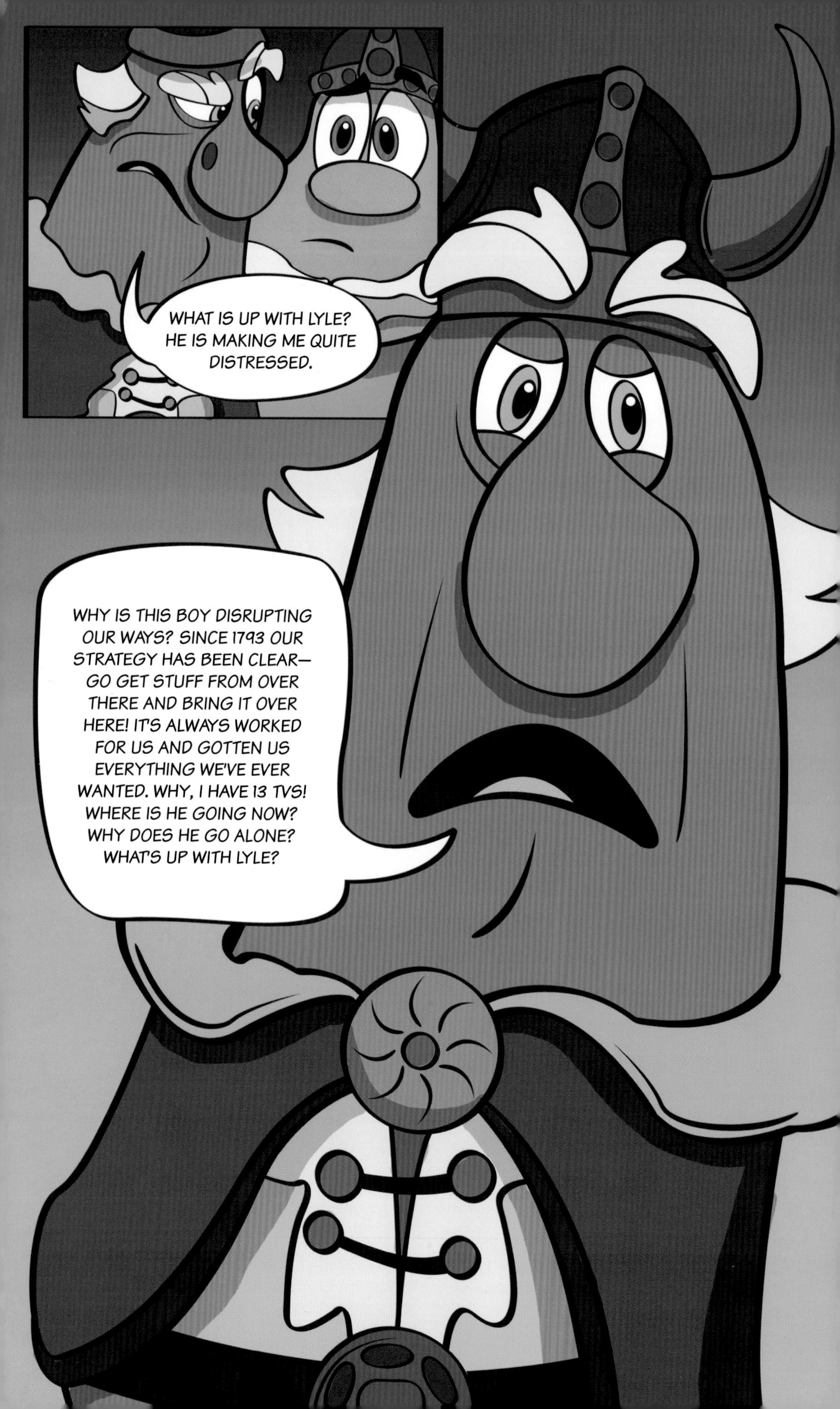
WHAT IS UP WITH LYLE? HE IS MAKING ME QUITE DISTRESSED.
WHY IS THIS BOY DISRUPTING OUR WAYS? SINCE 1793 OUR STRATEGY HAS BEEN CLEAR— GO GET STUFF FROM OVER THERE AND BRING IT OVER HERE! IT'S ALWAYS WORKED FOR US AND GOTTEN US EVERYTHING WE'VE EVER WANTED. WHY, I HAVE 13 TVS! WHERE IS HE GOING NOW? WHY DOES HE GO ALONE? WHAT'S UP WITH LYLE?

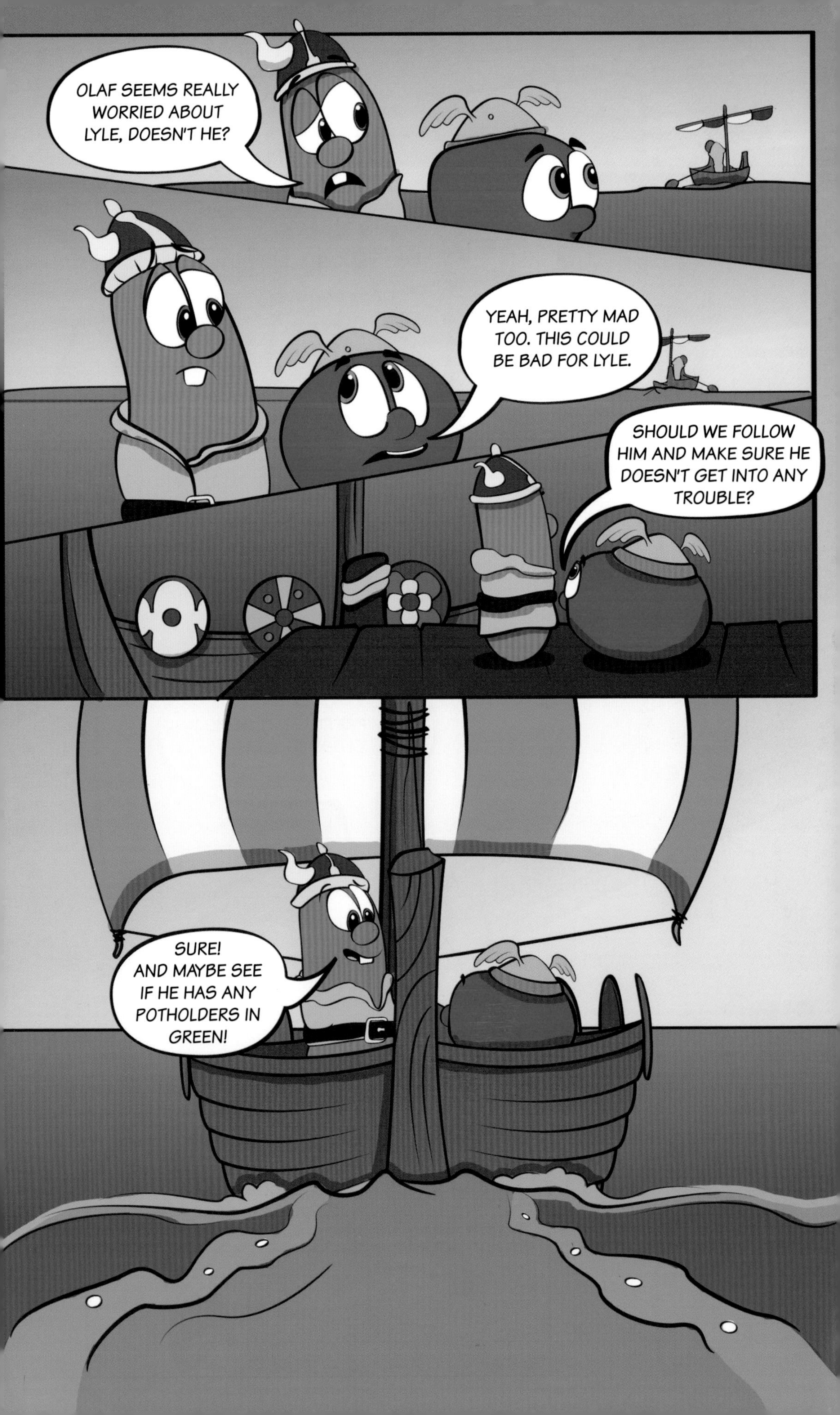
OLAF SEEMS REALLY WORRIED ABOUT LYLE, DOESN'T HE?
YEAH, PRETTY MAD TOO. THIS COULD BE BAD FOR LYLE.
SHOULD WE FOLLOW HIM AND MAKE SURE HE DOESN'T GET INTO ANY TROUBLE?
SURE! AND MAYBE SEE IF HE HAS ANY POTHOLDERS IN GREEN!

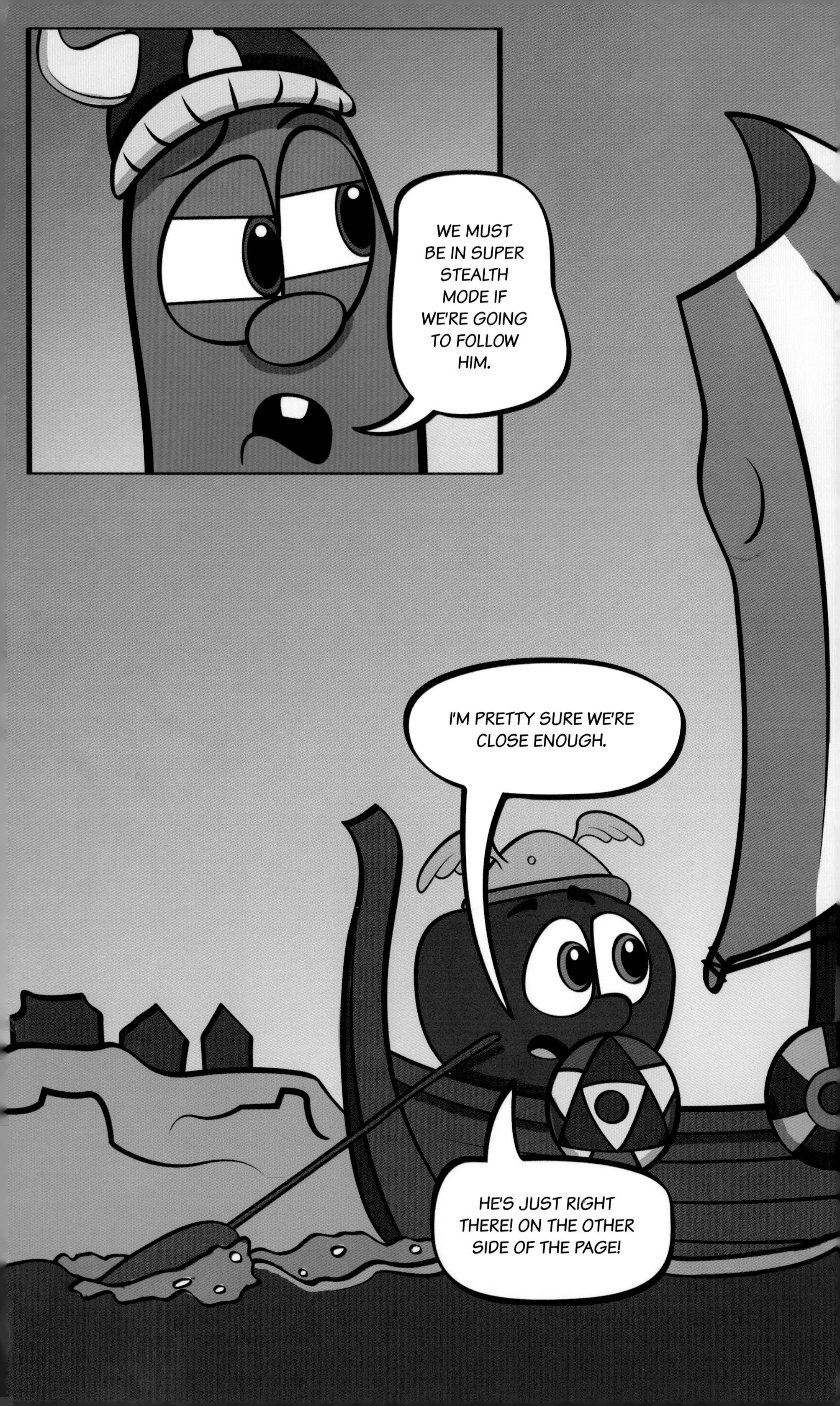
WE MUST BE IN SUPER STEALTH MODE IF WE'RE GOING TO FOLLOW HIM.
I'M PRETTY SURE WE'RE CLOSE ENOUGH.
HE'S JUST RIGHT THERE! ON THE OTHER SIDE OF THE PAGE!

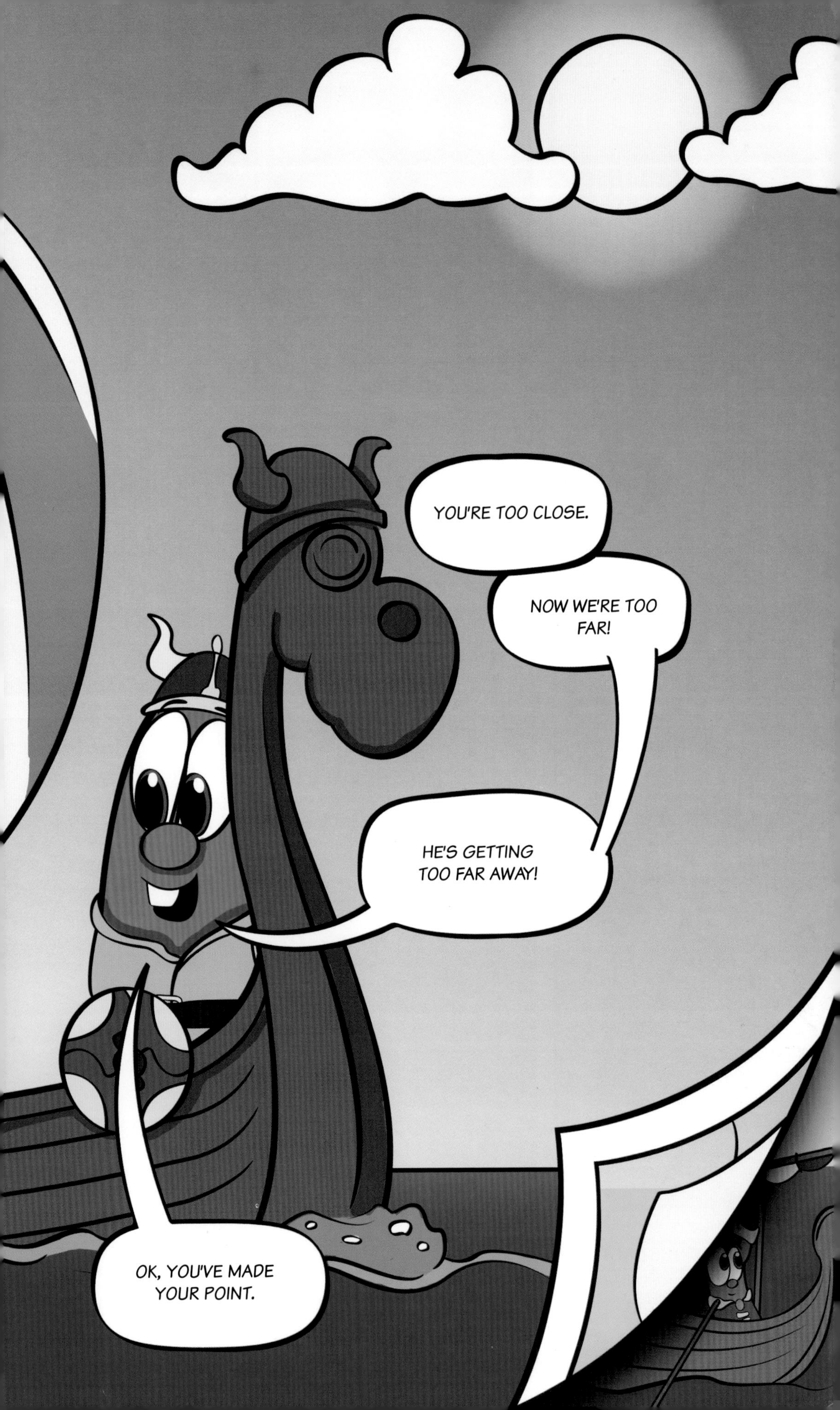
YOU'RE TOO CLOSE.
NOW WE'RE TOO FAR!
HE'S GETTING TOO FAR AWAY!
OK, YOU'VE MADE YOUR POINT.

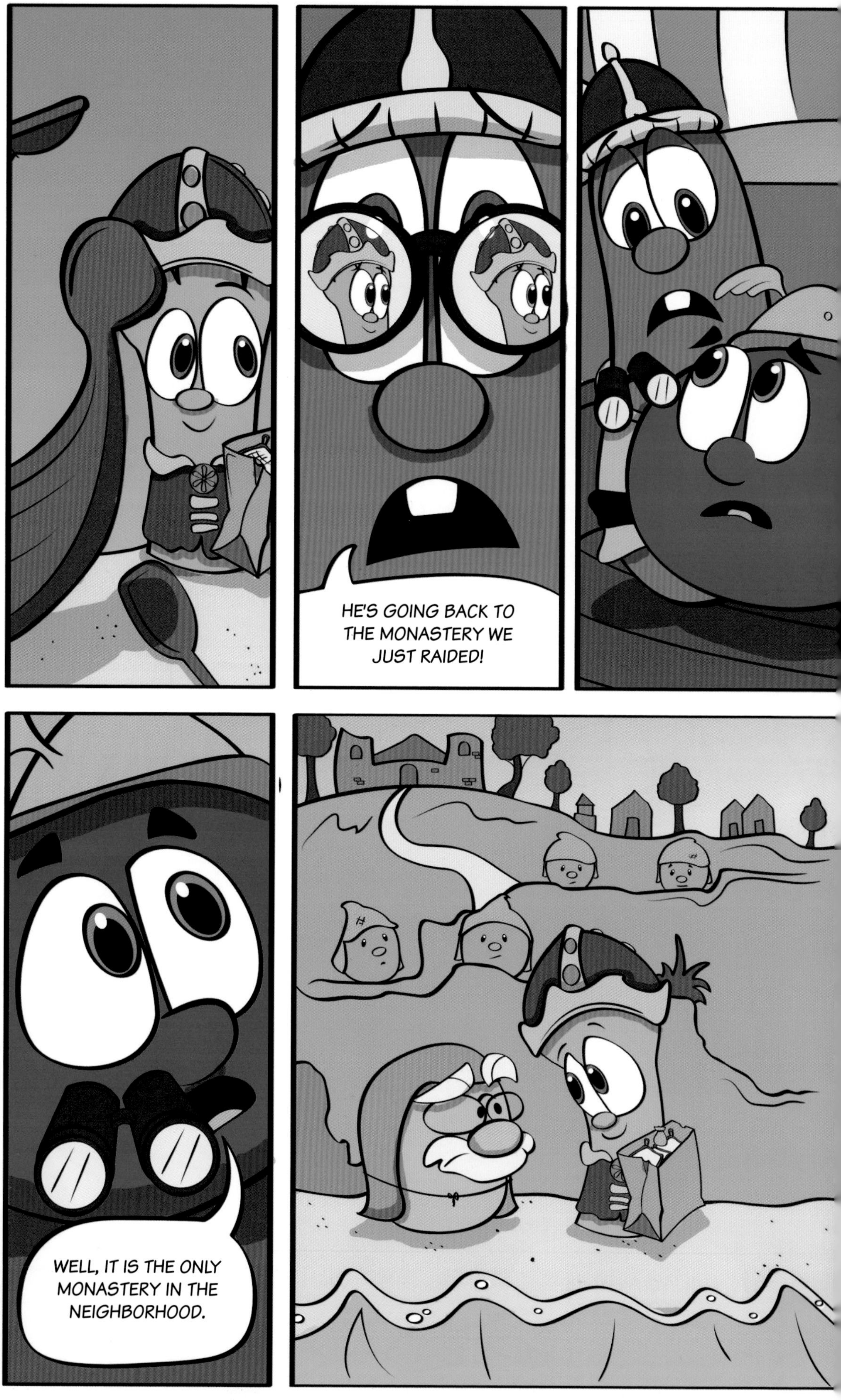
HE'S GOING BACK TO THE MONASTERY WE JUST RAIDED!
WELL, IT IS THE ONLY MONASTERY IN THE NEIGHBORHOOD.

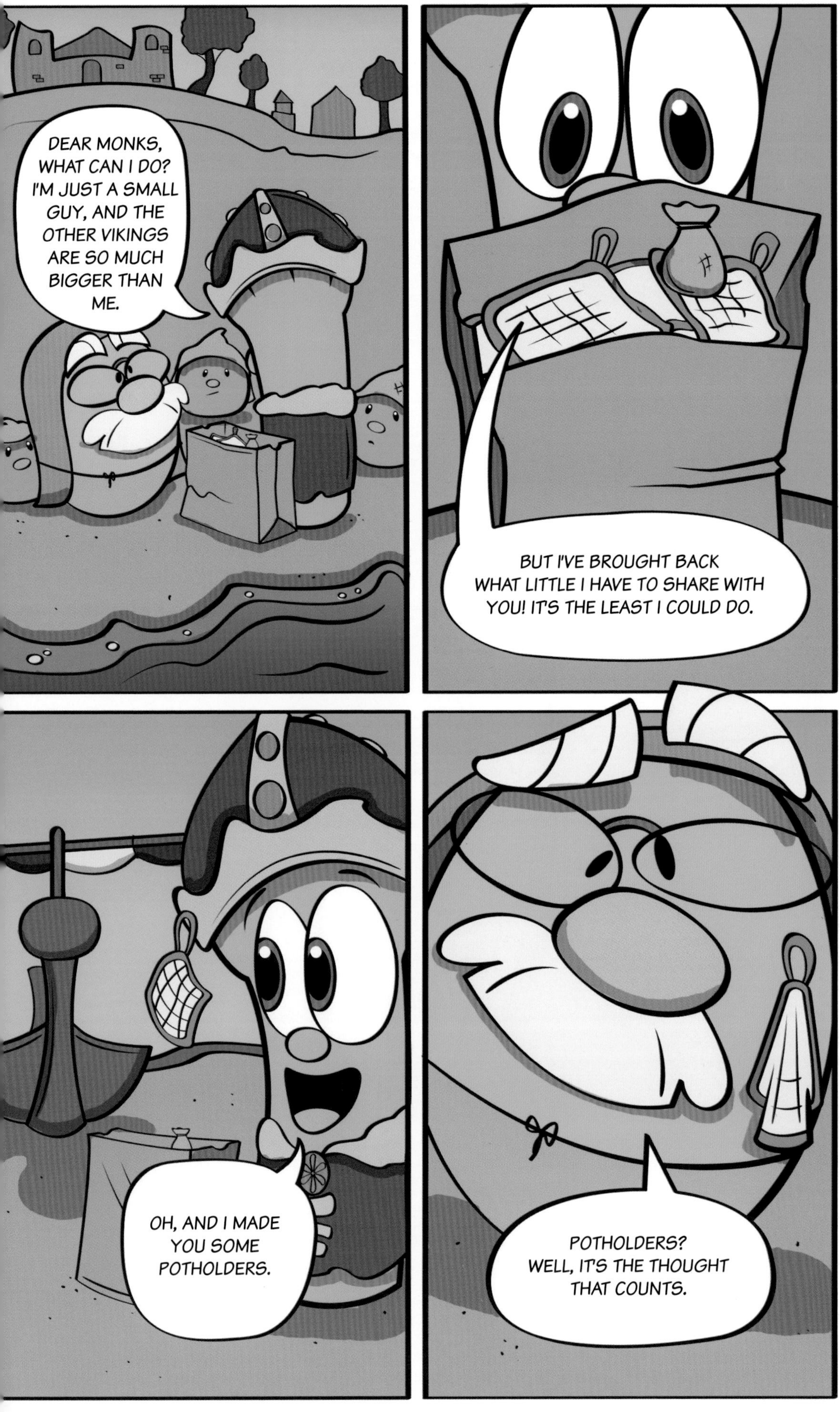
DEAR MONKS, WHAT CAN I DO? I'M JUST A SMALL GUY, AND THE OTHER VIKINGS ARE SO MUCH BIGGER THAN ME.
BUT I'VE BROUGHT BACK WHAT LITTLE I HAVE TO SHARE WITH YOU! IT'S THE LEAST I COULD DO.
OH, AND I MADE YOU SOME POTHOLDERS.
POTHOLDERS? WELL, IT'S THE THOUGHT THAT COUNTS.

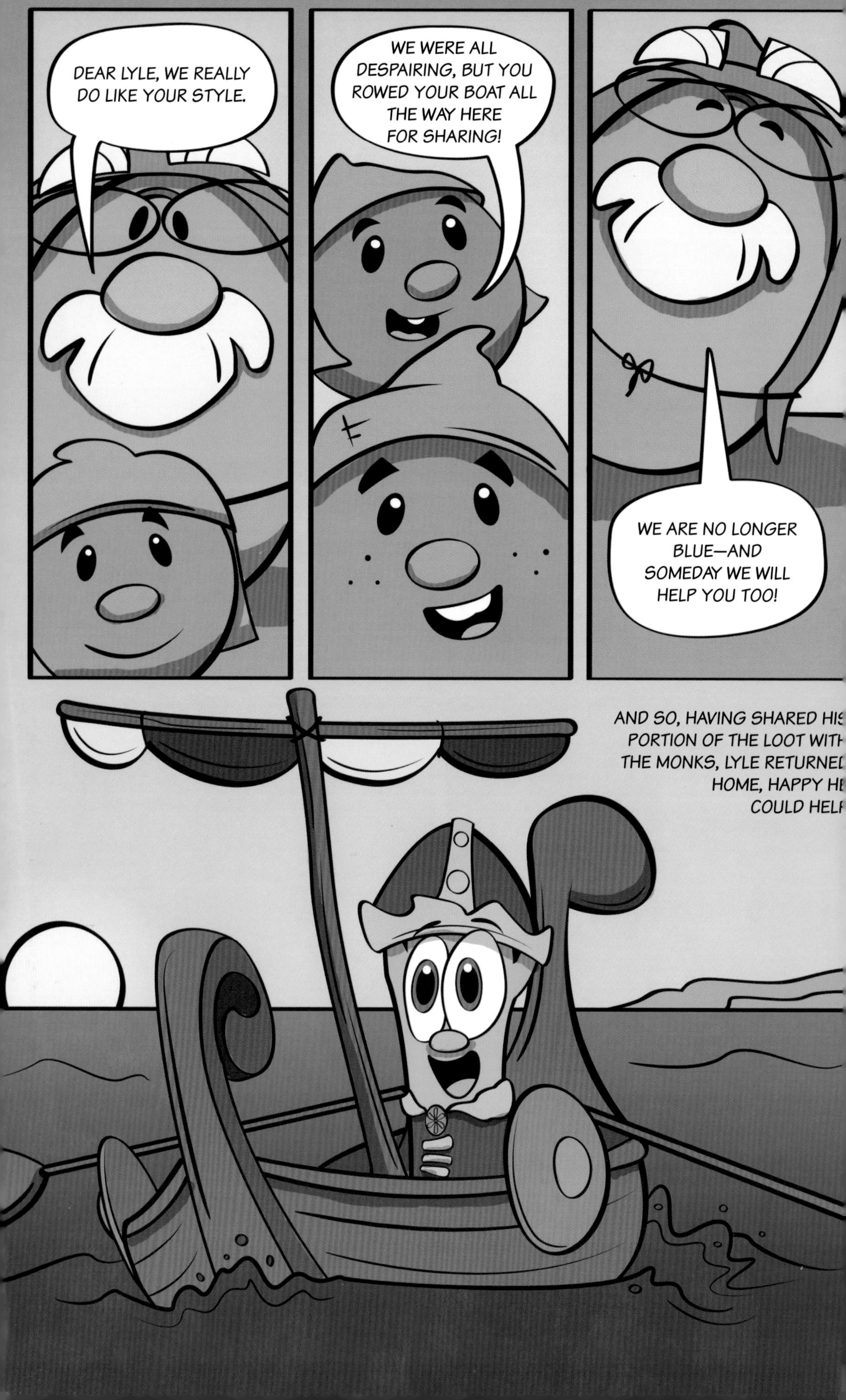
DEAR LYLE, WE REALLY DO LIKE YOUR STYLE.
WE WERE ALL DESPAIRING, BUT YOU ROWED YOUR BOAT ALL THE WAY HERE FOR SHARING!
WE ARE NO LONGER BLUE—AND SOMEDAY WE WILL HELP YOU TOO!
AND SO, HAVING SHARED HIS PORTION OF THE LOOT WITH THE MONKS, LYLE RETURNED HOME, HAPPY HE COULD HELP

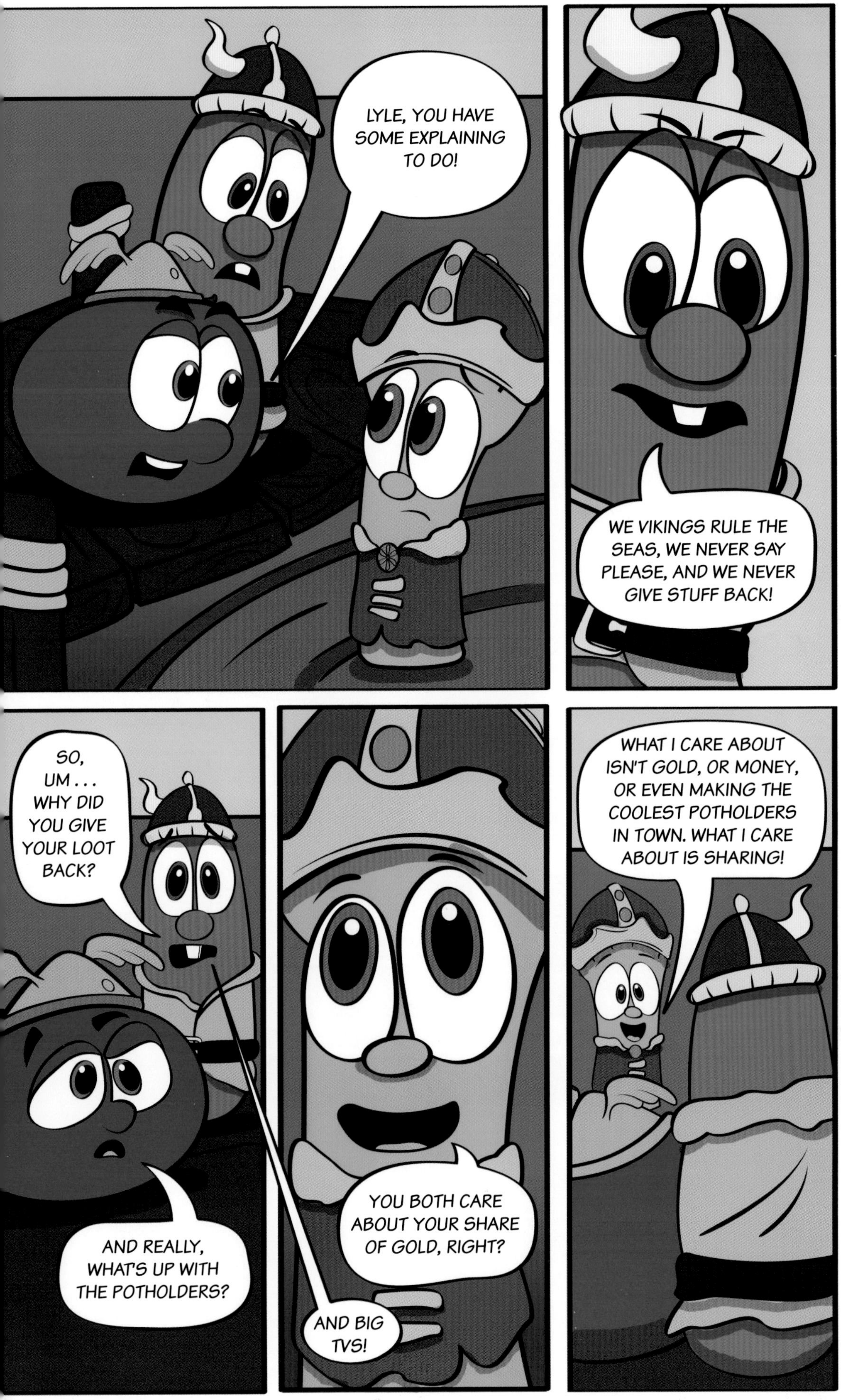
LYLE, YOU HAVE SOME EXPLAINING TO DO!
WE VIKINGS RULE THE SEAS, WE NEVER SAY PLEASE, AND WE NEVER GIVE STUFF BACK!
SO, UM . . . WHY DID YOU GIVE YOUR LOOT BACK?
AND REALLY, WHAT'S UP WITH THE POTHOLDERS?
YOU BOTH CARE ABOUT YOUR SHARE OF GOLD, RIGHT?
AND BIG TVS!
WHAT I CARE ABOUT ISN'T GOLD, OR MONEY, OR EVEN MAKING THE COOLEST POTHOLDERS IN TOWN. WHAT I CARE ABOUT IS SHARING!

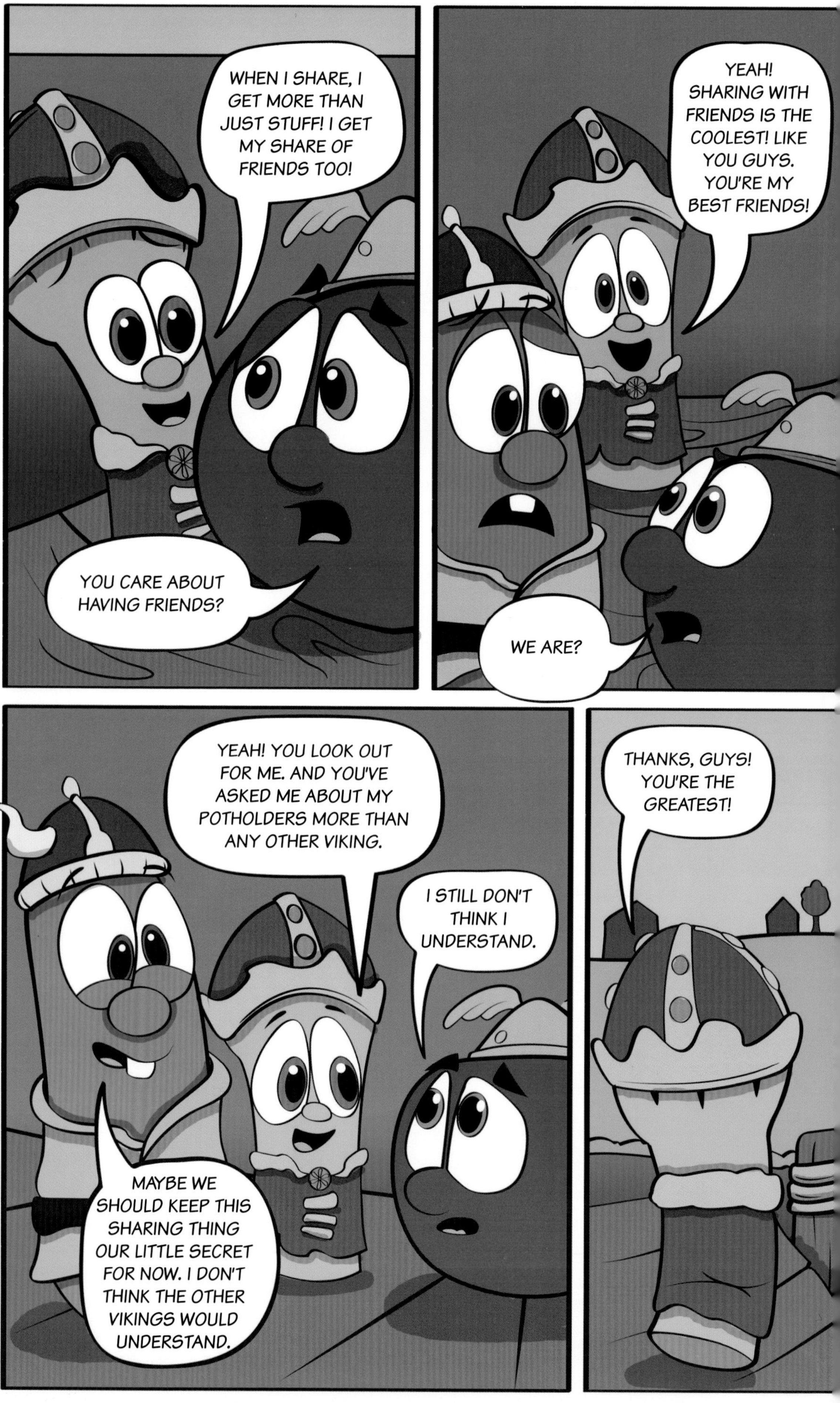
WHEN I SHARE, I GET MORE THAN JUST STUFF! I GET MY SHARE OF FRIENDS TOO!
YOU CARE ABOUT HAVING FRIENDS?
YEAH! SHARING WITH FRIENDS IS THE COOLEST! LIKE YOU GUYS. YOU'RE MY BEST FRIENDS!
WE ARE?
YEAH! YOU LOOK OUT FOR ME. AND YOU'VE ASKED ME ABOUT MY POTHOLDERS MORE THAN ANY OTHER VIKING.
I STILL DON'T THINK I UNDERSTAND.
MAYBE WE SHOULD KEEP THIS SHARING THING OUR LITTLE SECRET FOR NOW. I DON'T THINK THE OTHER VIKINGS WOULD UNDERSTAND.
THANKS, GUYS! YOU'RE THE GREATEST!

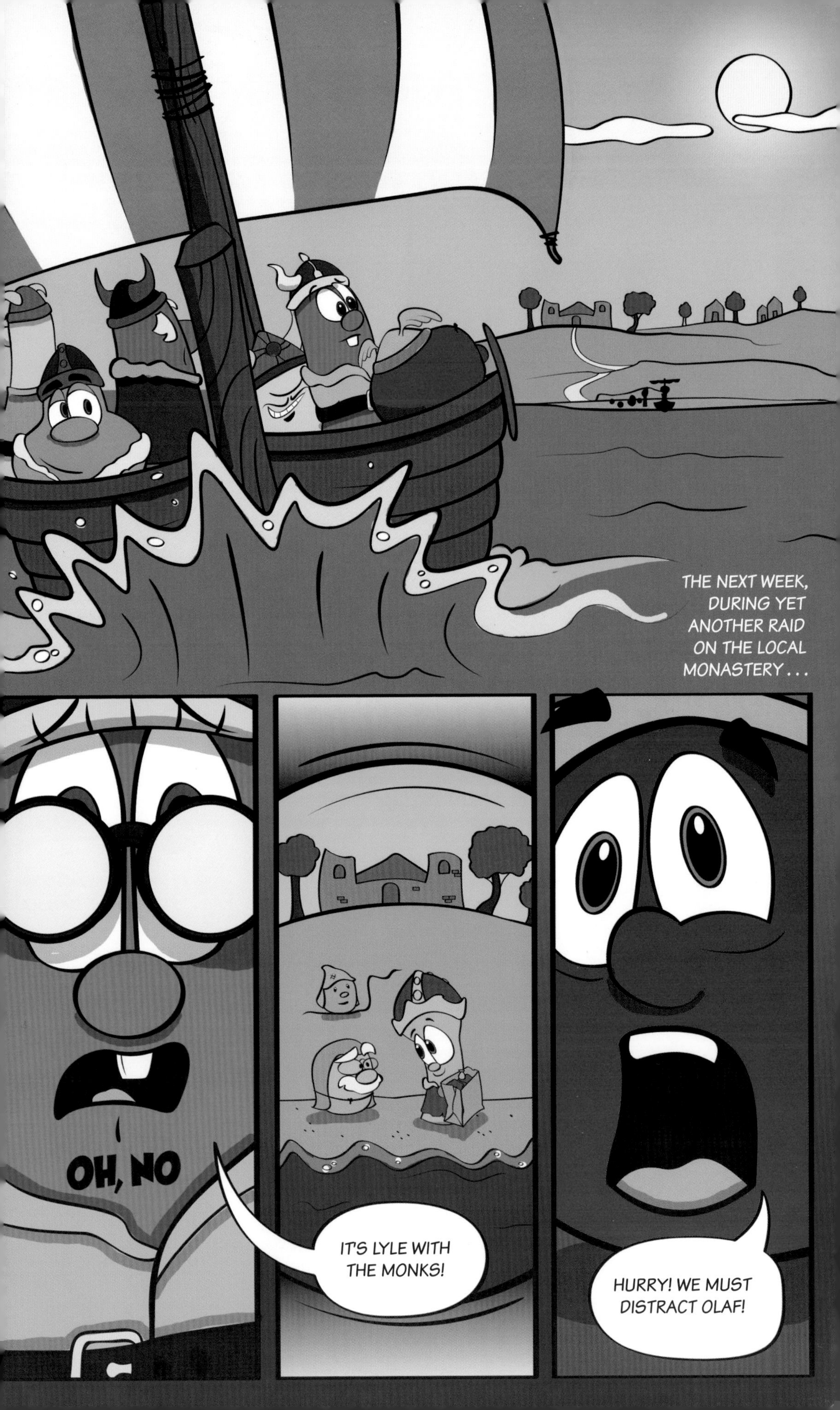
THE NEXT WEEK, DURING YET ANOTHER RAID ON THE LOCAL MONASTERY . . .
OH, NO
IT'S LYLE WITH THE MONKS!
HURRY! WE MUST DISTRACT OLAF!

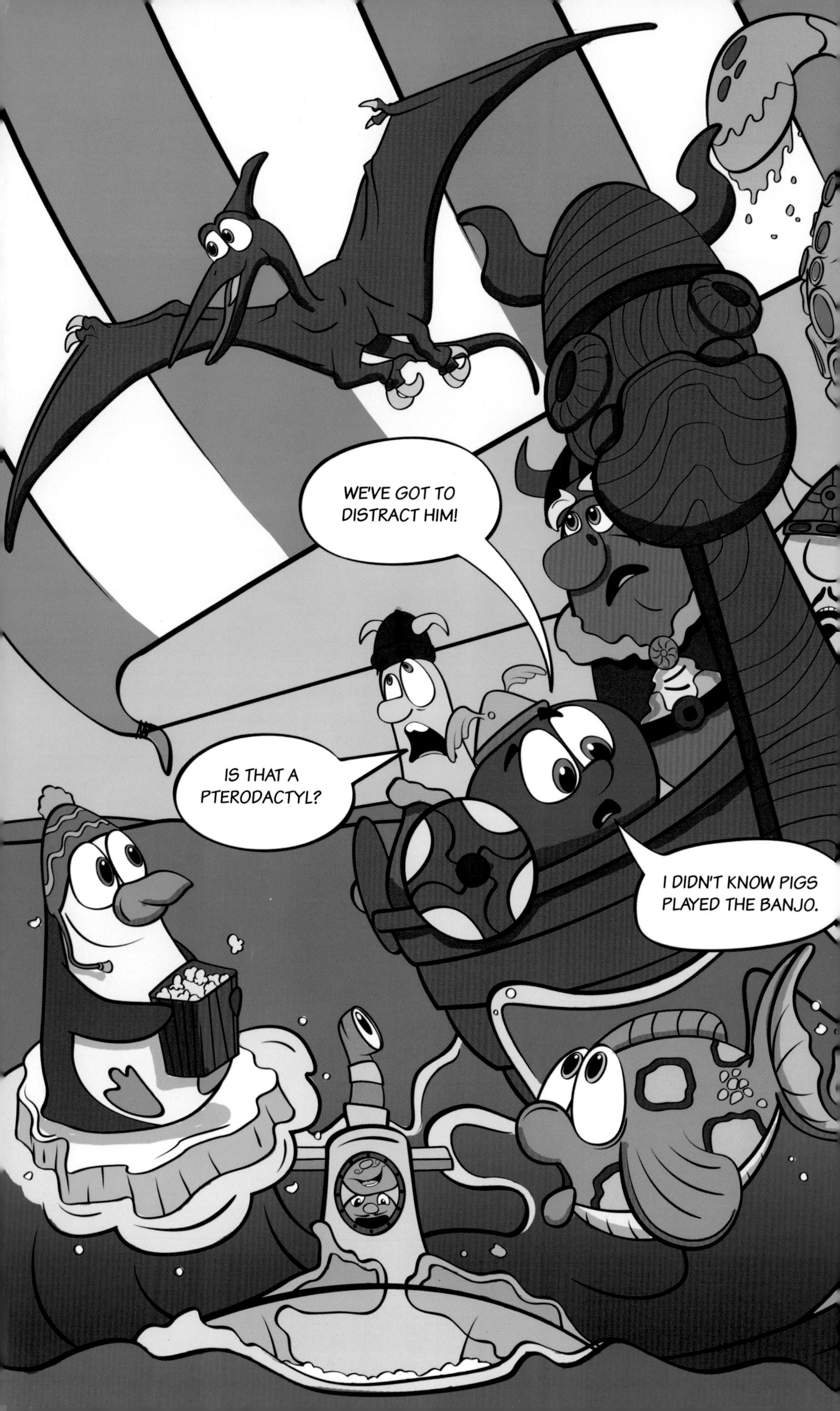
WE'VE GOT TO DISTRACT HIM!
IS THAT A PTERODACTYL?
I DIDN'T KNOW PIGS PLAYED THE BANJO.

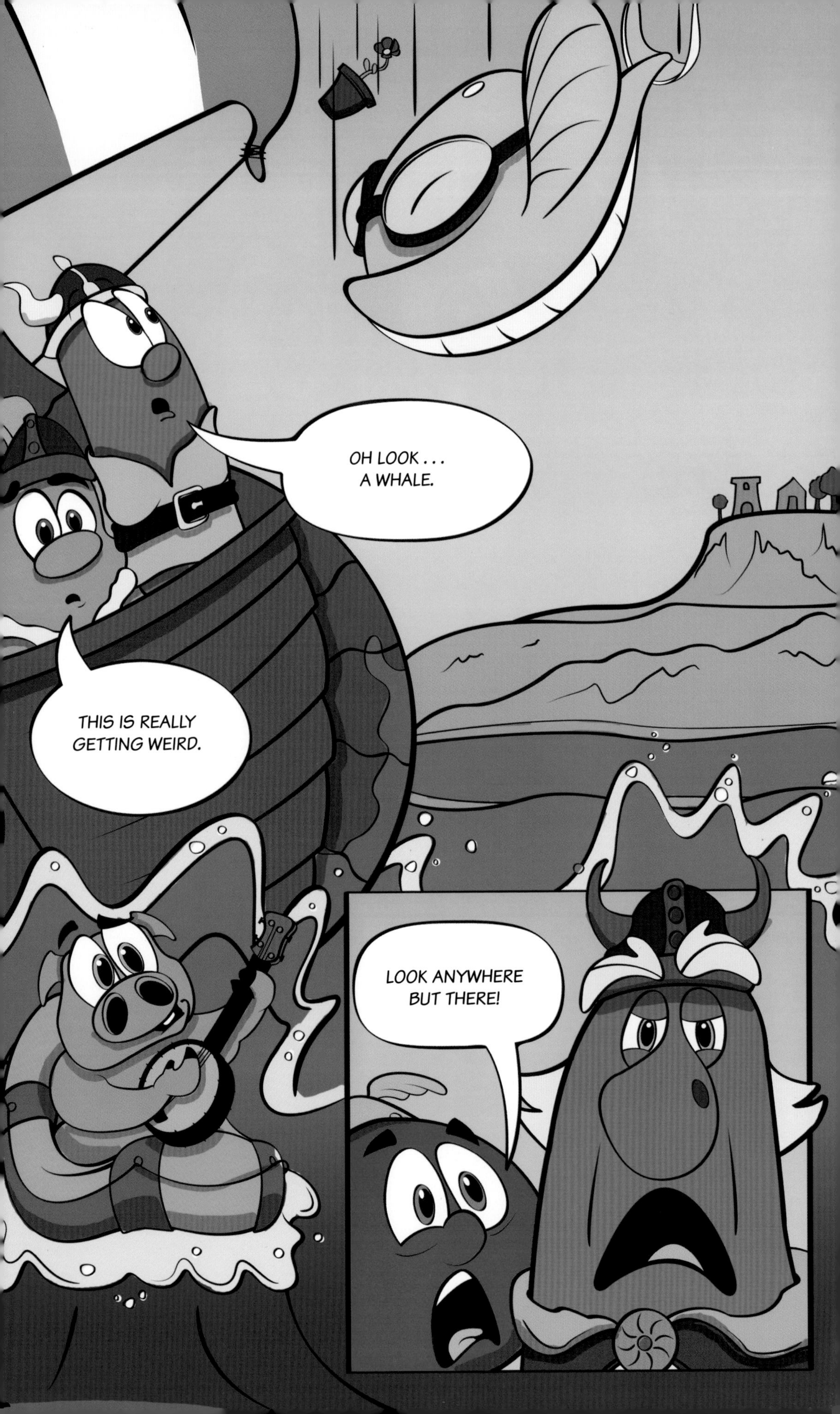
OH LOOK . . . A WHALE.
THIS IS REALLY GETTING WEIRD.
LOOK ANYWHERE BUT THERE!

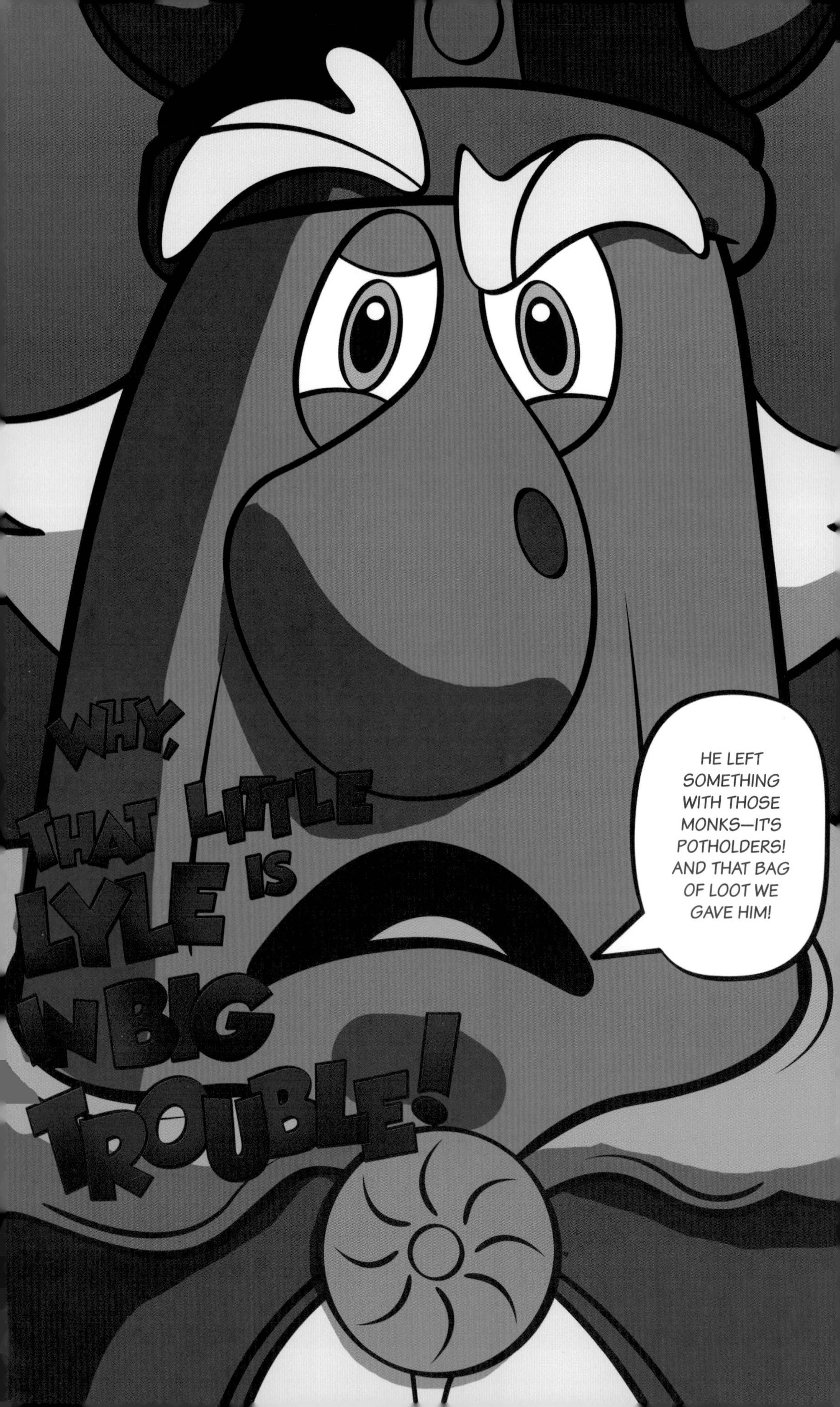

WHY, THAT LITTLE LYLE IS IN BIG TROUBLE!
HE LEFT SOMETHING WITH THOSE MONKS—IT'S POTHOLDERS! AND THAT BAG OF LOOT WE GAVE HIM!

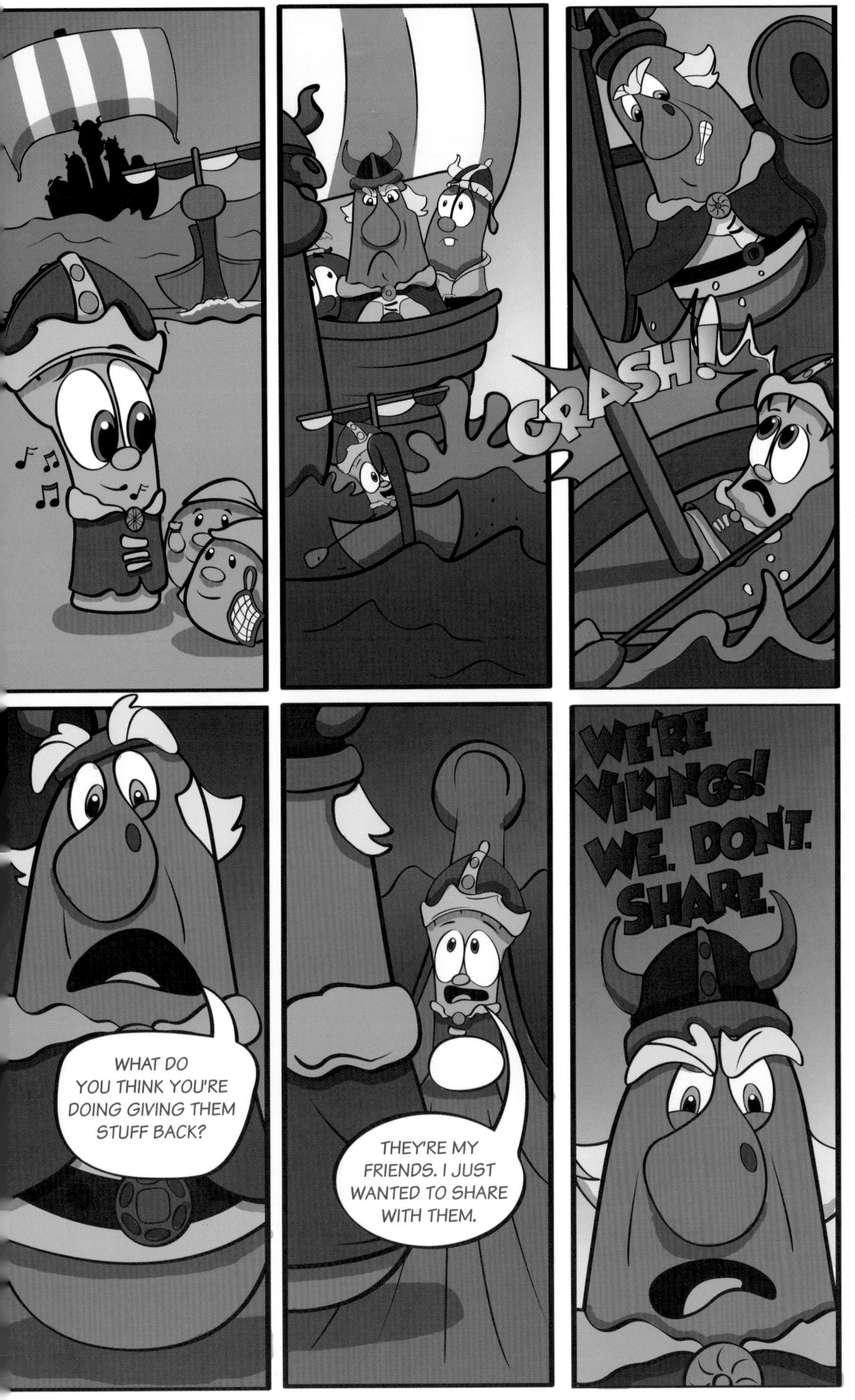
CRASH!
WHAT DO YOU THINK YOU'RE DOING GIVING THEM STUFF BACK?
THEY'RE MY FRIENDS. I JUST WANTED TO SHARE WITH THEM.
WE'RE VIKINGS! WE. DON'T. SHARE.

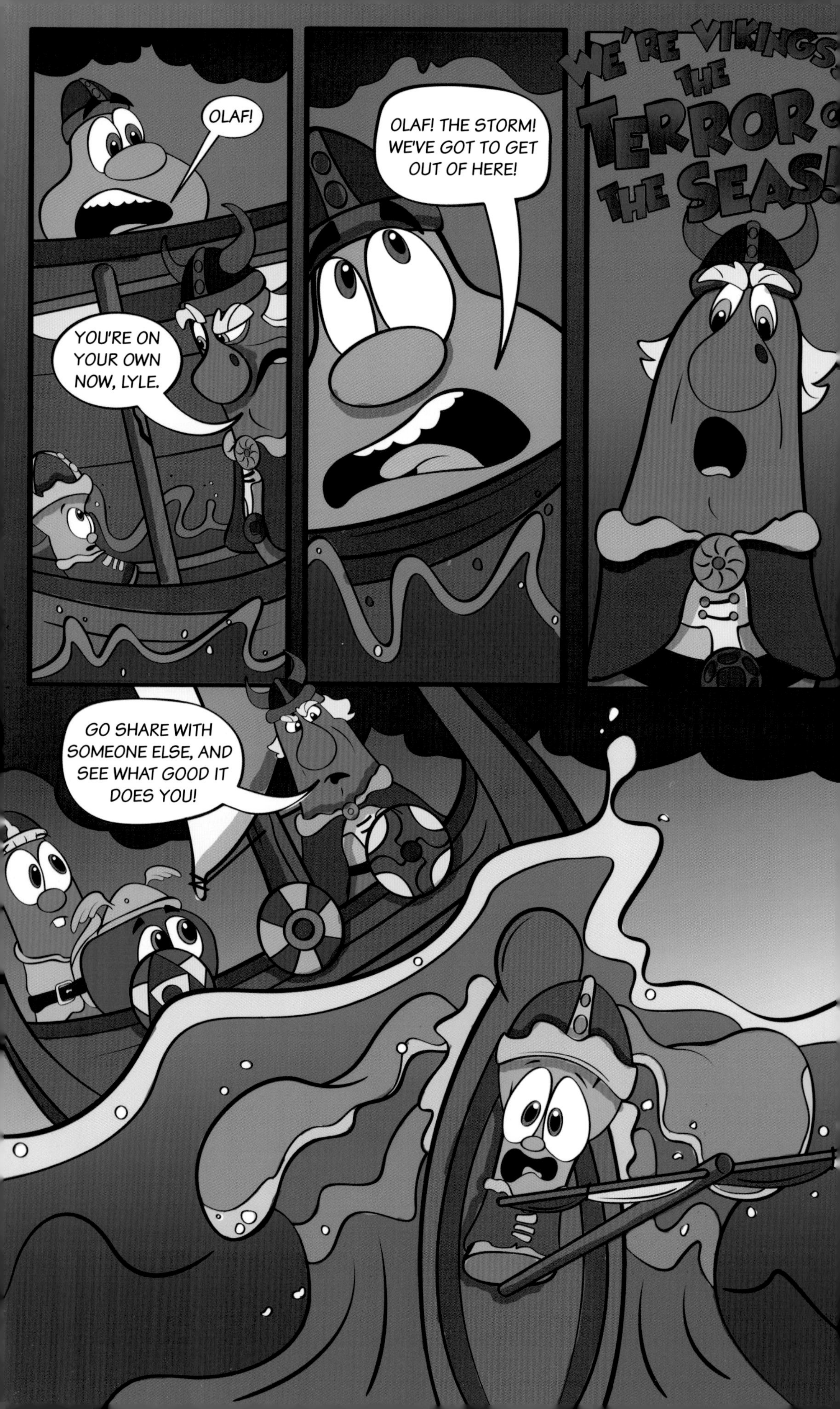
OLAF!
YOU'RE ON YOUR OWN NOW, LYLE.
OLAF! THE STORM! WE'VE GOT TO GET OUT OF HERE!
WE'RE VIKINGS, THE TERROR OF THE SEAS!
GO SHARE WITH SOMEONE ELSE, AND SEE WHAT GOOD IT DOES YOU!

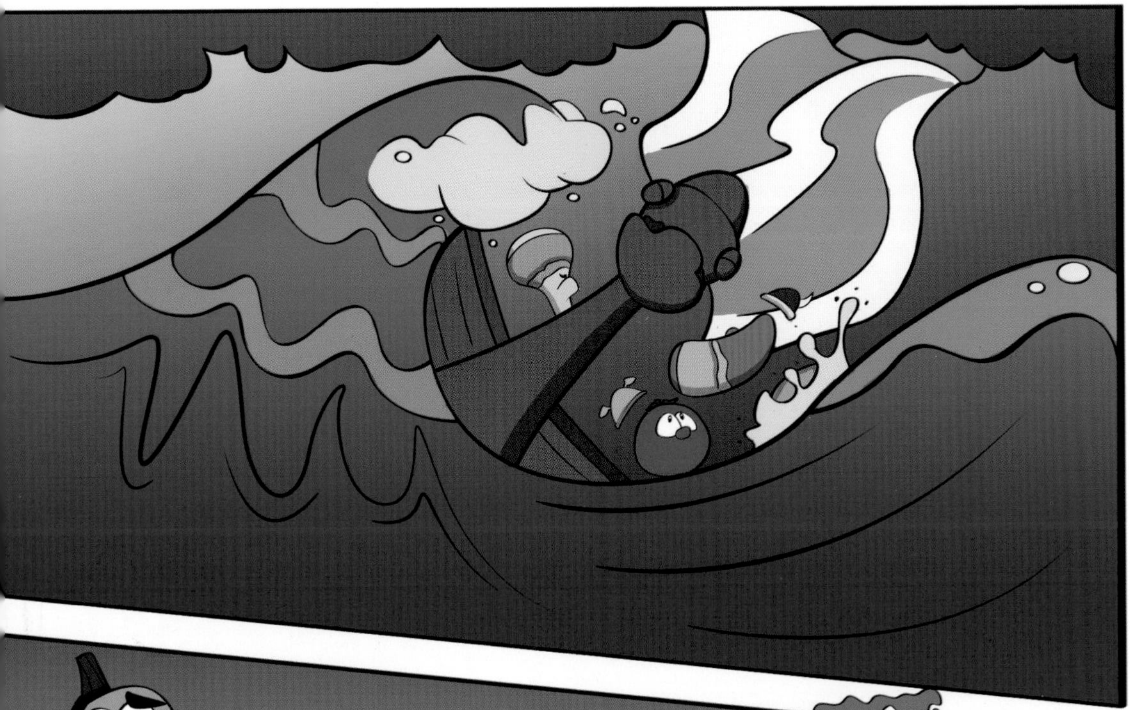

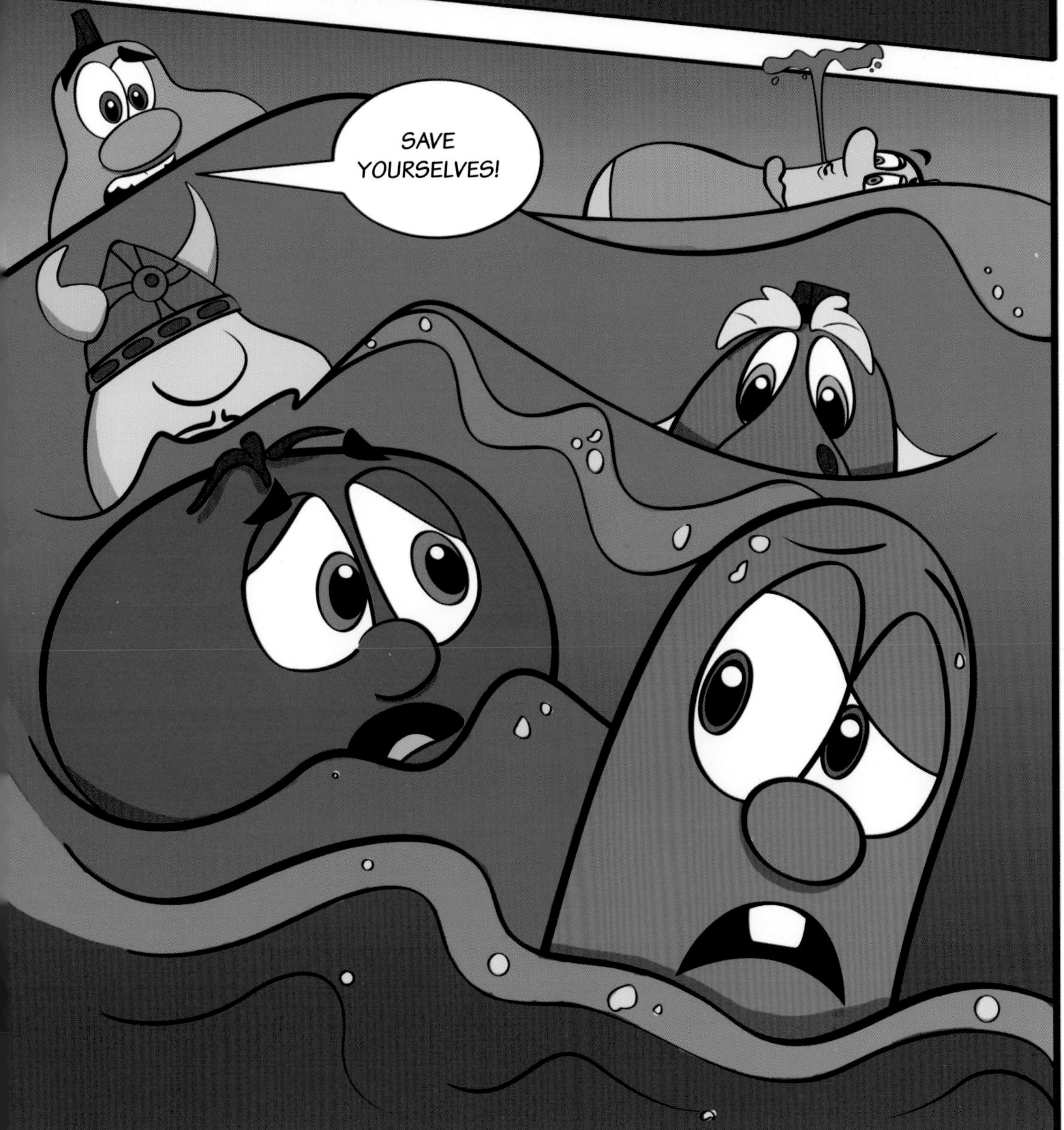
SAVE
YOURSELVES!

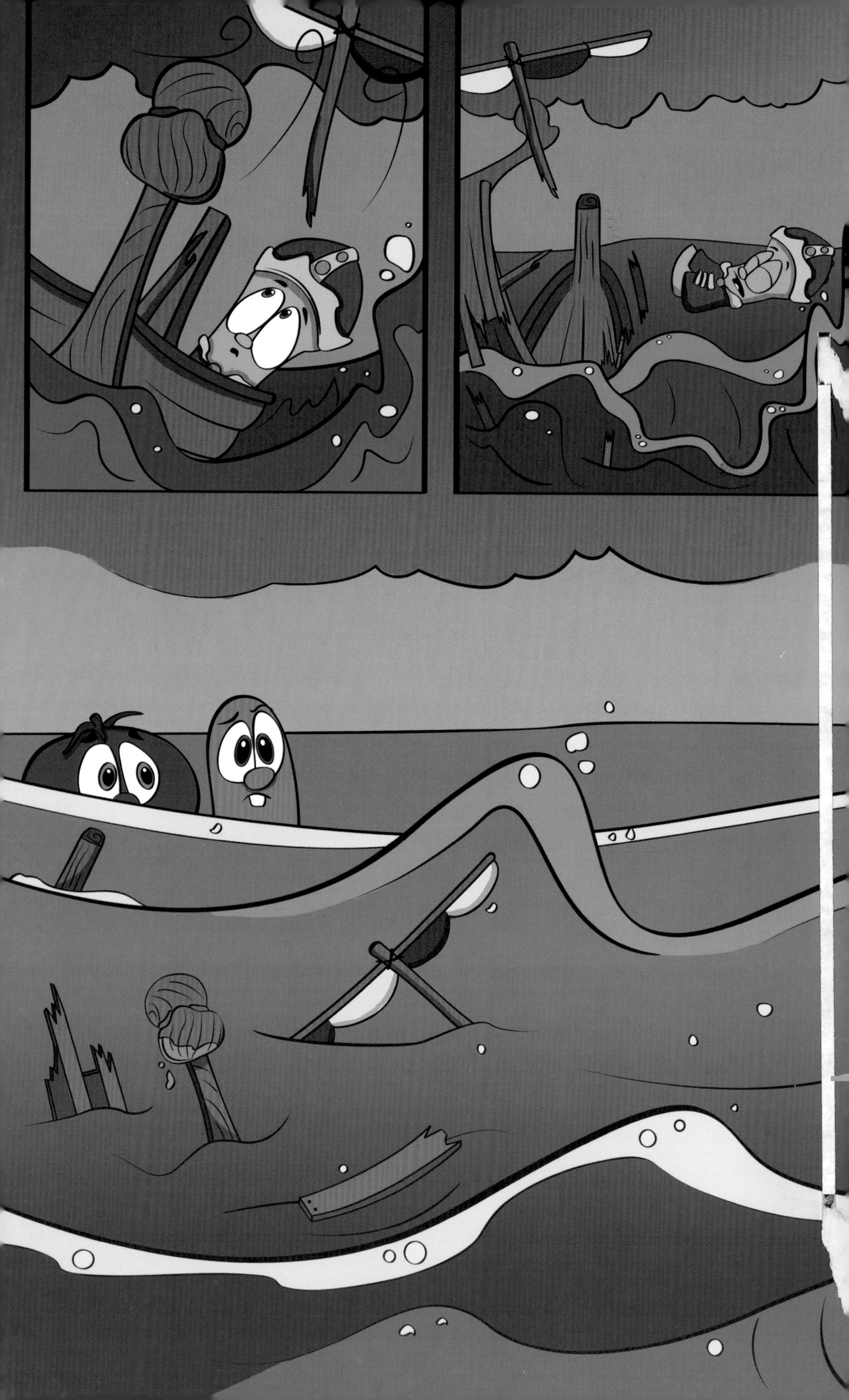

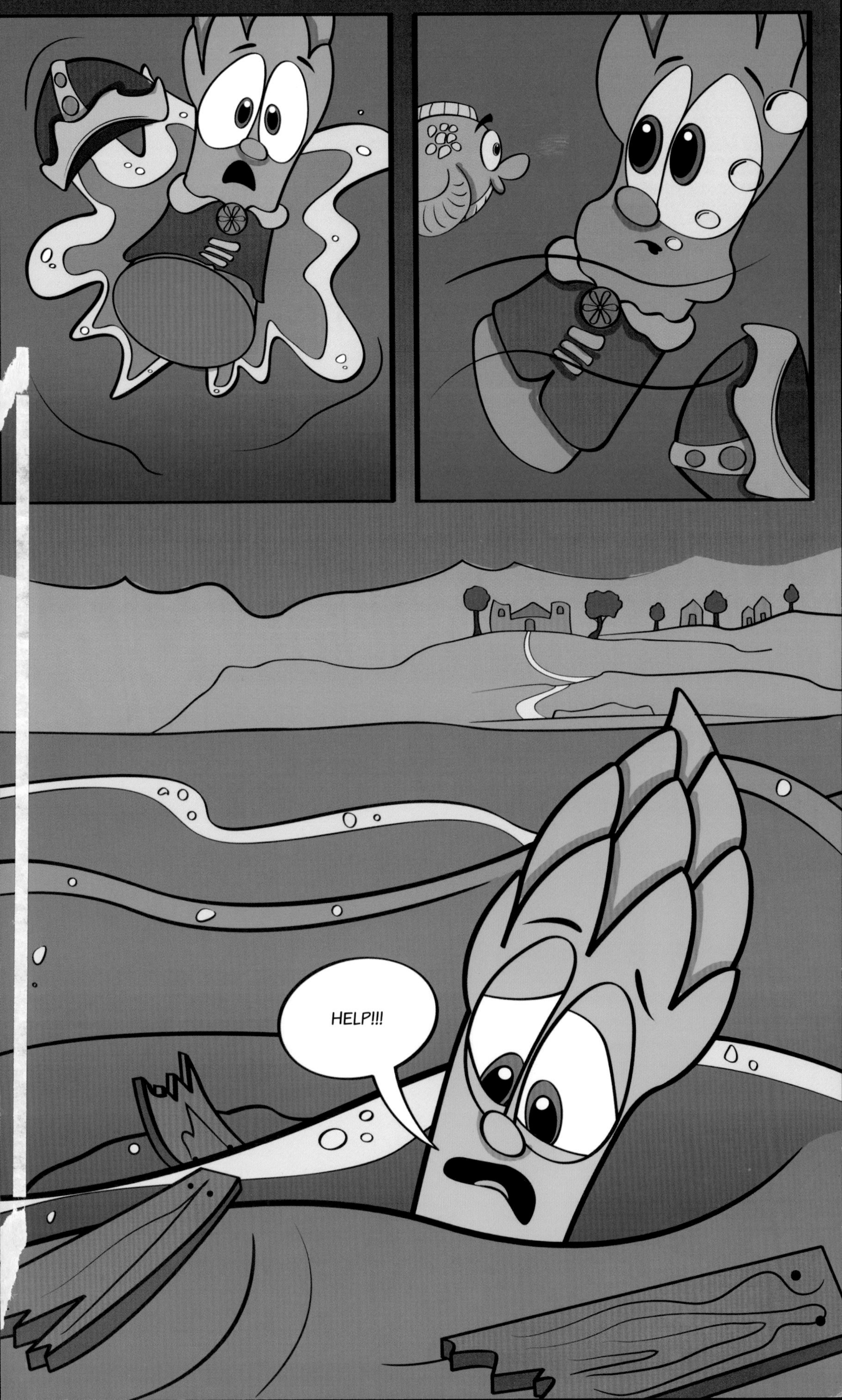
HELP!!!

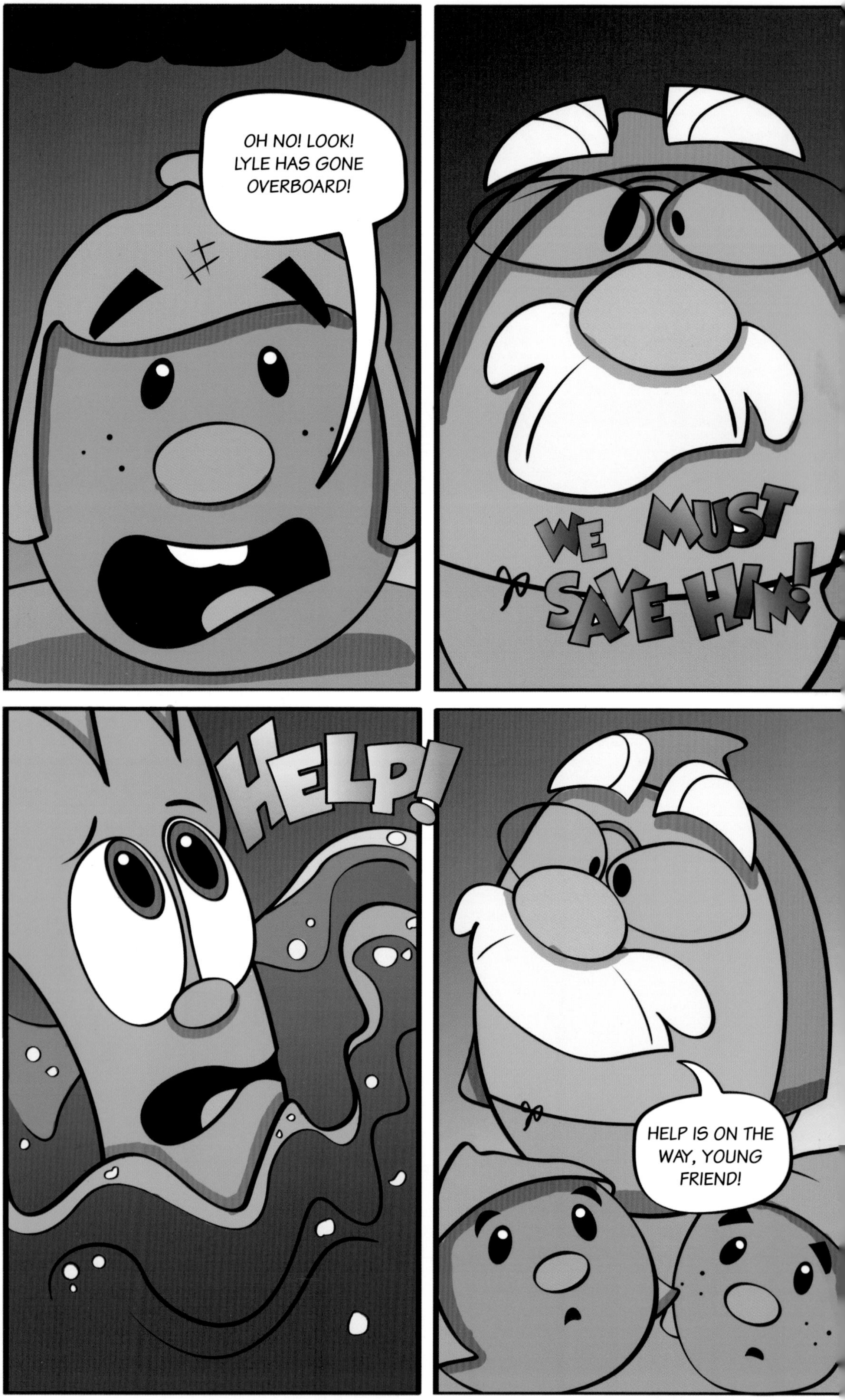

OH NO! LOOK! LYLE HAS GONE OVERBOARD!
WE MUST SAVE HIM!
HELP!
HELP IS ON THE WAY, YOUNG FRIEND!

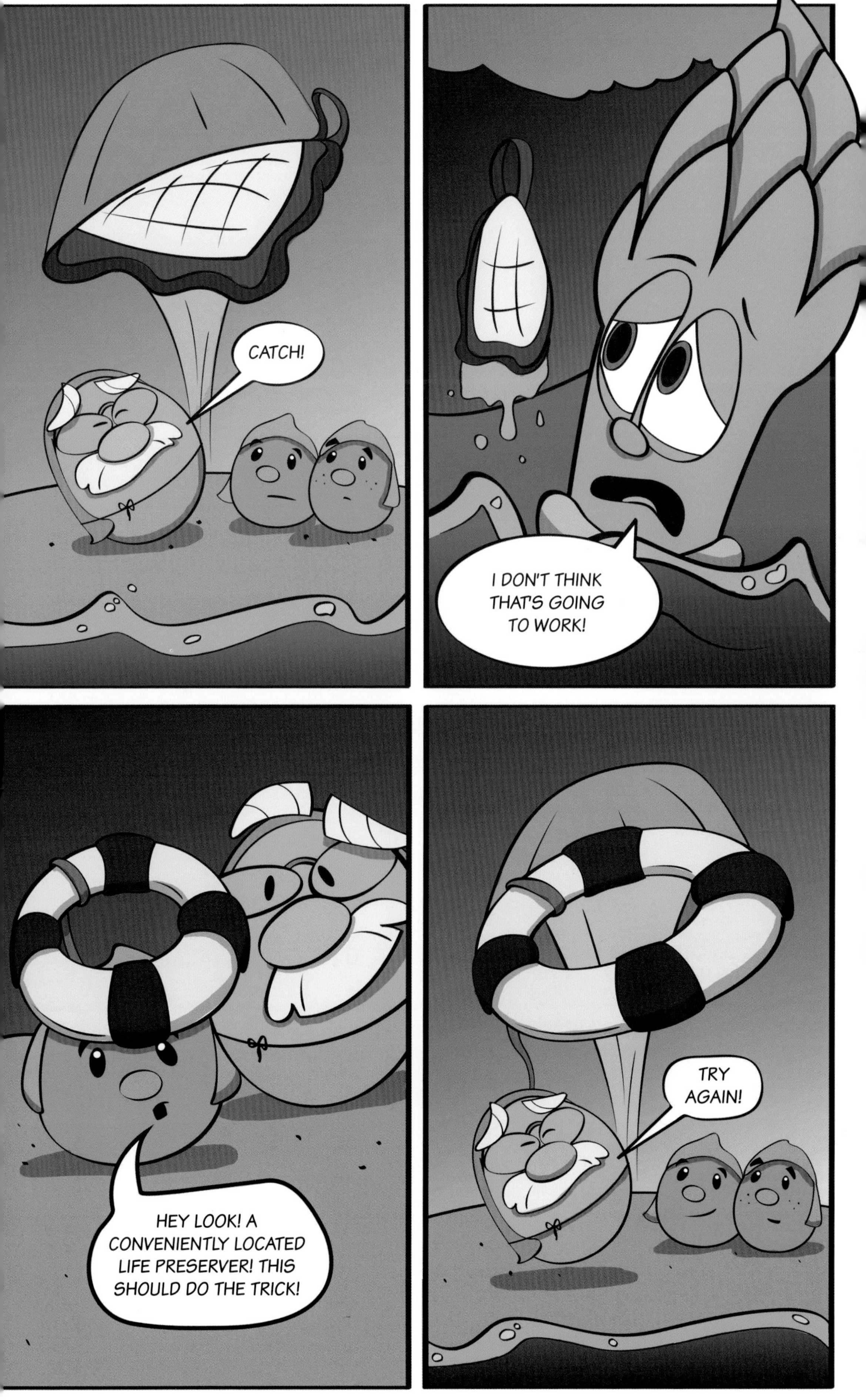
CATCH!
I DON'T THINK THAT'S GOING TO WORK!
HEY LOOK! A CONVENIENTLY LOCATED LIFE PRESERVER! THIS SHOULD DO THE TRICK!
TRY AGAIN!

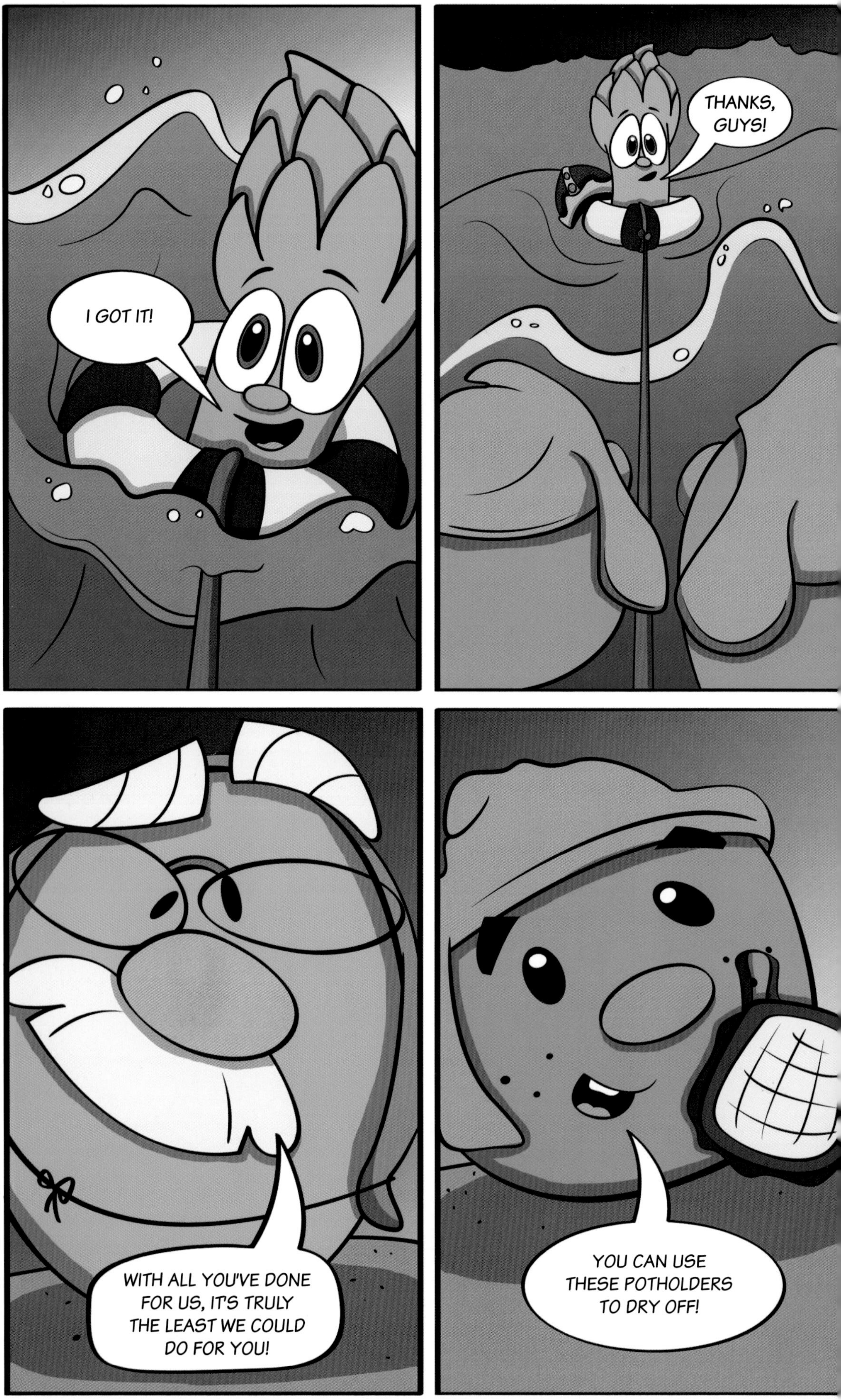
I GOT IT!
THANKS, GUYS!
WITH ALL YOU'VE DONE FOR US, IT'S TRULY THE LEAST WE COULD DO FOR YOU!
YOU CAN USE THESE POTHOLDERS TO DRY OFF!

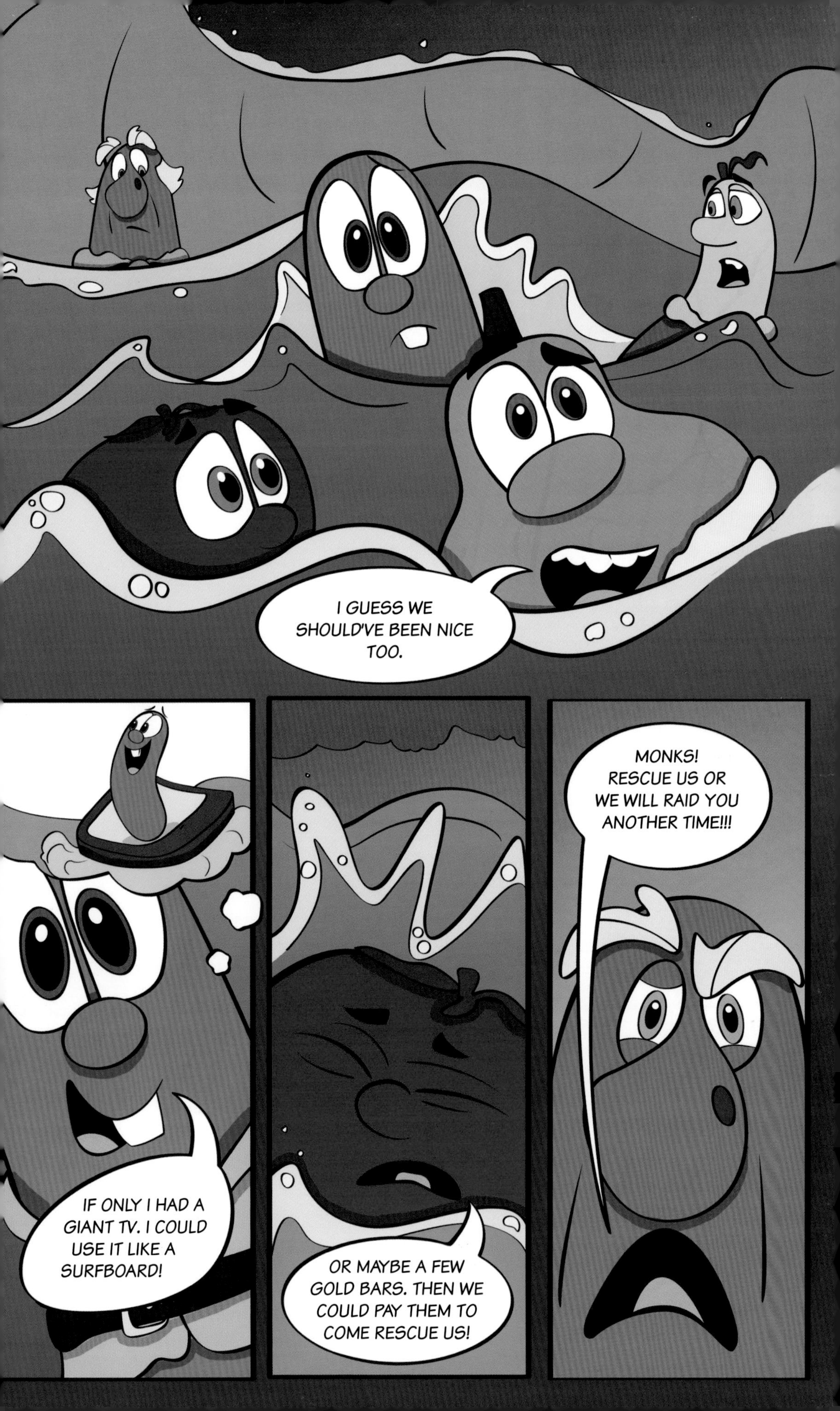
I GUESS WE SHOULD'VE BEEN NICE TOO.
IF ONLY I HAD A GIANT TV. I COULD USE IT LIKE A SURFBOARD!
OR MAYBE A FEW GOLD BARS. THEN WE COULD PAY THEM TO COME RESCUE US!
MONKS! RESCUE US OR WE WILL RAID YOU ANOTHER TIME!!!

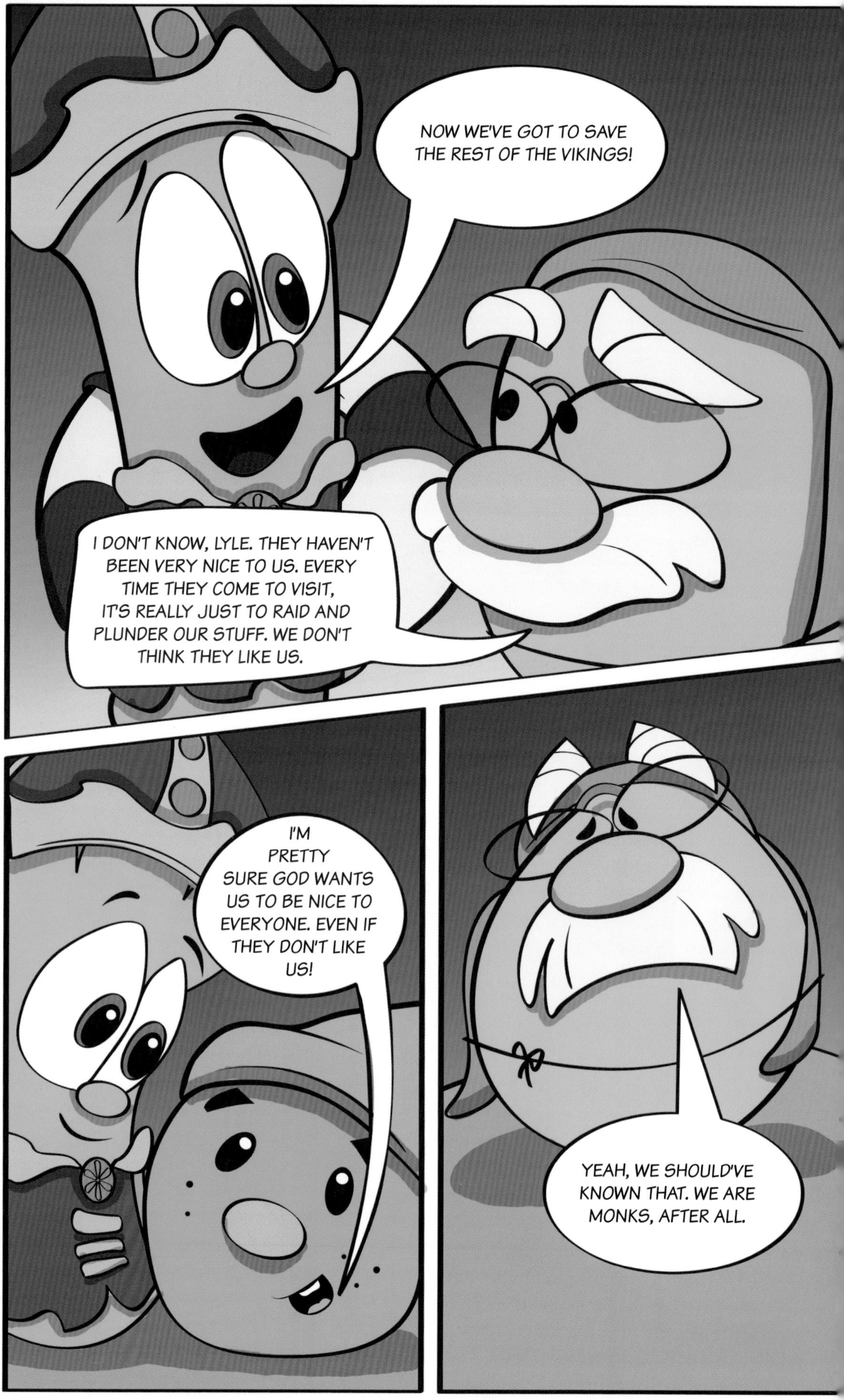
NOW WE'VE GOT TO SAVE THE REST OF THE VIKINGS!
I DON'T KNOW, LYLE. THEY HAVEN'T BEEN VERY NICE TO US. EVERY TIME THEY COME TO VISIT, IT'S REALLY JUST TO RAID AND PLUNDER OUR STUFF. WE DON'T THINK THEY LIKE US.
I'M PRETTY SURE GOD WANTS US TO BE NICE TO EVERYONE. EVEN IF THEY DON'T LIKE US!
YEAH, WE SHOULD'VE KNOWN THAT. WE ARE MONKS, AFTER ALL.

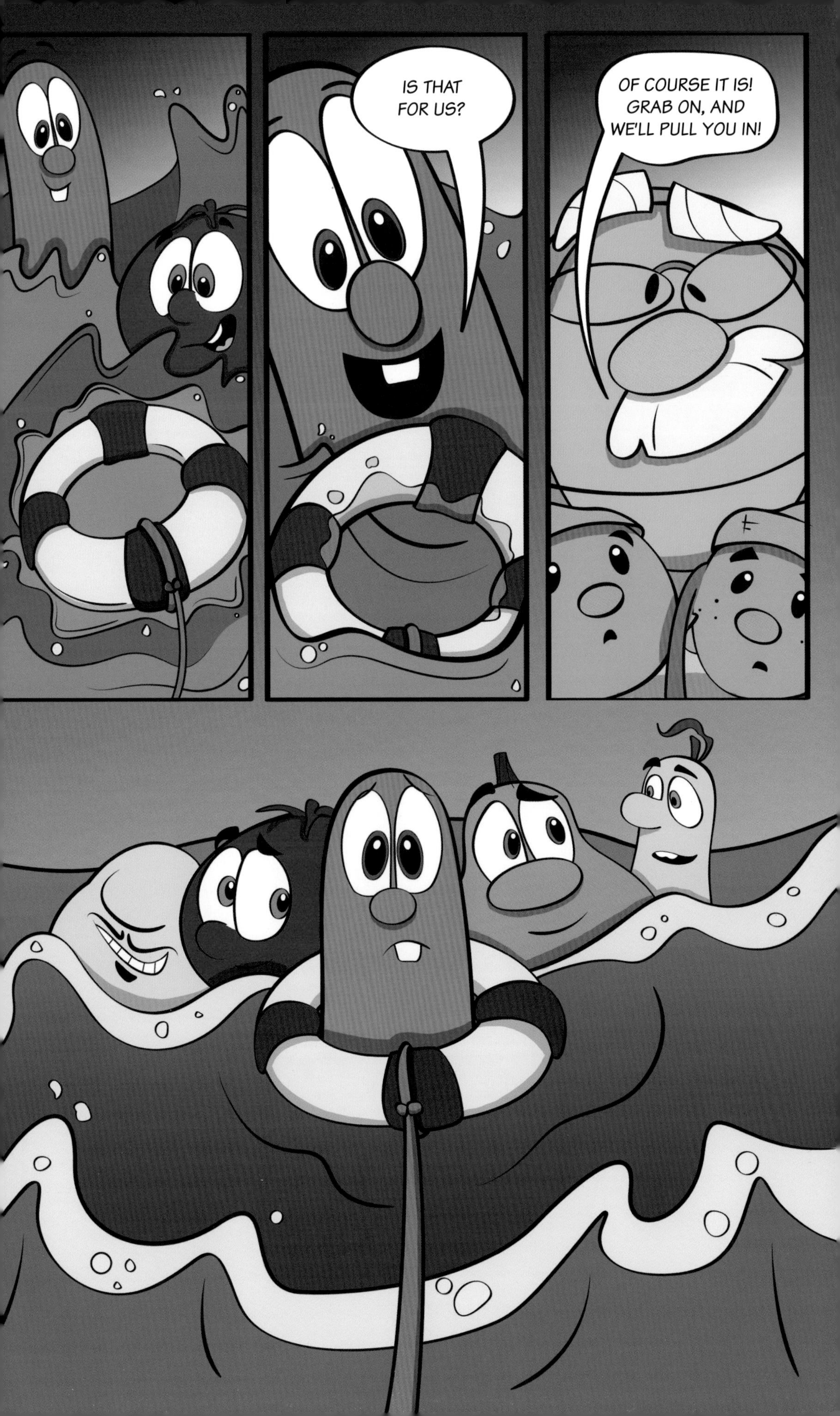
IS THAT FOR US?
OF COURSE IT IS! GRAB ON, AND WE'LL PULL YOU IN!

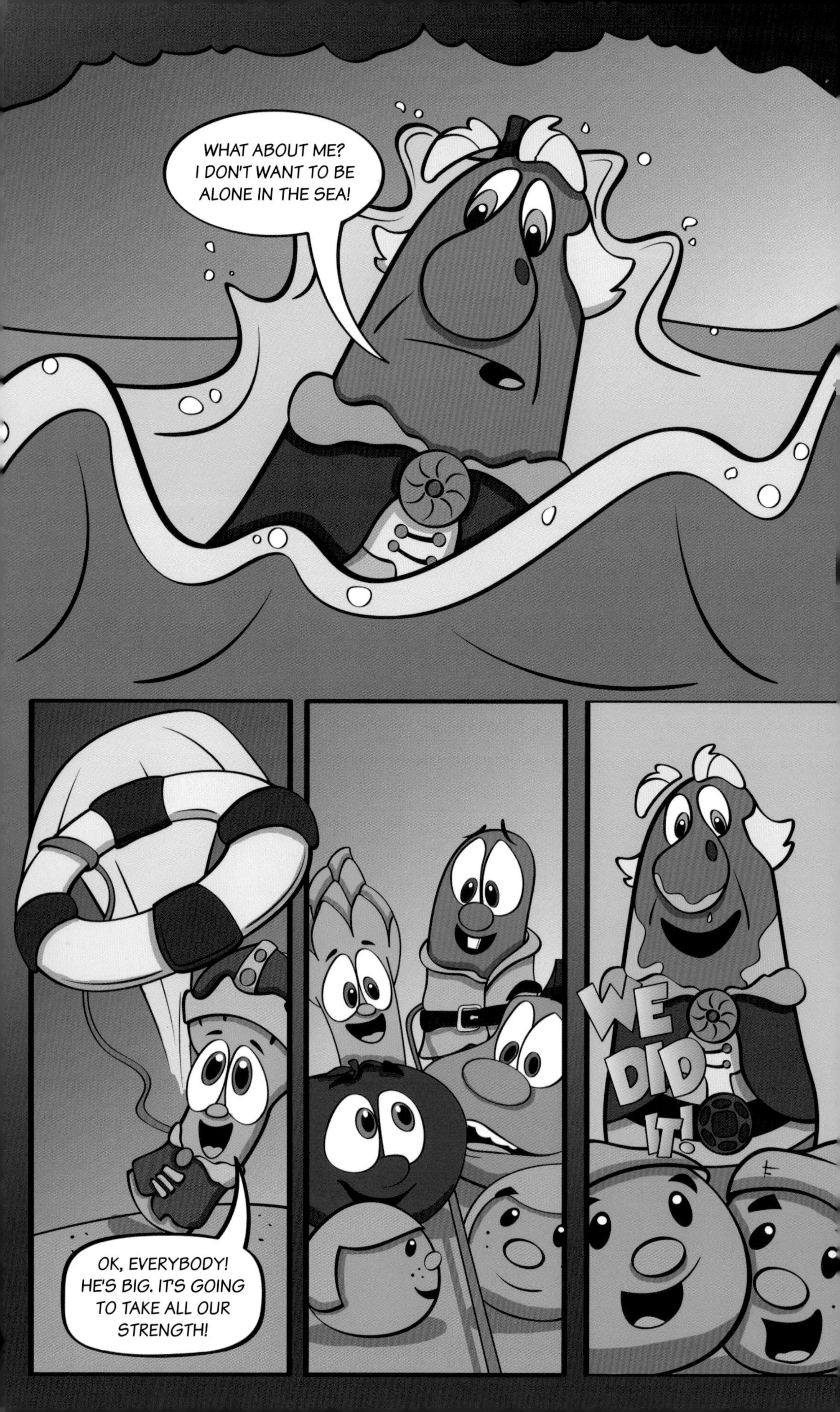
WHAT ABOUT ME? I DON'T WANT TO BE ALONE IN THE SEA!
OK, EVERYBODY! HE'S BIG. IT'S GOING TO TAKE ALL OUR STRENGTH!
WE DID IT!

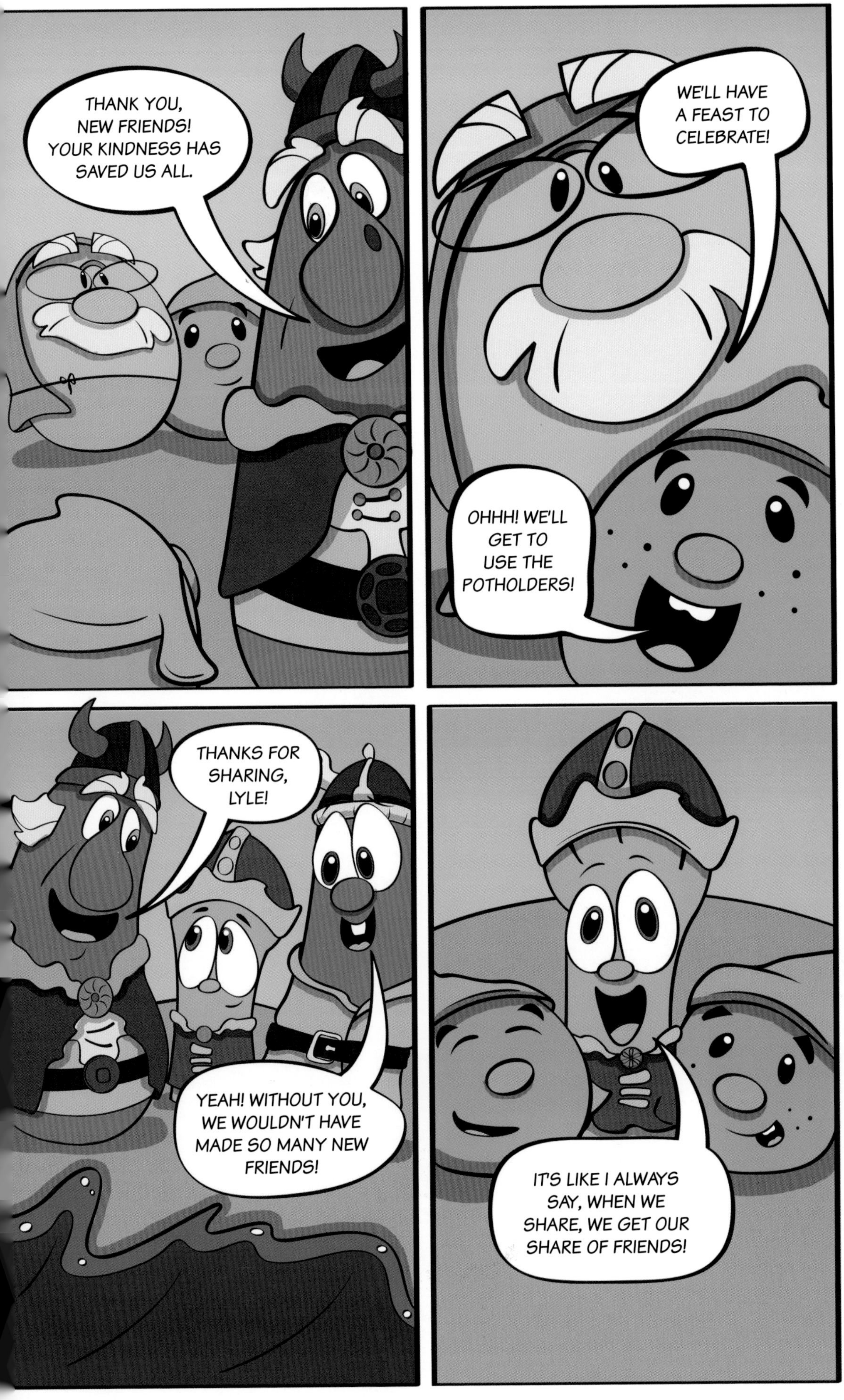
THANK YOU, NEW FRIENDS! YOUR KINDNESS HAS SAVED US ALL.
WE'LL HAVE A FEAST TO CELEBRATE!
OHHH! WE'LL GET TO USE THE POTHOLDERS!
THANKS FOR SHARING, LYLE!
YEAH! WITHOUT YOU, WE WOULDN'T HAVE MADE SO MANY NEW FRIENDS!
IT'S LIKE I ALWAYS SAY, WHEN WE SHARE, WE GET OUR SHARE OF FRIENDS!

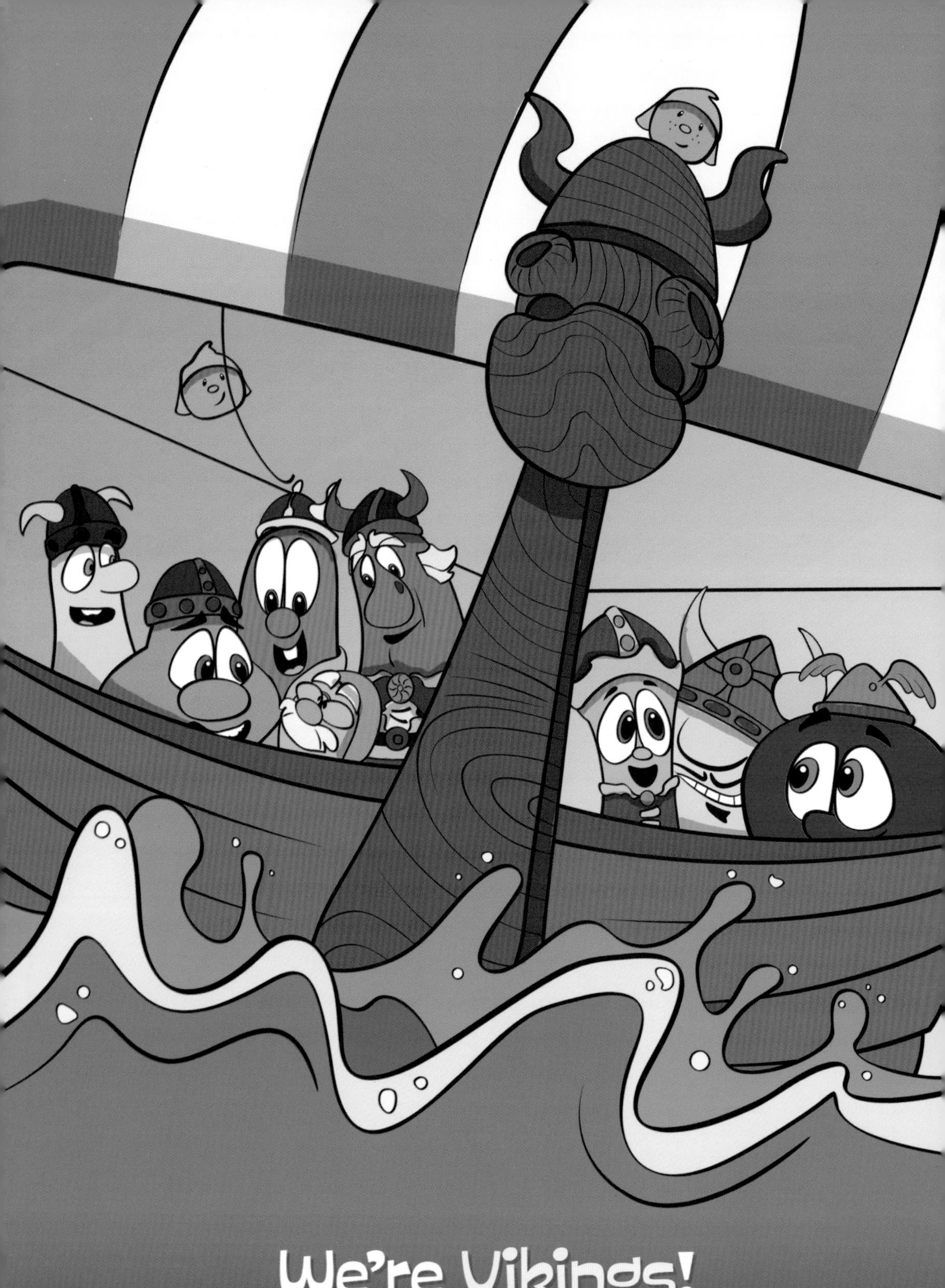

We're Vikings! The sharers of the sea!

. . . AND DO NOT FORGET TO DO GOOD AND TO SHARE WITH OTHERS, FOR WITH SUCH SACRIFICES GOD IS PLEASED.—HEBREWS 13:16 (NIV)

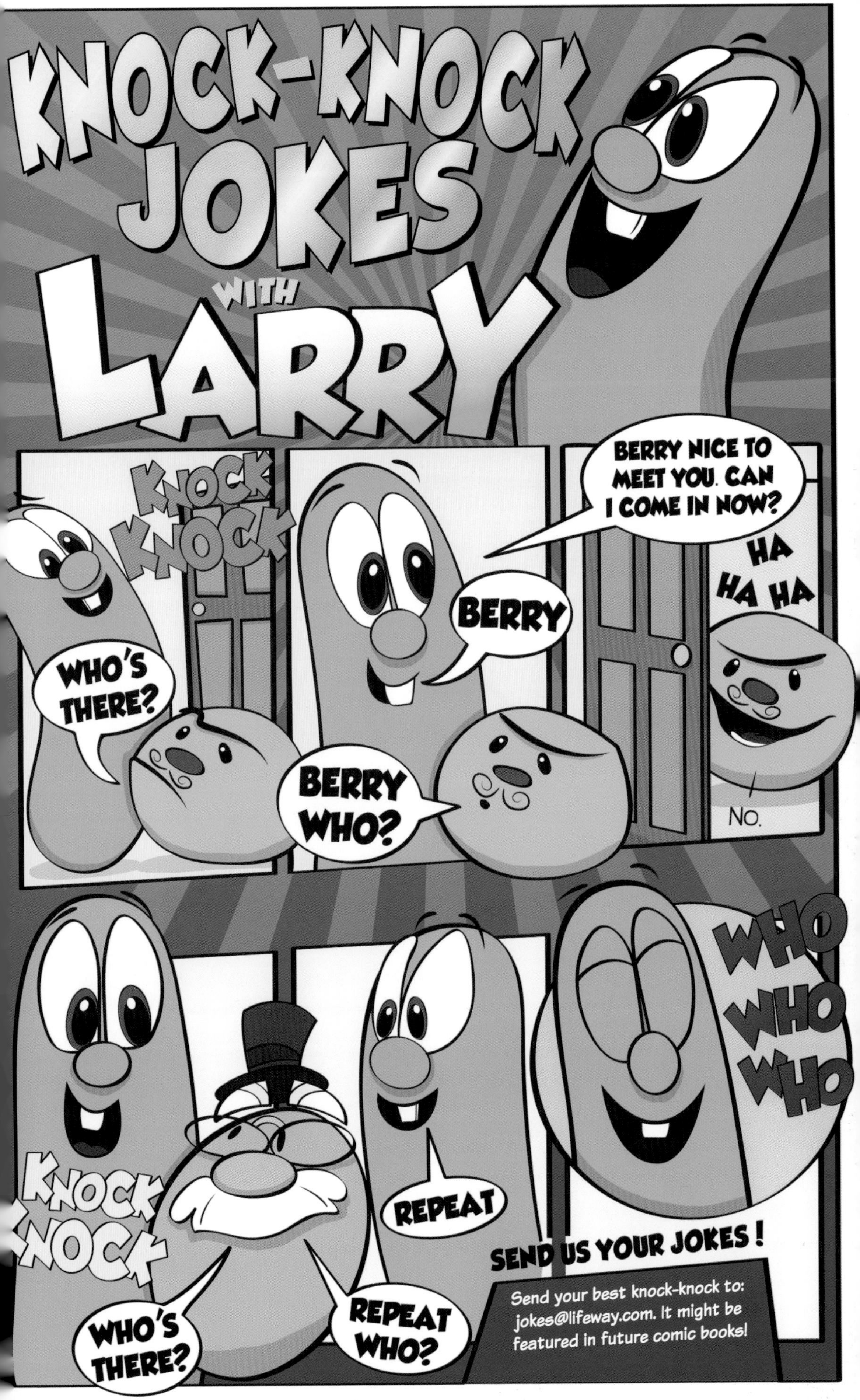
KNOCK-KNOCK JOKES WITH LARRY
KNOCK KNOCK
WHO'S THERE?
BERRY
BERRY WHO?
BERRY NICE TO MEET YOU. CAN I COME IN NOW?
HA HA HA
NO.
KNOCK KNOCK
WHO'S THERE?
REPEAT
REPEAT WHO?
WHO WHO WHO
SEND US YOUR JOKES !
Send your best knock-knock to: jokes@lifeway.com. It might be featured in future comic books!

NETFLIX

ALL-NEW ORIGINAL SERIES
COMING TO NETFLIX IN NOVEMBER

Visit VeggieTales.com for
downloadable coloring sheets,
activities and more!

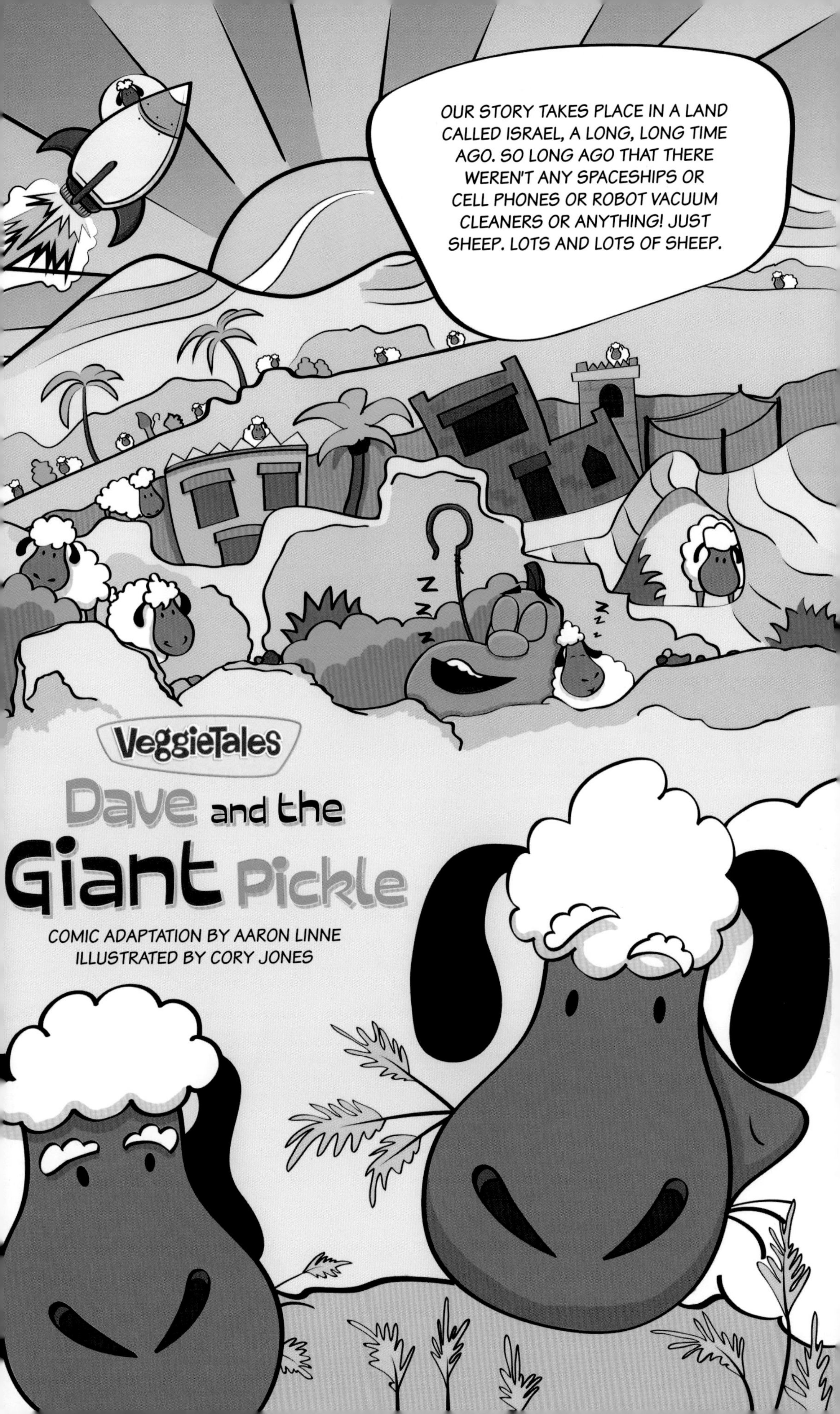
OUR STORY TAKES PLACE IN A LAND CALLED ISRAEL, A LONG, LONG TIME AGO. SO LONG AGO THAT THERE WEREN'T ANY SPACESHIPS OR CELL PHONES OR ROBOT VACUUM CLEANERS OR ANYTHING! JUST SHEEP. LOTS AND LOTS OF SHEEP.
VeggieTales
Dave and the Giant Pickle
COMIC ADAPTATION BY AARON LINNE
ILLUSTRATED BY CORY JONES

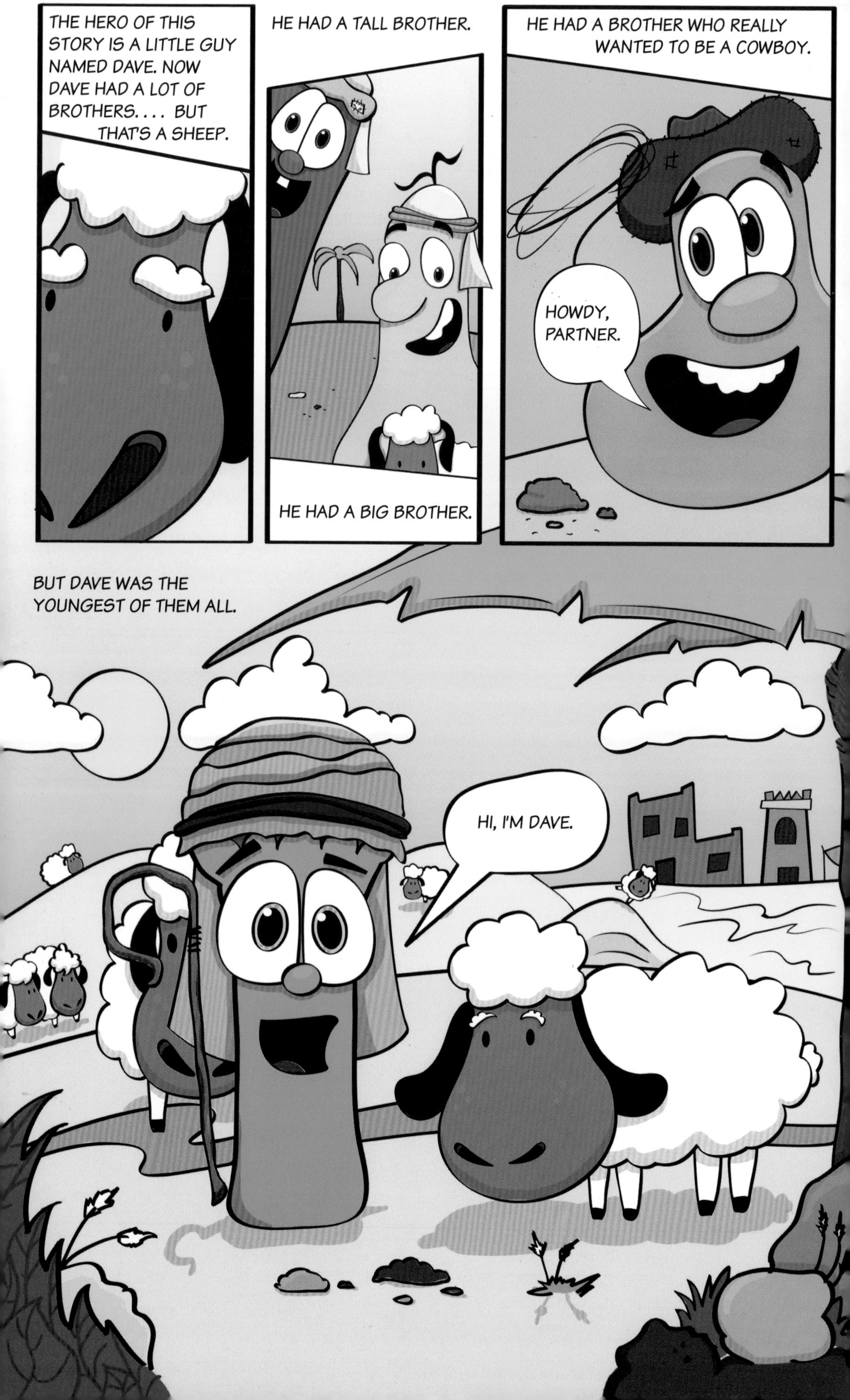
THE HERO OF THIS STORY IS A LITTLE GUY NAMED DAVE. NOW DAVE HAD A LOT OF BROTHERS. . . . BUT THAT'S A SHEEP.
HE HAD A TALL BROTHER.
HE HAD A BIG BROTHER.
HE HAD A BROTHER WHO REALLY WANTED TO BE A COWBOY.
HOWDY, PARTNER.
BUT DAVE WAS THE YOUNGEST OF THEM ALL.
HI, I'M DAVE.

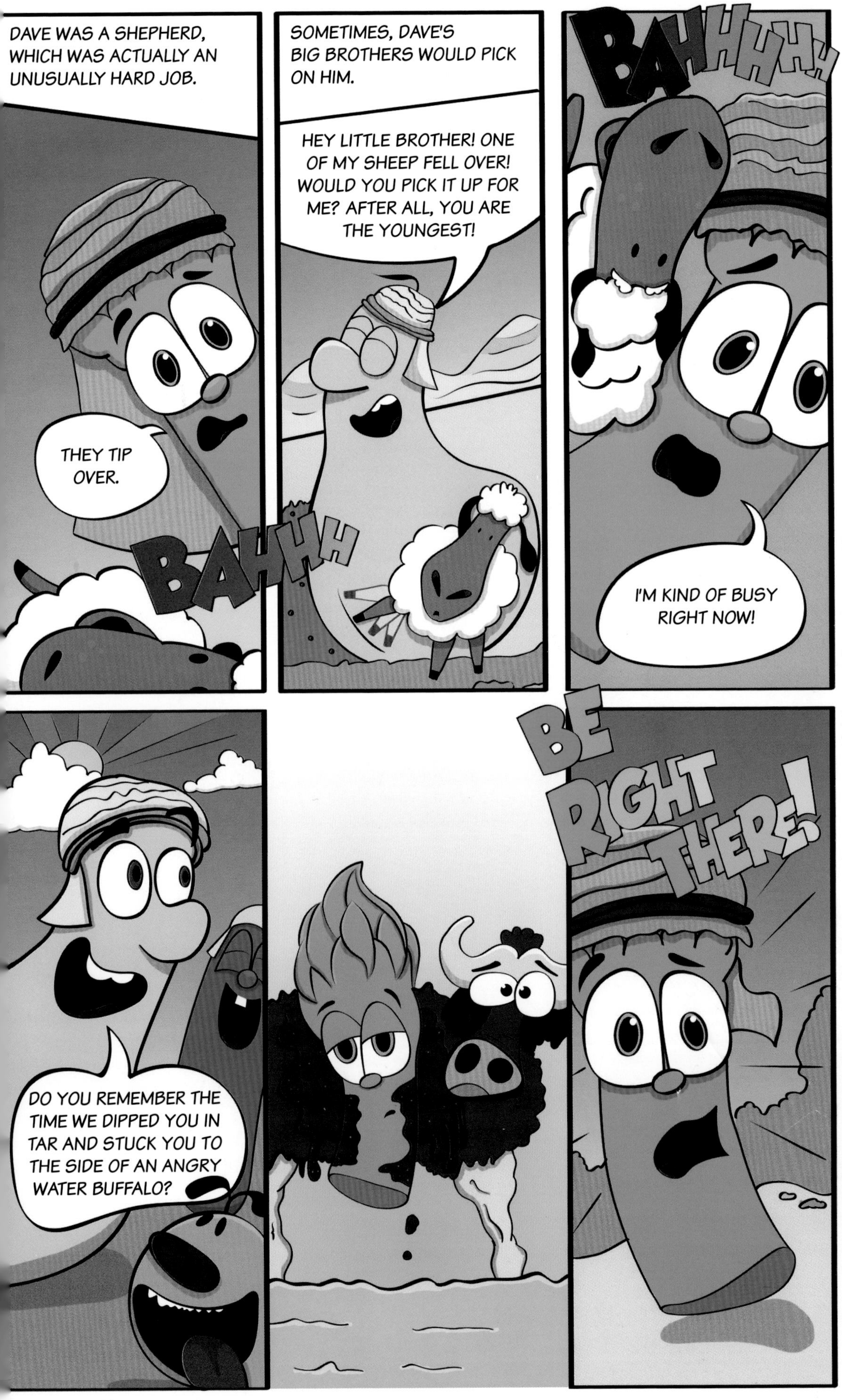
DAVE WAS A SHEPHERD, WHICH WAS ACTUALLY AN UNUSUALLY HARD JOB.
THEY TIP OVER.
BAHHH
SOMETIMES, DAVE'S BIG BROTHERS WOULD PICK ON HIM.
HEY LITTLE BROTHER! ONE OF MY SHEEP FELL OVER! WOULD YOU PICK IT UP FOR ME? AFTER ALL, YOU ARE THE YOUNGEST!
BAHHHHHH
I'M KIND OF BUSY RIGHT NOW!
DO YOU REMEMBER THE TIME WE DIPPED YOU IN TAR AND STUCK YOU TO THE SIDE OF AN ANGRY WATER BUFFALO?
BE RIGHT THERE!

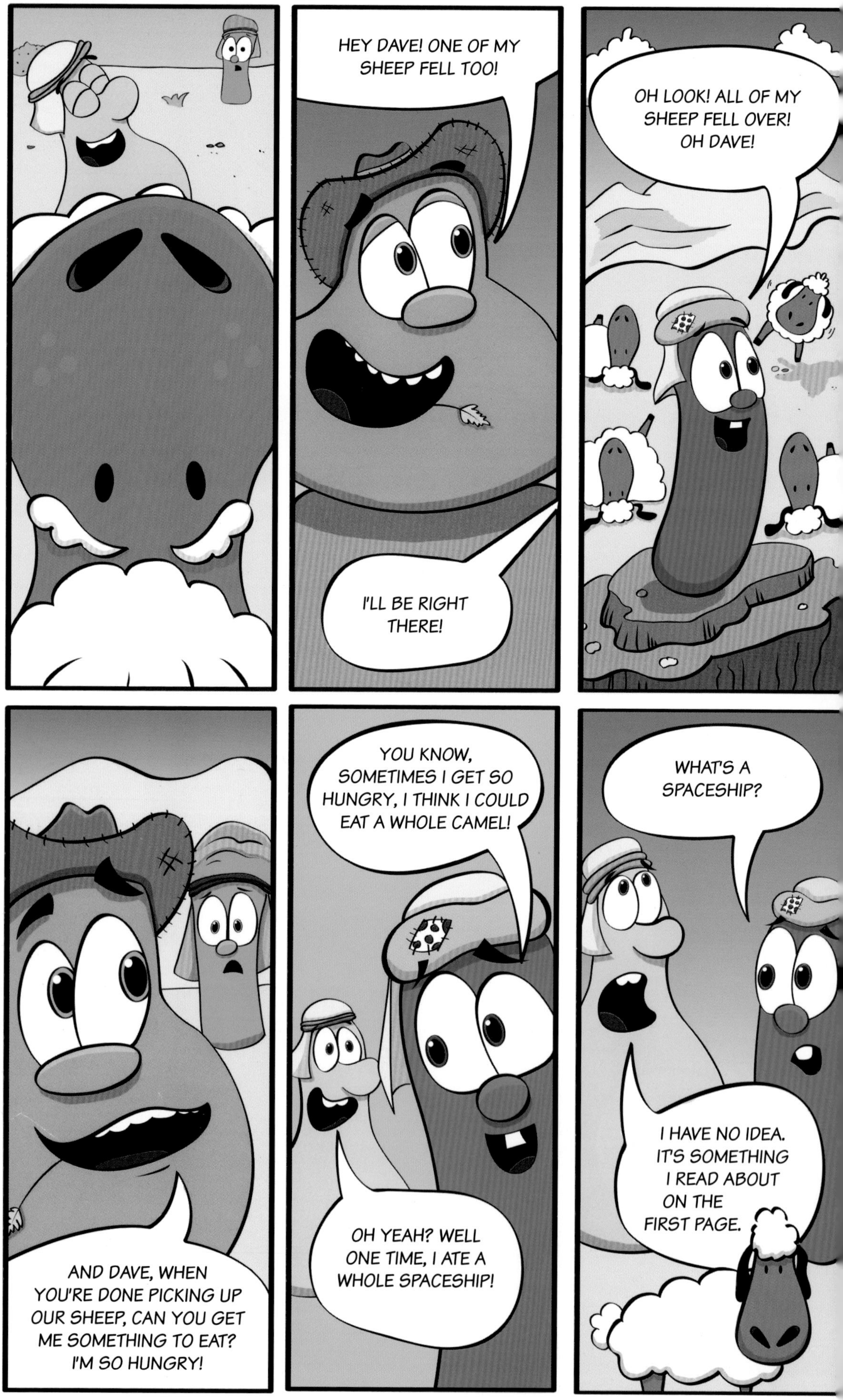
HEY DAVE! ONE OF MY SHEEP FELL TOO!
I'LL BE RIGHT THERE!
OH LOOK! ALL OF MY SHEEP FELL OVER! OH DAVE!
AND DAVE, WHEN YOU'RE DONE PICKING UP OUR SHEEP, CAN YOU GET ME SOMETHING TO EAT? I'M SO HUNGRY!
YOU KNOW, SOMETIMES I GET SO HUNGRY, I THINK I COULD EAT A WHOLE CAMEL!
OH YEAH? WELL ONE TIME, I ATE A WHOLE SPACESHIP!
WHAT'S A SPACESHIP?
I HAVE NO IDEA. IT'S SOMETHING I READ ABOUT ON THE FIRST PAGE.

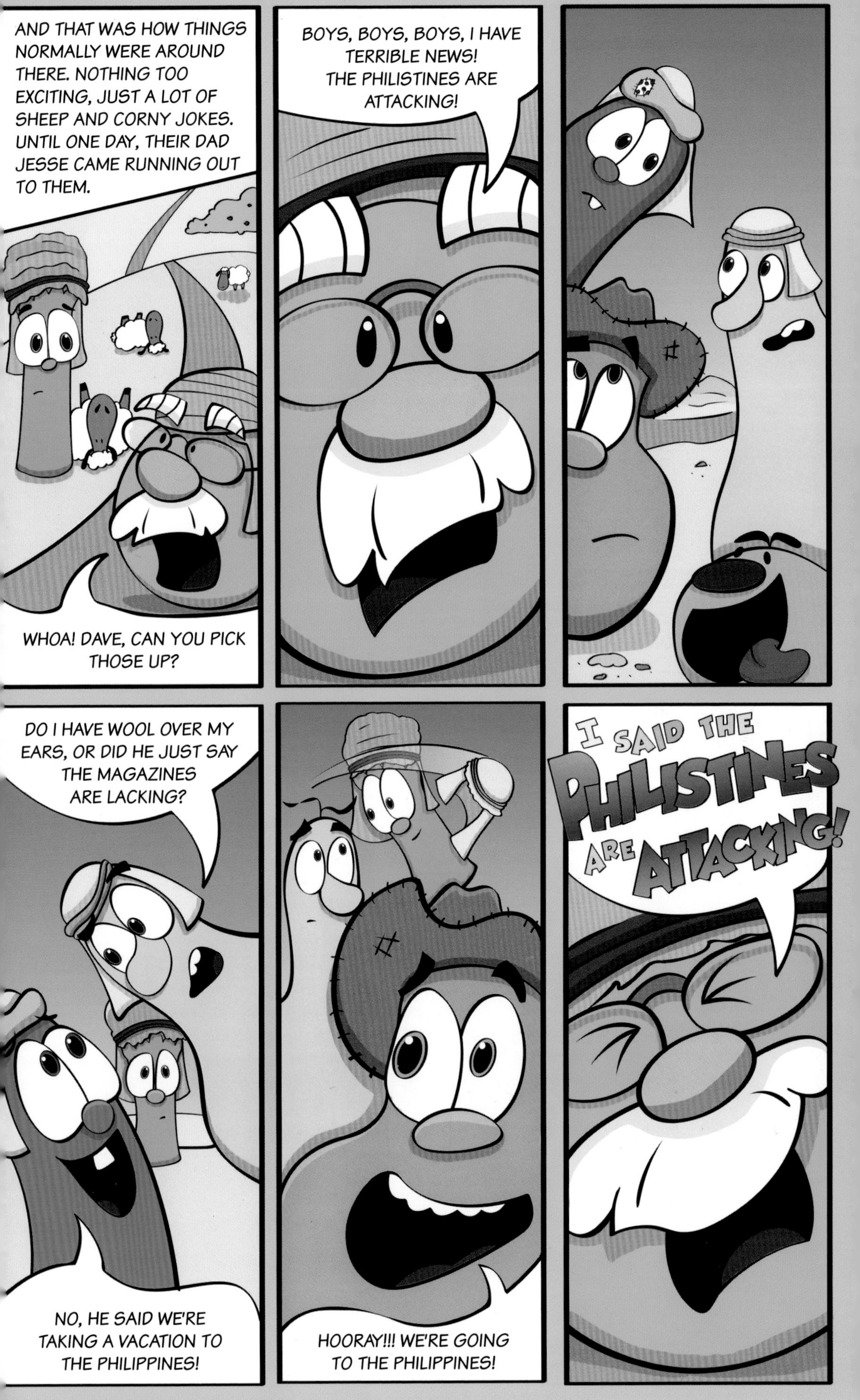
AND THAT WAS HOW THINGS NORMALLY WERE AROUND THERE. NOTHING TOO EXCITING, JUST A LOT OF SHEEP AND CORNY JOKES. UNTIL ONE DAY, THEIR DAD JESSE CAME RUNNING OUT TO THEM.
WHOA! DAVE, CAN YOU PICK THOSE UP?
BOYS, BOYS, BOYS, I HAVE TERRIBLE NEWS! THE PHILISTINES ARE ATTACKING!
DO I HAVE WOOL OVER MY EARS, OR DID HE JUST SAY THE MAGAZINES ARE LACKING?
NO, HE SAID WE'RE TAKING A VACATION TO THE PHILIPPINES!
HOORAY!!! WE'RE GOING TO THE PHILIPPINES!
I SAID THE PHILISTINES ARE ATTACKING!

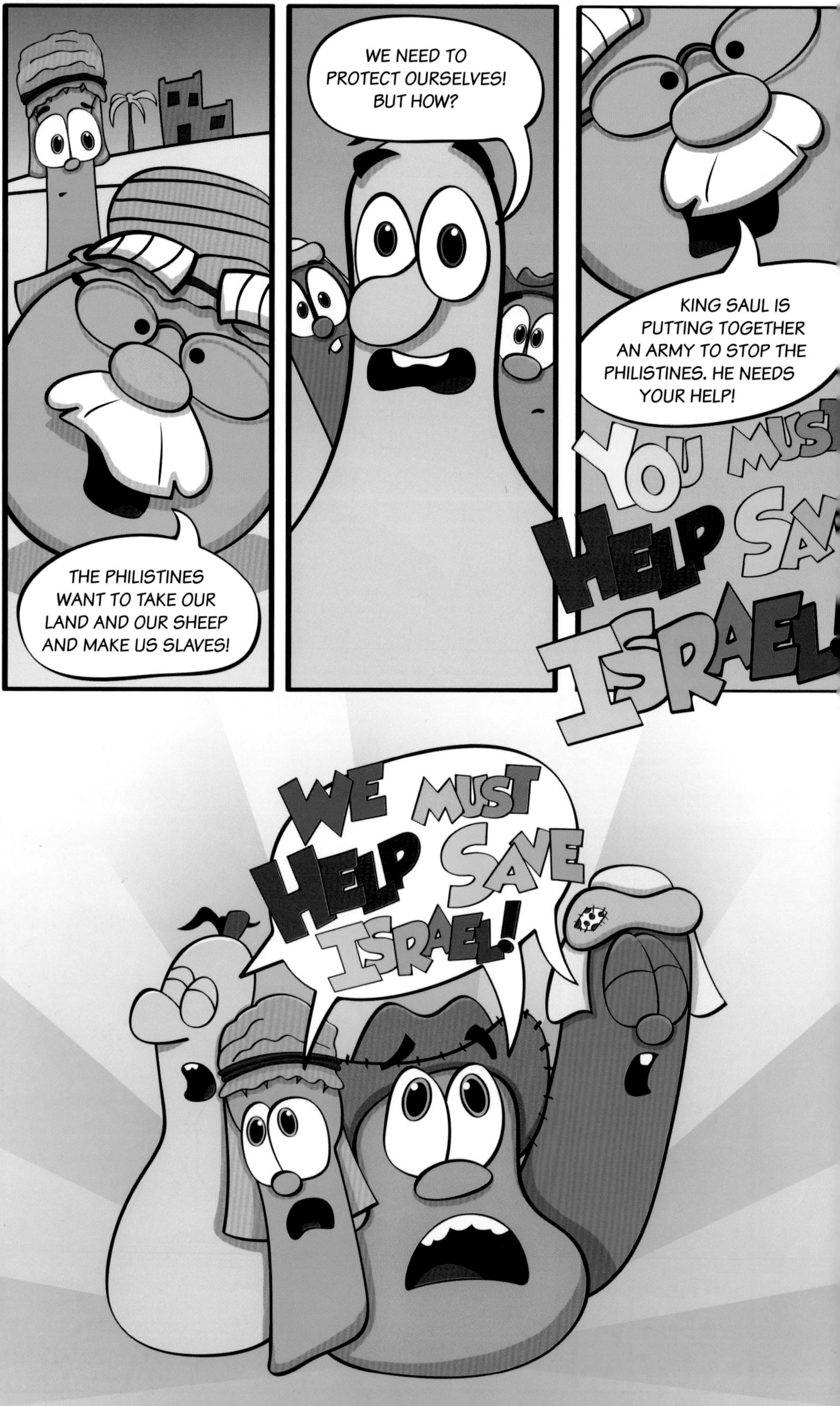
THE PHILISTINES WANT TO TAKE OUR LAND AND OUR SHEEP AND MAKE US SLAVES!
WE NEED TO PROTECT OURSELVES! BUT HOW?
KING SAUL IS PUTTING TOGETHER AN ARMY TO STOP THE PHILISTINES. HE NEEDS YOUR HELP!
YOU MUST HELP SAVE ISRAEL!
WE MUST HELP SAVE ISRAEL!

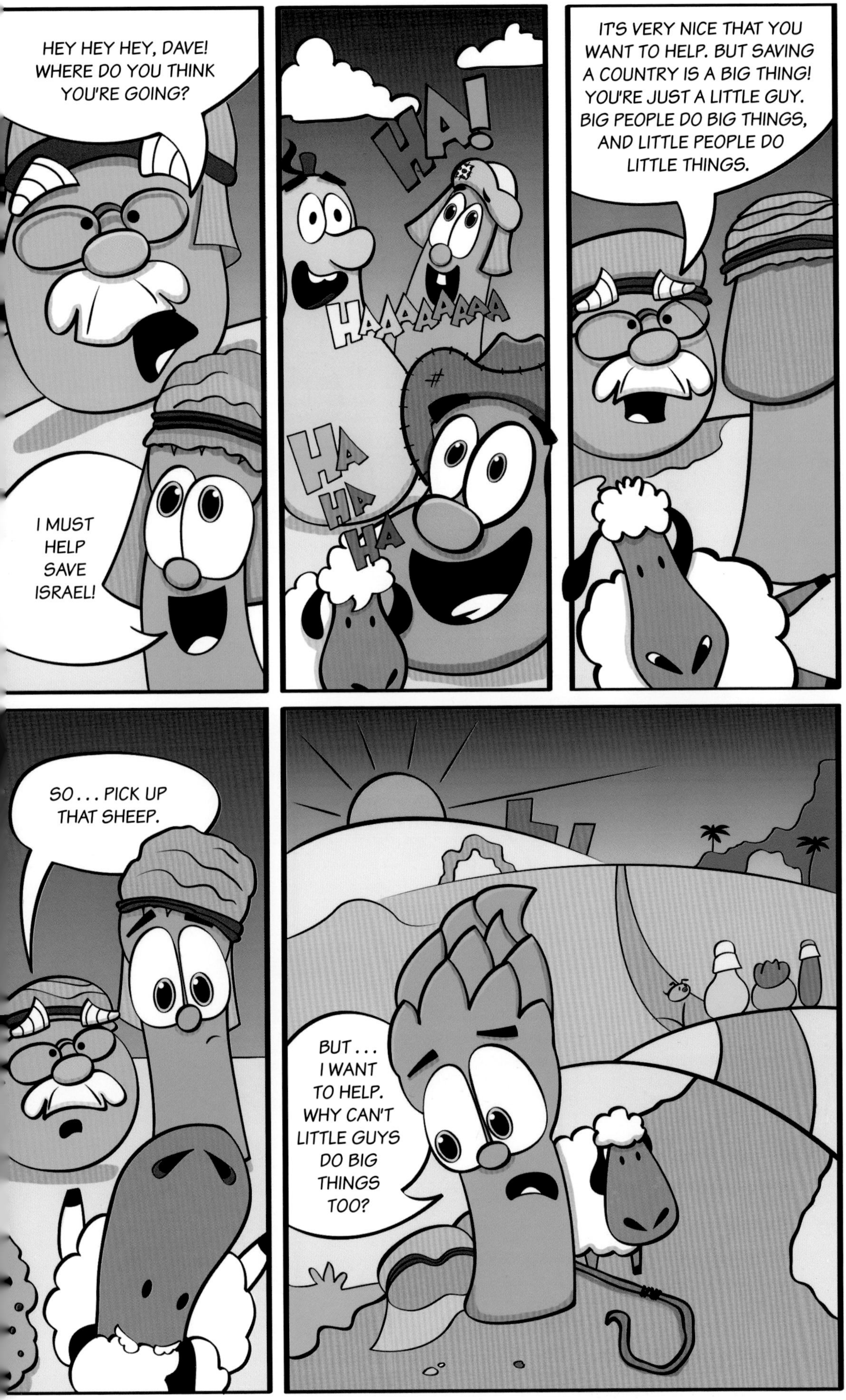
HEY HEY HEY, DAVE! WHERE DO YOU THINK YOU'RE GOING?
I MUST HELP SAVE ISRAEL!
HA!
HAAAAAAA
HA HA HA HA
IT'S VERY NICE THAT YOU WANT TO HELP. BUT SAVING A COUNTRY IS A BIG THING! YOU'RE JUST A LITTLE GUY. BIG PEOPLE DO BIG THINGS, AND LITTLE PEOPLE DO LITTLE THINGS.
SO . . . PICK UP THAT SHEEP.
BUT . . . I WANT TO HELP. WHY CAN'T LITTLE GUYS DO BIG THINGS TOO?

BY THE TIME DAVE'S BROTHERS REACHED THE BATTLEFIELD, THE PHILISTINES WERE ALREADY PREPARING FOR BATTLE WITH THE ISRAELITES.

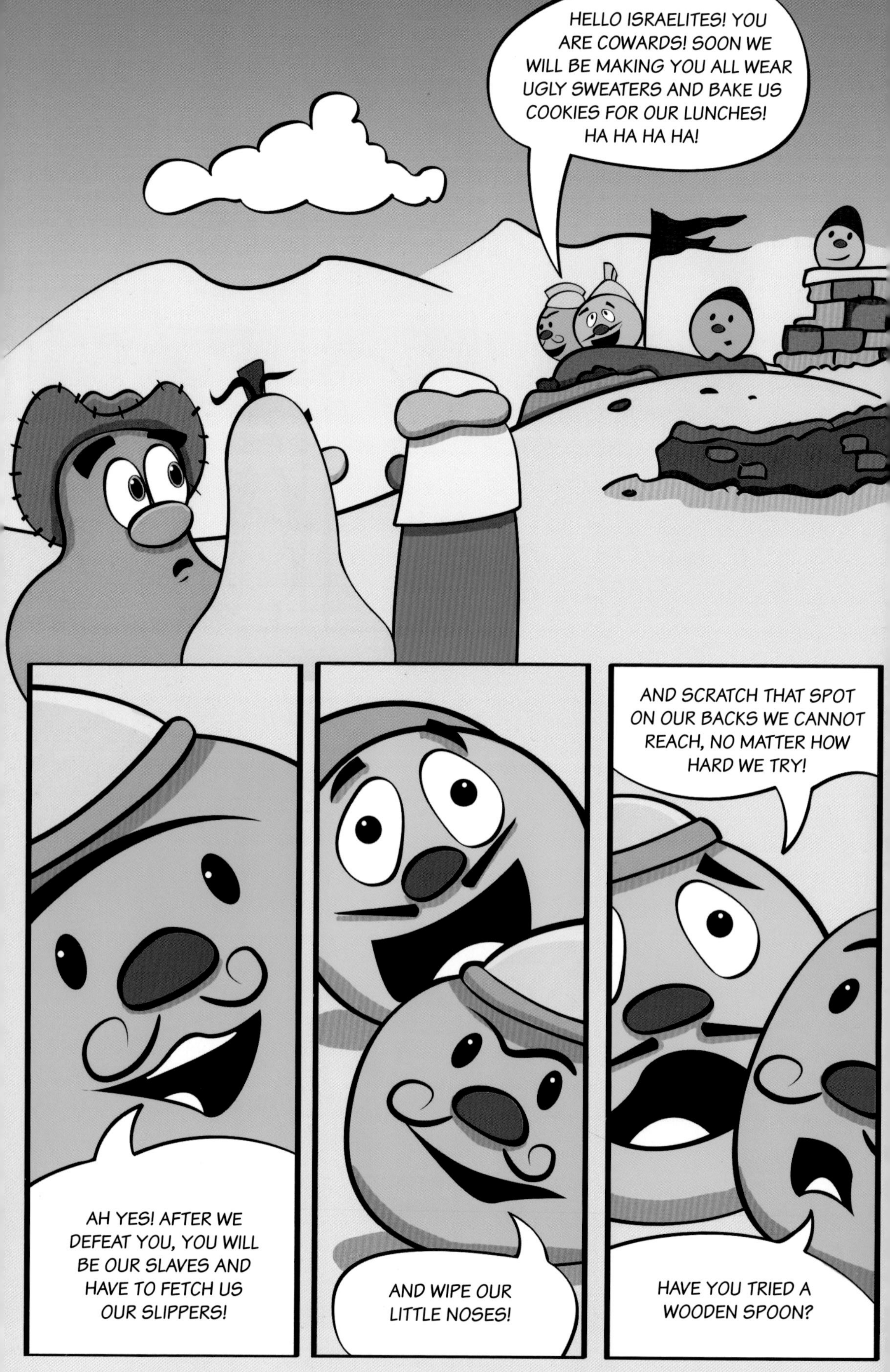

HELLO ISRAELITES! YOU ARE COWARDS! SOON WE WILL BE MAKING YOU ALL WEAR UGLY SWEATERS AND BAKE US COOKIES FOR OUR LUNCHES! HA HA HA HA!
AH YES! AFTER WE DEFEAT YOU, YOU WILL BE OUR SLAVES AND HAVE TO FETCH US OUR SLIPPERS!
AND WIPE OUR LITTLE NOSES!
AND SCRATCH THAT SPOT ON OUR BACKS WE CANNOT REACH, NO MATTER HOW HARD WE TRY!
HAVE YOU TRIED A WOODEN SPOON?

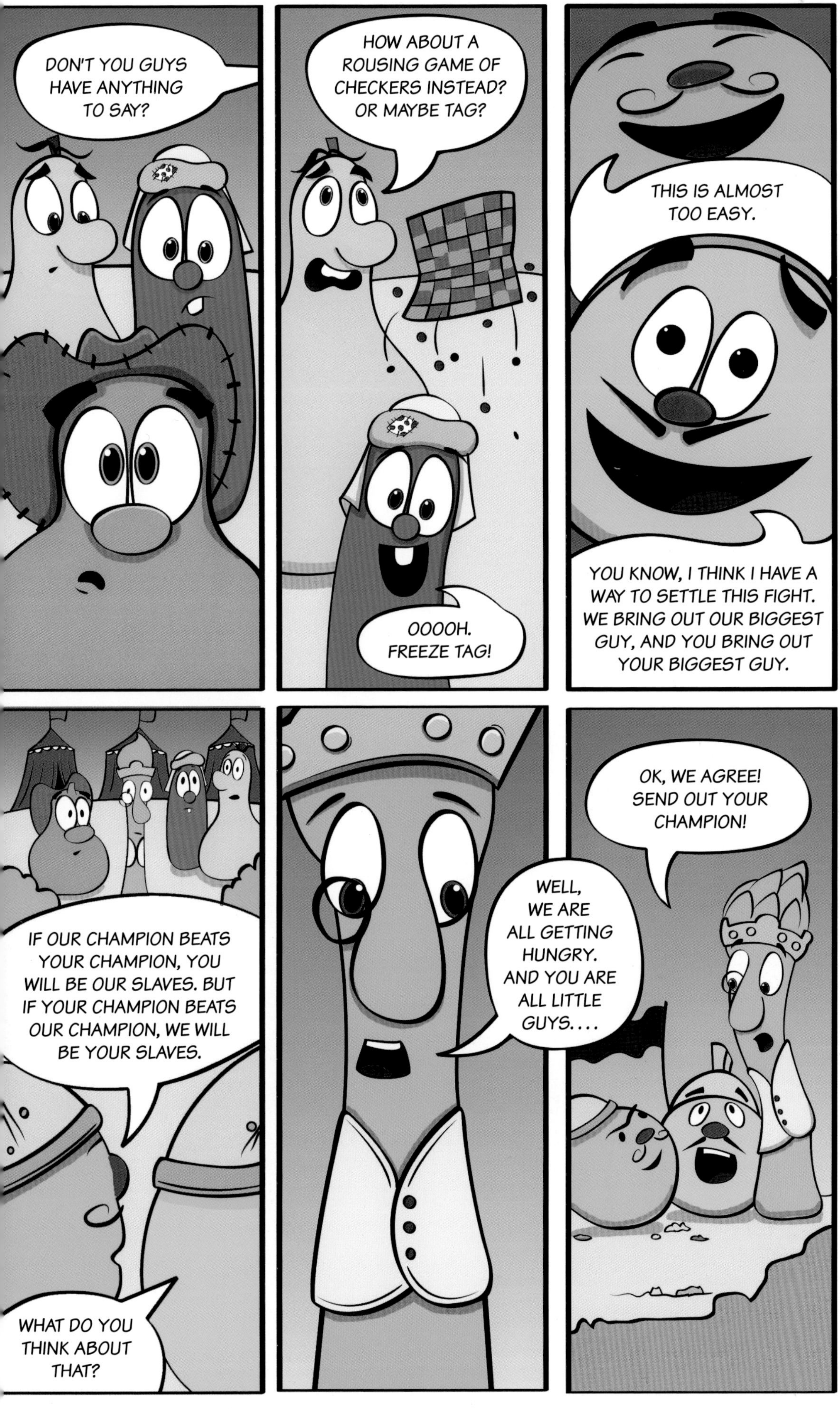
DON'T YOU GUYS HAVE ANYTHING TO SAY?
HOW ABOUT A ROUSING GAME OF CHECKERS INSTEAD? OR MAYBE TAG?
OOOOH. FREEZE TAG!
THIS IS ALMOST TOO EASY.
YOU KNOW, I THINK I HAVE A WAY TO SETTLE THIS FIGHT. WE BRING OUT OUR BIGGEST GUY, AND YOU BRING OUT YOUR BIGGEST GUY.
IF OUR CHAMPION BEATS YOUR CHAMPION, YOU WILL BE OUR SLAVES. BUT IF YOUR CHAMPION BEATS OUR CHAMPION, WE WILL BE YOUR SLAVES.
WHAT DO YOU THINK ABOUT THAT?
WELL, WE ARE ALL GETTING HUNGRY. AND YOU ARE ALL LITTLE GUYS....
OK, WE AGREE! SEND OUT YOUR CHAMPION!

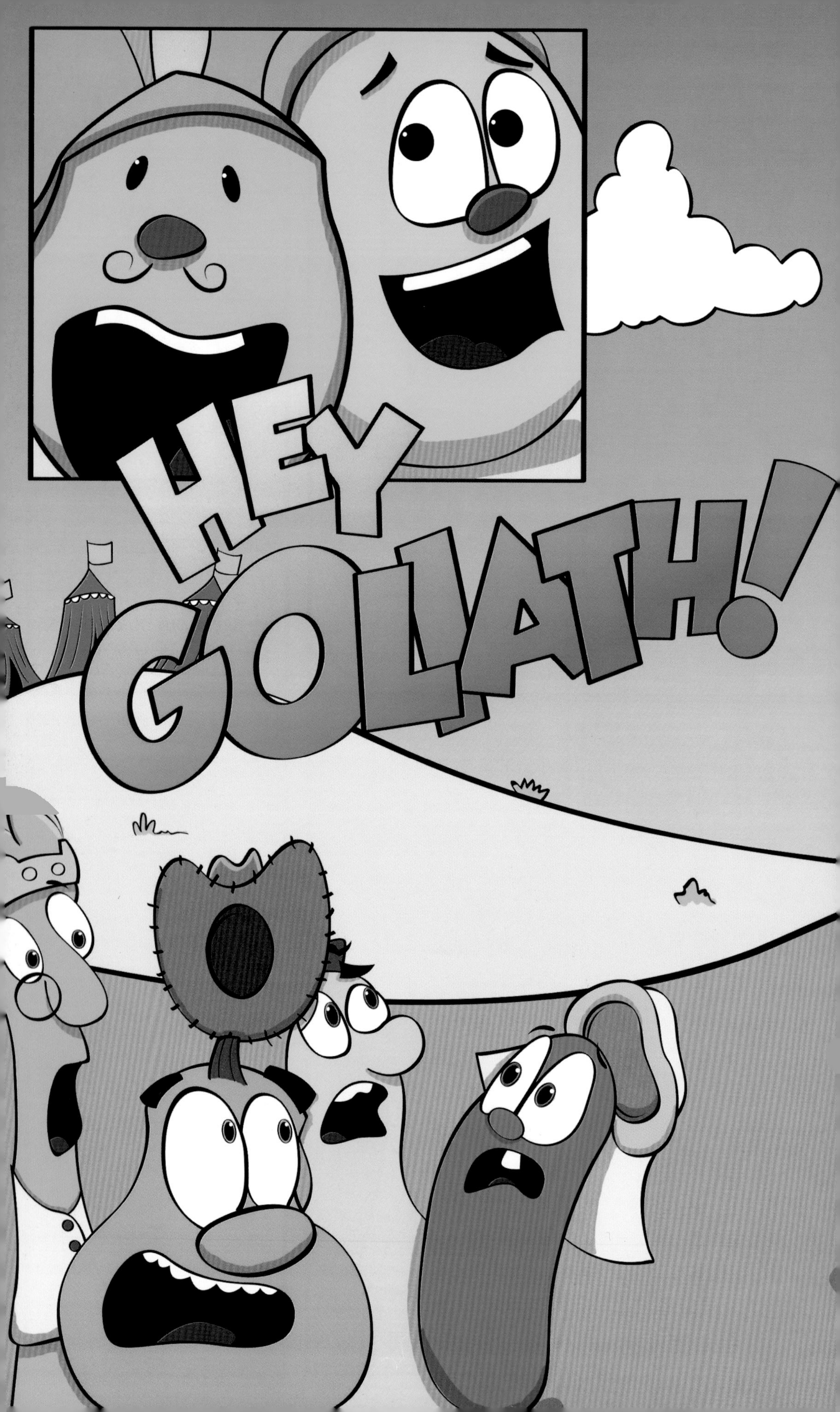
HEY GOLIATH!

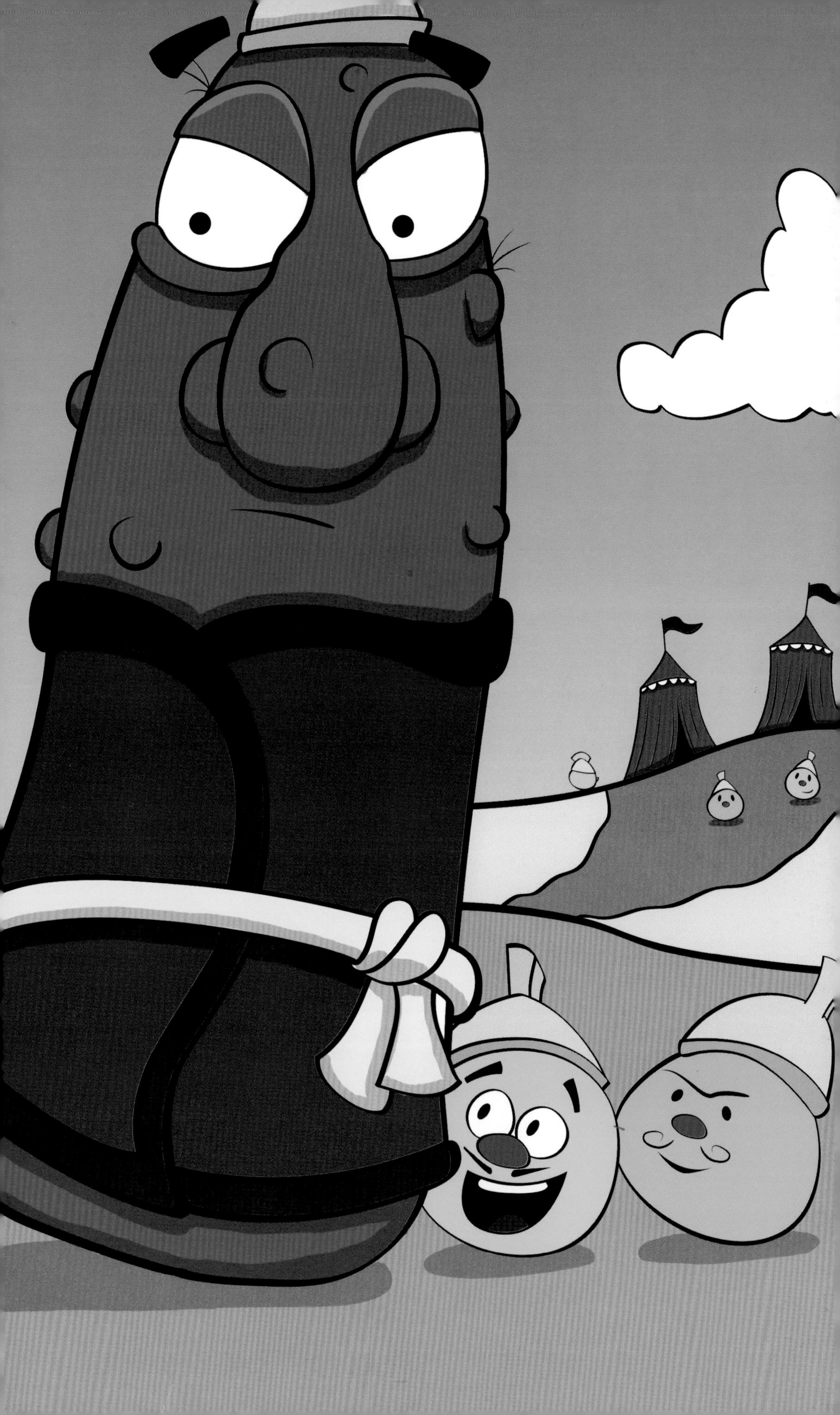

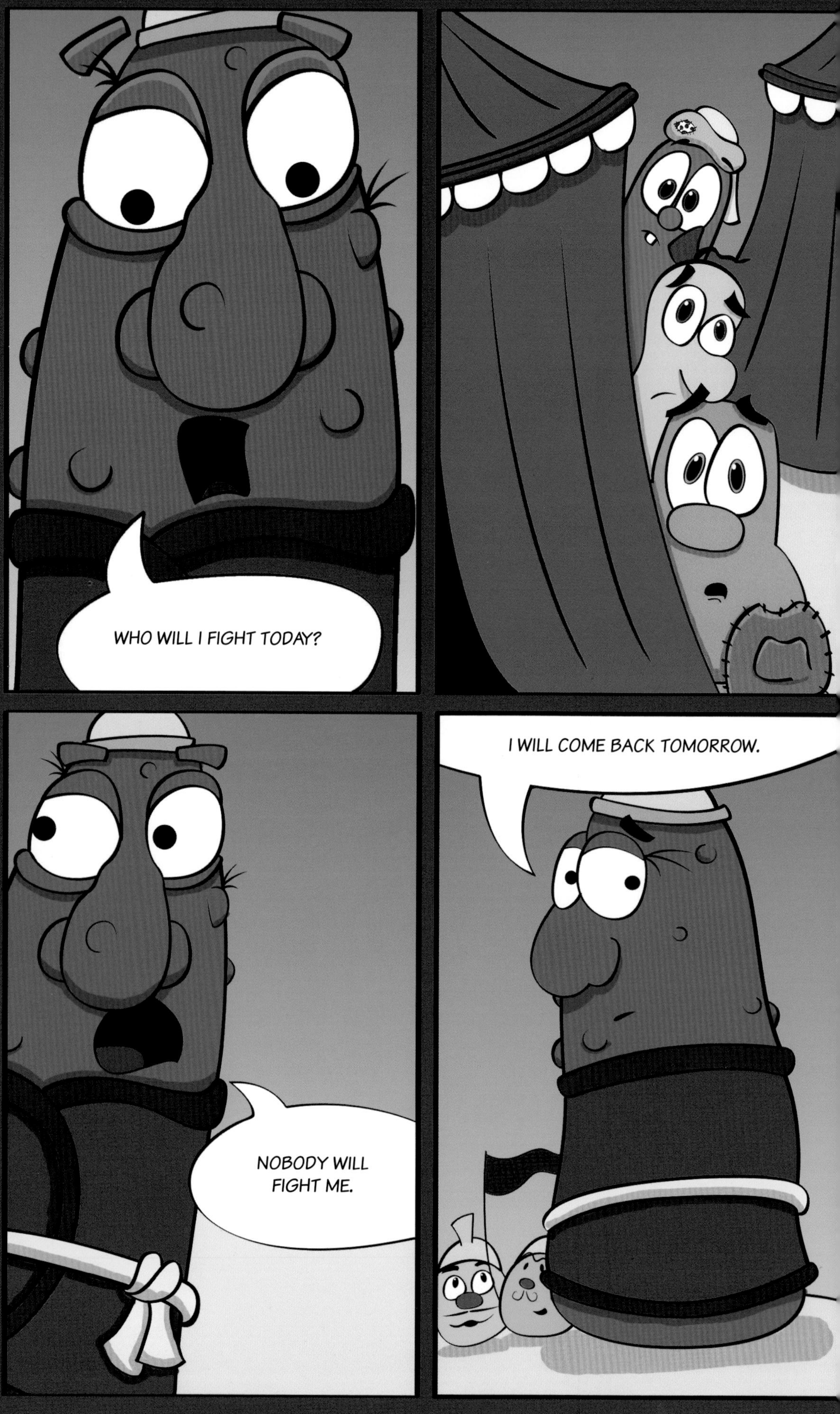
WHO WILL I FIGHT TODAY?
NOBODY WILL FIGHT ME.
I WILL COME BACK TOMORROW.

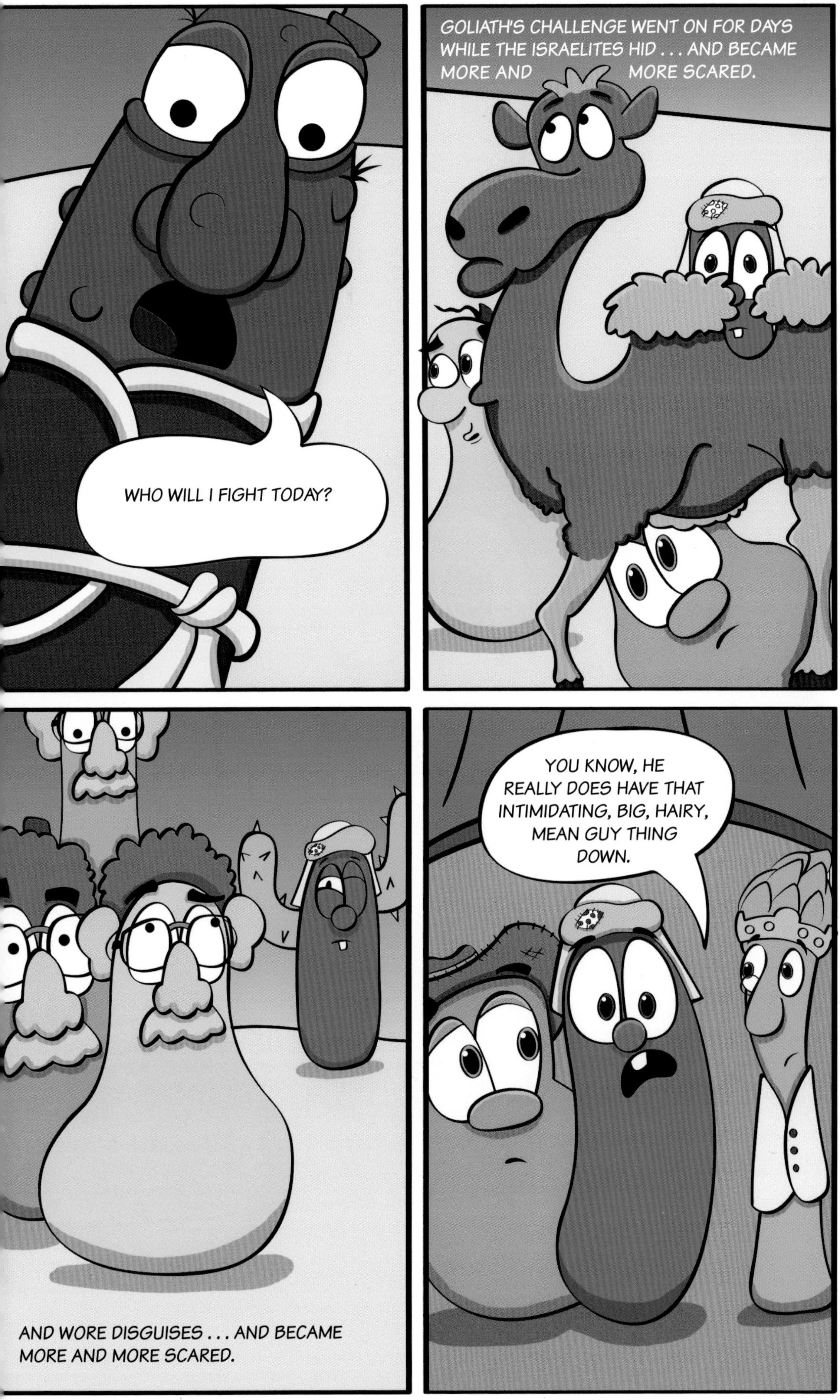
WHO WILL I FIGHT TODAY?
GOLIATH'S CHALLENGE WENT ON FOR DAYS WHILE THE ISRAELITES HID . . . AND BECAME MORE AND MORE SCARED.
AND WORE DISGUISES . . . AND BECAME MORE AND MORE SCARED.
YOU KNOW, HE REALLY DOES HAVE THAT INTIMIDATING, BIG, HAIRY, MEAN GUY THING DOWN.

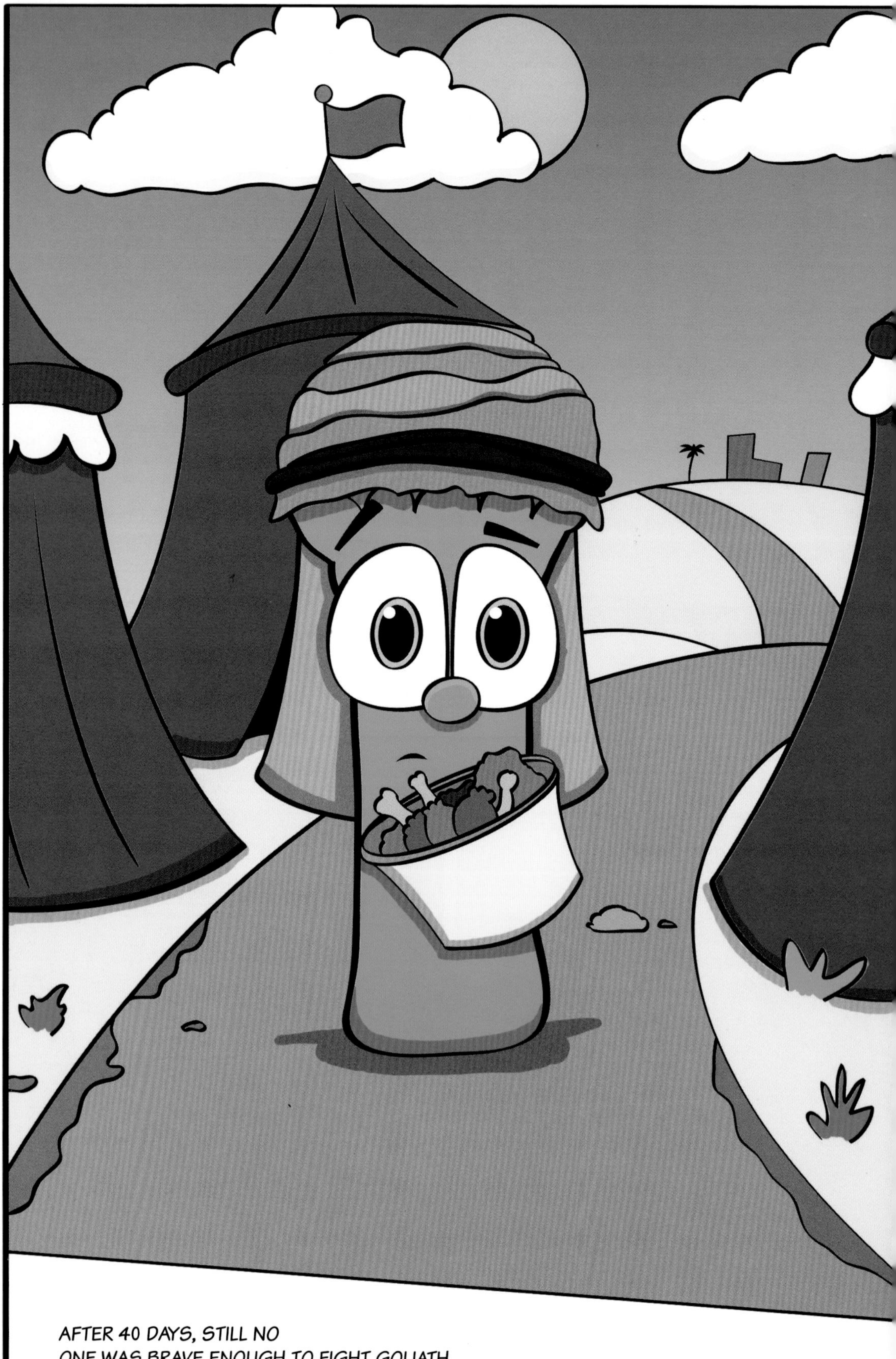

AFTER 40 DAYS, STILL NO
ONE WAS BRAVE ENOUGH TO FIGHT GOLIATH.

WORD HAD GOTTEN BACK TO DAVE THAT HIS BROTHERS WERE REALLY WANTING SOME FRIED CHICKEN, SO HE BROUGHT SOME RIGHT TO THE BATTLE LINES.

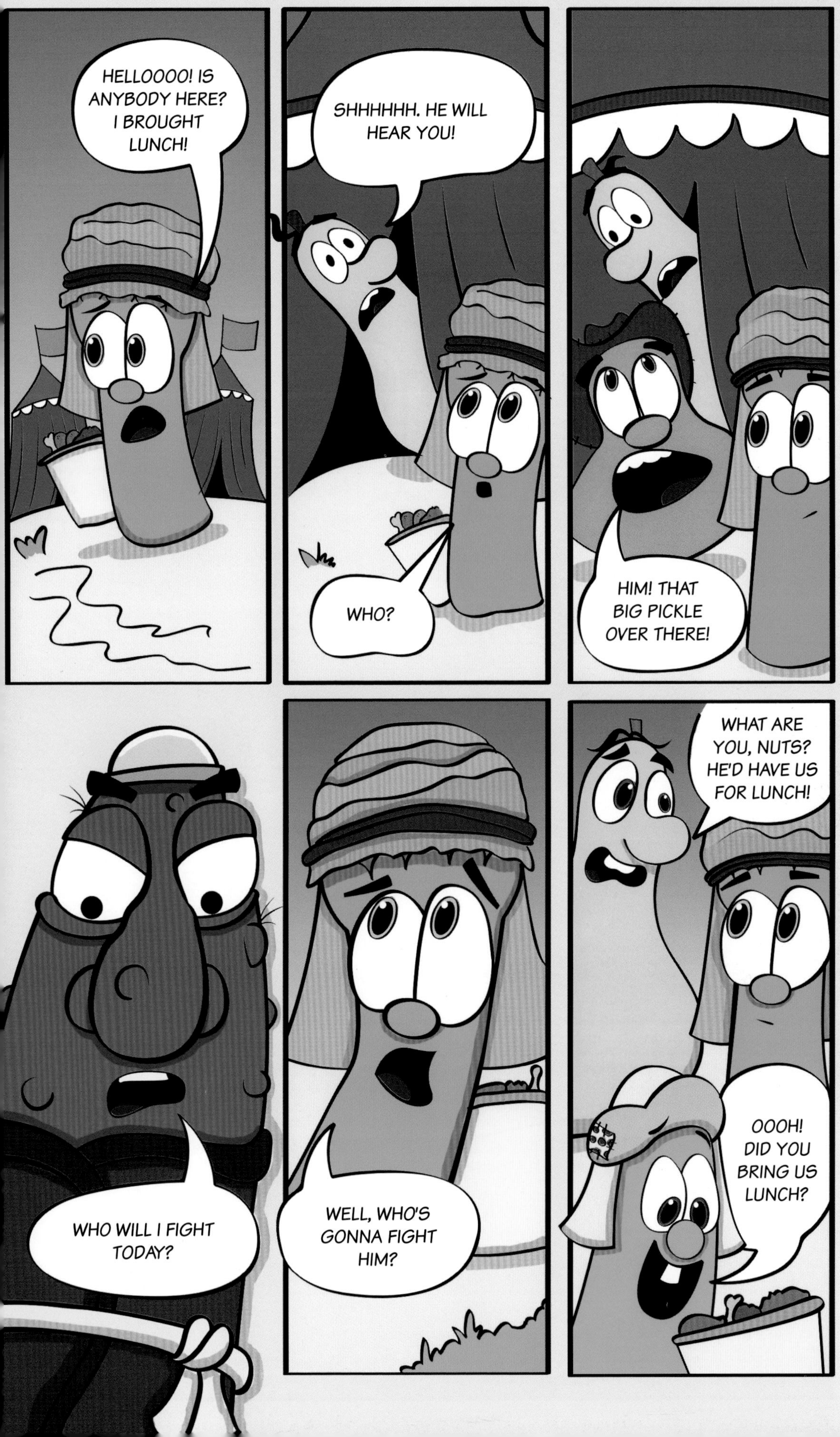

HELLOOOO! IS ANYBODY HERE? I BROUGHT LUNCH!
SHHHHHH. HE WILL HEAR YOU!
WHO?
HIM! THAT BIG PICKLE OVER THERE!
WHO WILL I FIGHT TODAY?
WELL, WHO'S GONNA FIGHT HIM?
WHAT ARE YOU, NUTS? HE'D HAVE US FOR LUNCH!
OOOH! DID YOU BRING US LUNCH?

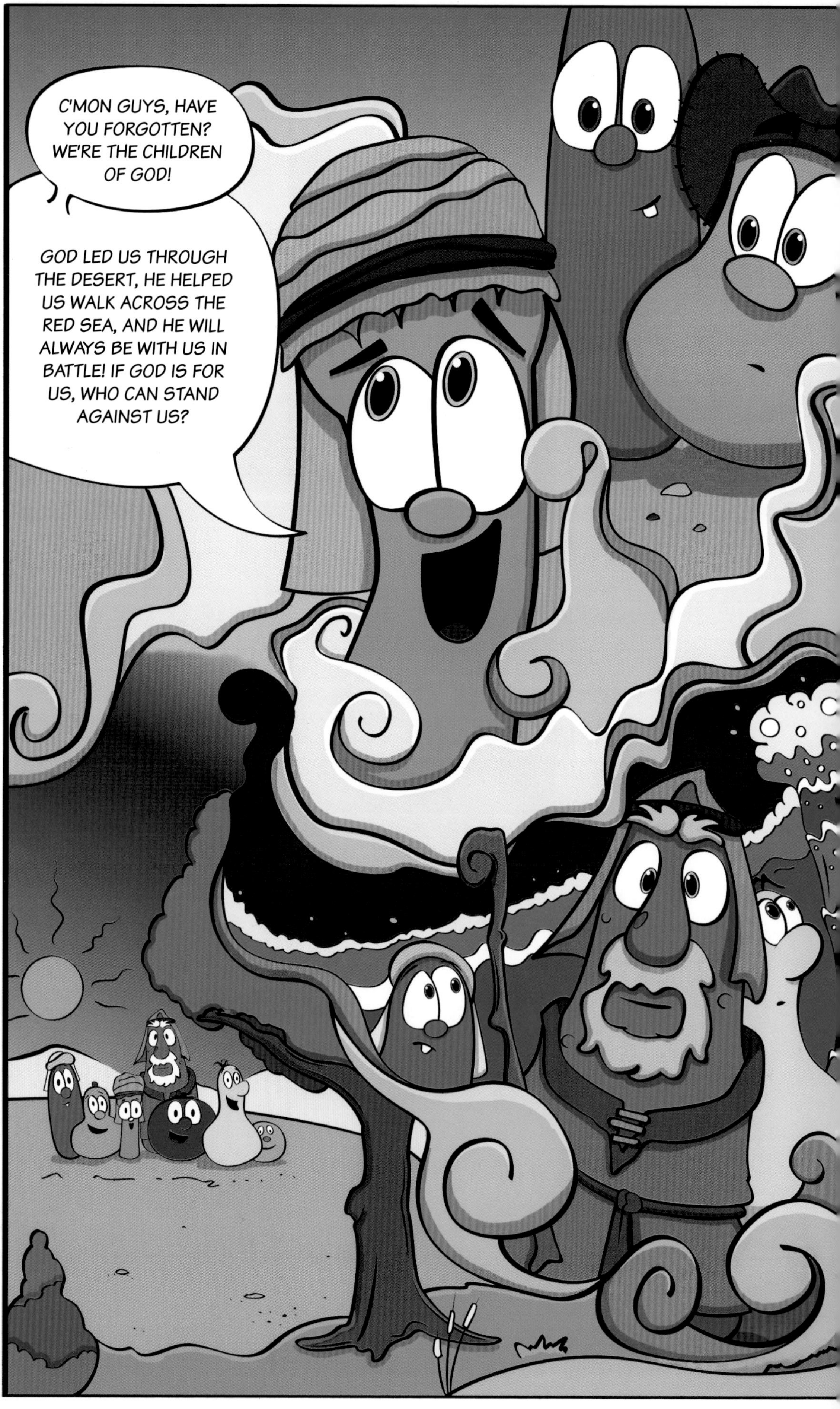
C'MON GUYS, HAVE YOU FORGOTTEN? WE'RE THE CHILDREN OF GOD!
GOD LED US THROUGH THE DESERT, HE HELPED US WALK ACROSS THE RED SEA, AND HE WILL ALWAYS BE WITH US IN BATTLE! IF GOD IS FOR US, WHO CAN STAND AGAINST US?

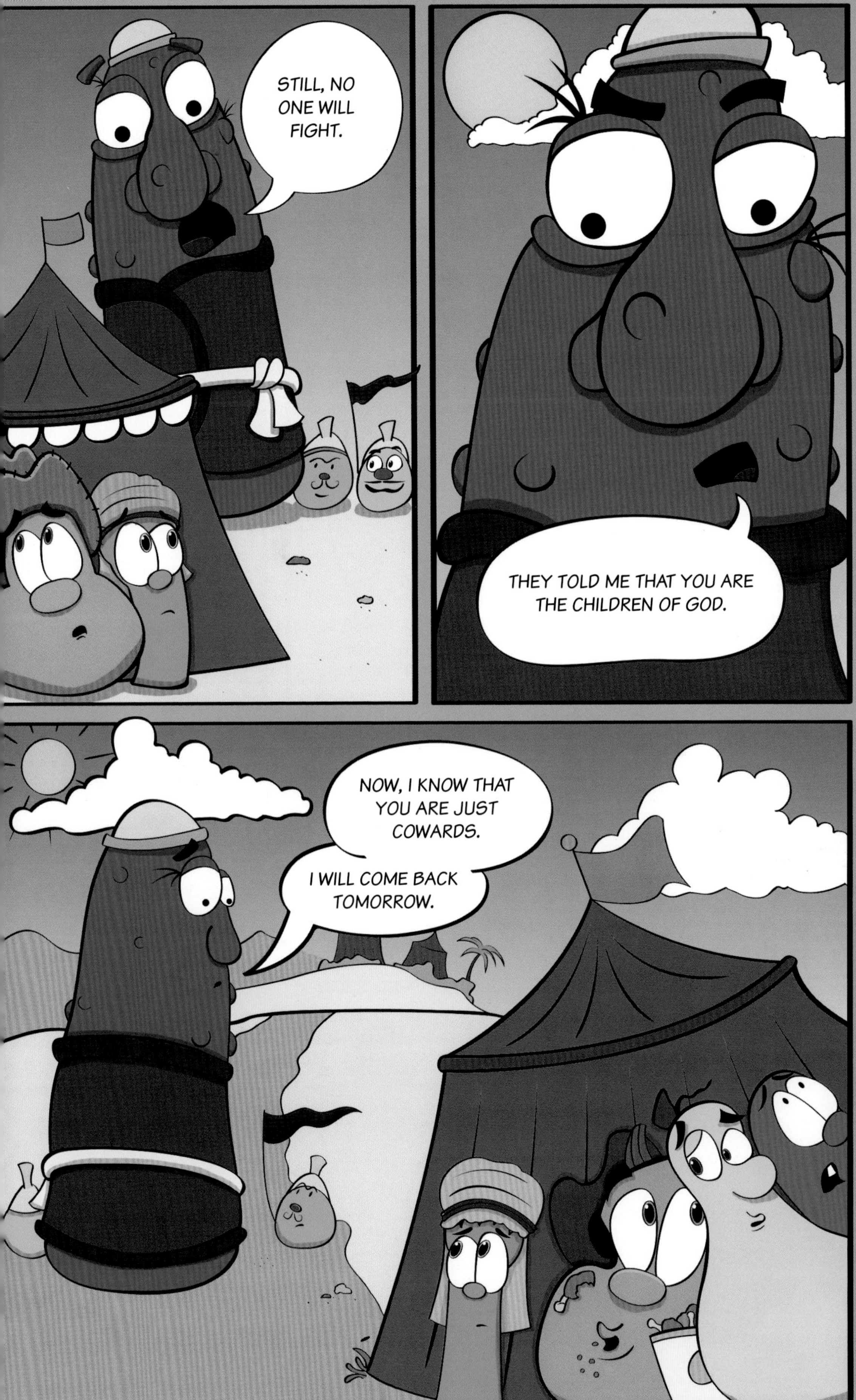
STILL, NO ONE WILL FIGHT.
THEY TOLD ME THAT YOU ARE THE CHILDREN OF GOD.
NOW, I KNOW THAT YOU ARE JUST COWARDS.
I WILL COME BACK TOMORROW.

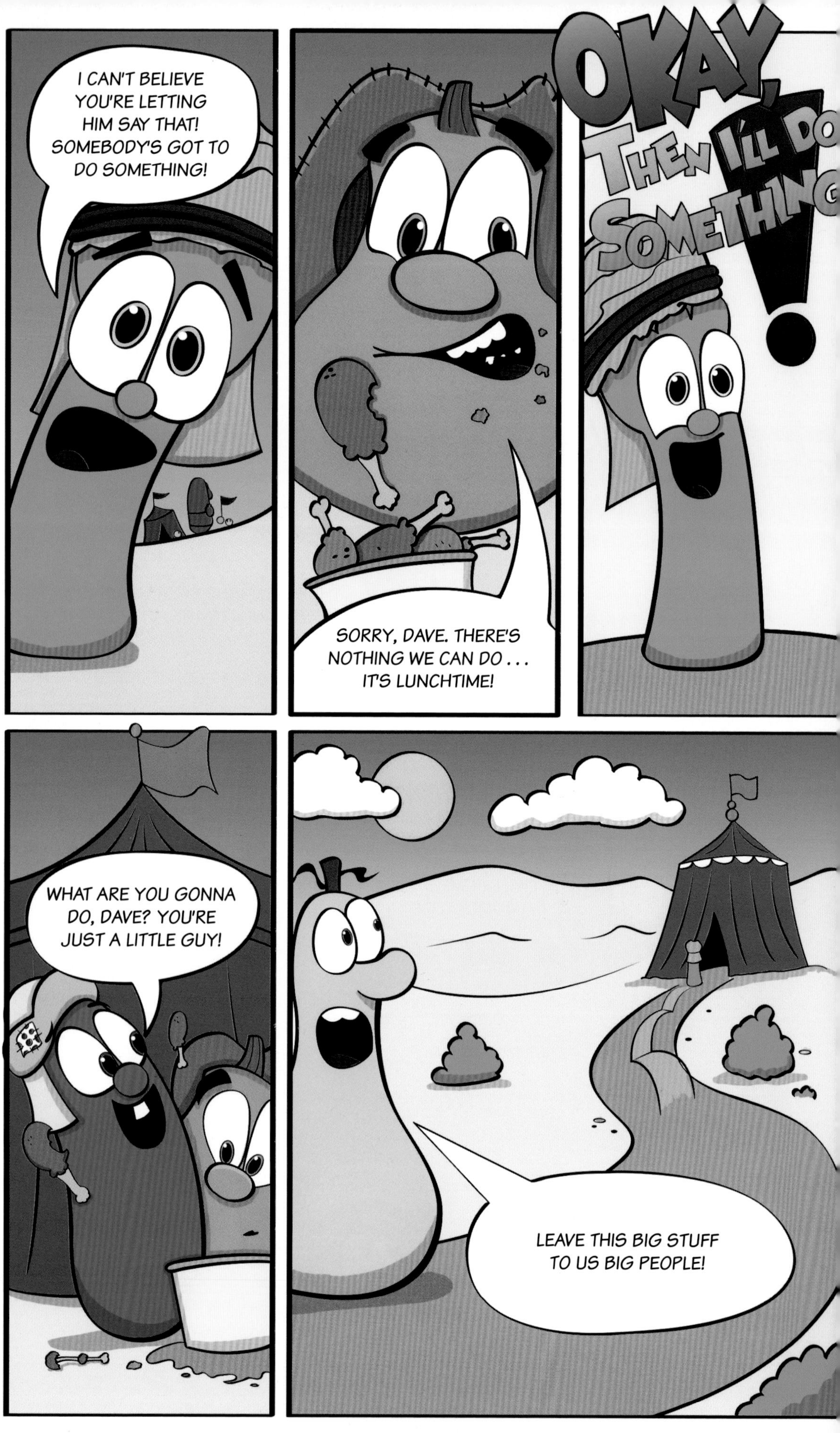
I CAN'T BELIEVE YOU'RE LETTING HIM SAY THAT! SOMEBODY'S GOT TO DO SOMETHING!
SORRY, DAVE. THERE'S NOTHING WE CAN DO . . . IT'S LUNCHTIME!
OKAY, THEN I'LL DO SOMETHING!
WHAT ARE YOU GONNA DO, DAVE? YOU'RE JUST A LITTLE GUY!
LEAVE THIS BIG STUFF TO US BIG PEOPLE!

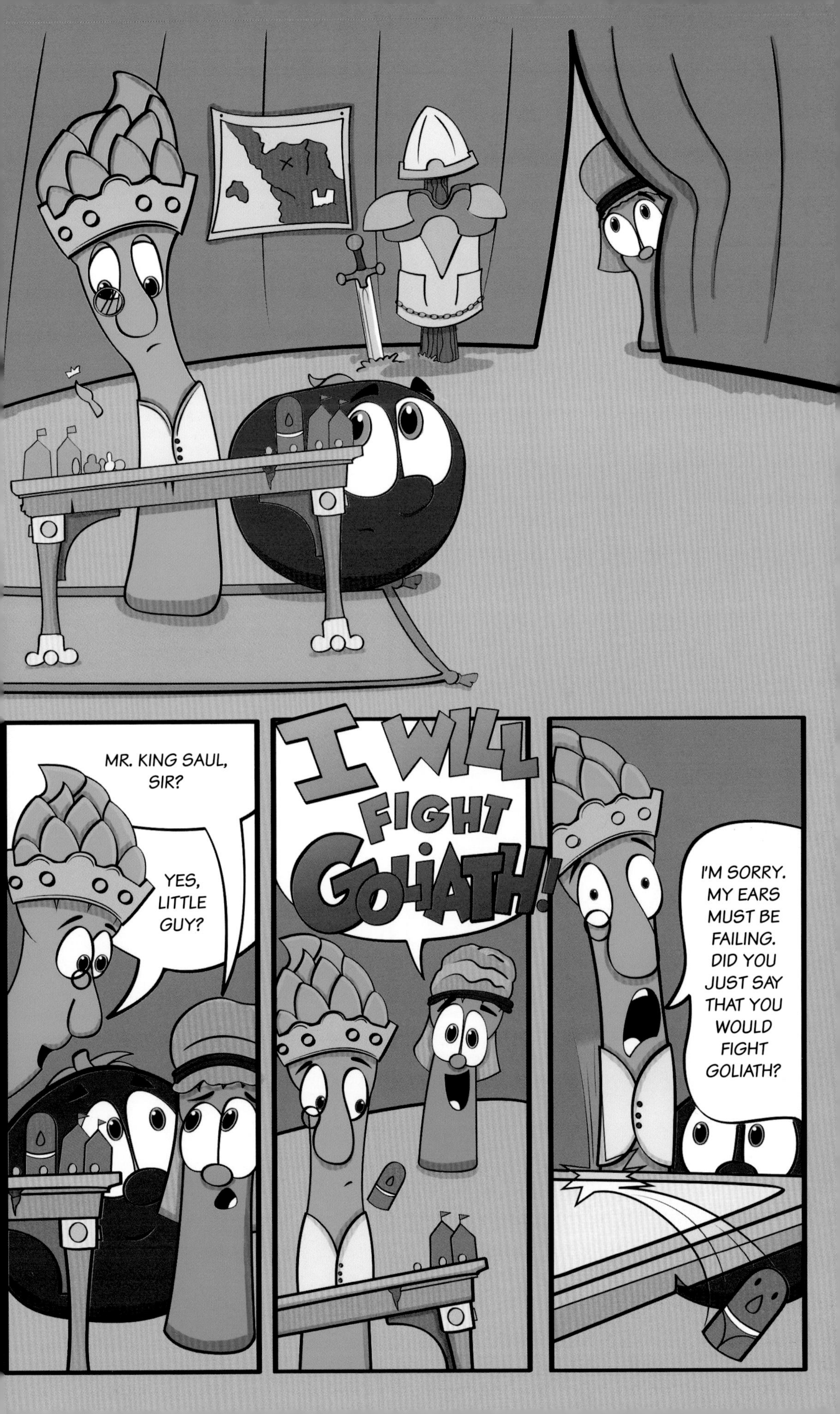
MR. KING SAUL, SIR?
YES, LITTLE GUY?
I WILL FIGHT GOLIATH!
I'M SORRY. MY EARS MUST BE FAILING. DID YOU JUST SAY THAT YOU WOULD FIGHT GOLIATH?

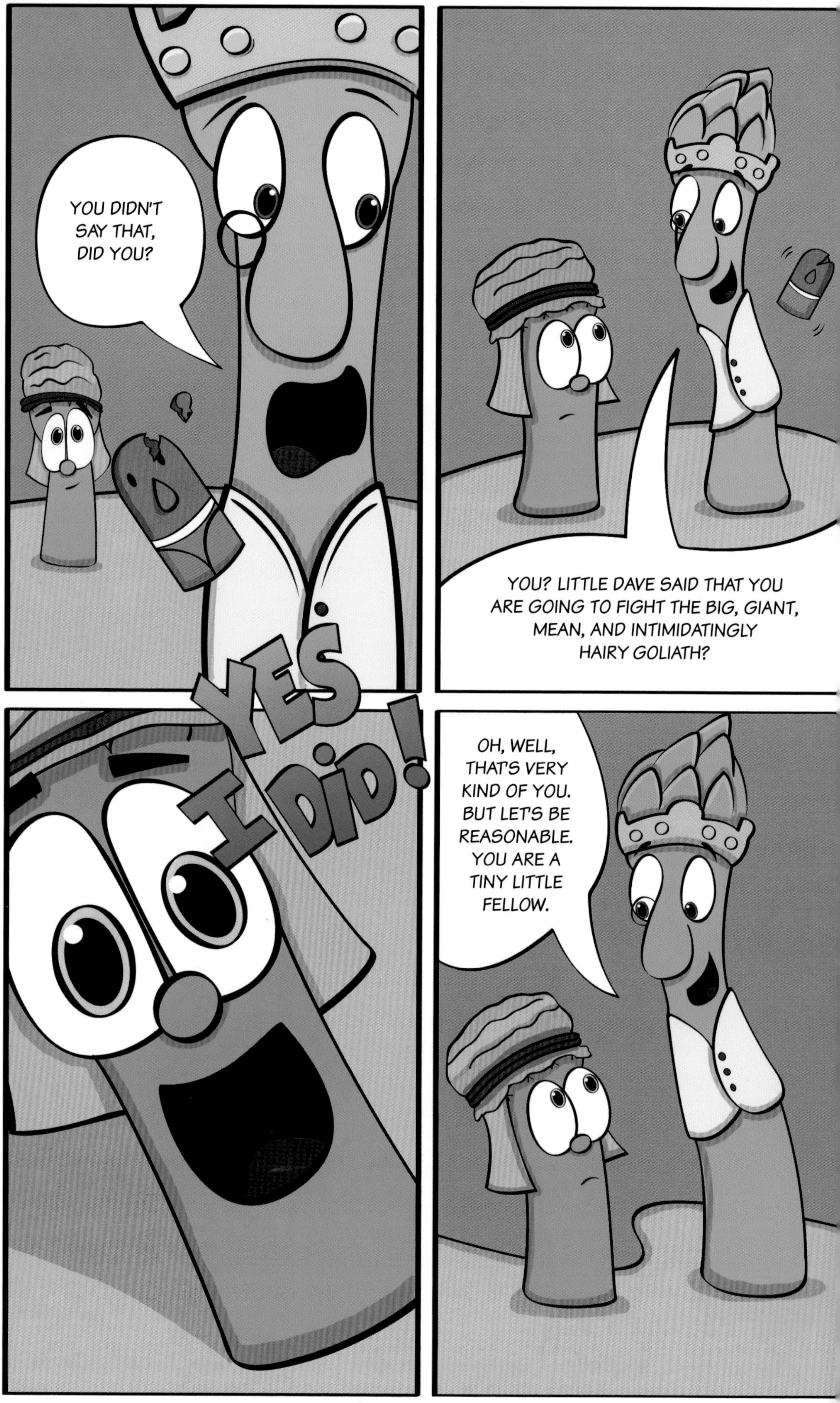
YOU DIDN'T SAY THAT, DID YOU?
YOU? LITTLE DAVE SAID THAT YOU ARE GOING TO FIGHT THE BIG, GIANT, MEAN, AND INTIMIDATINGLY HAIRY GOLIATH?
YES I DID!
OH, WELL, THAT'S VERY KIND OF YOU. BUT LET'S BE REASONABLE. YOU ARE A TINY LITTLE FELLOW.

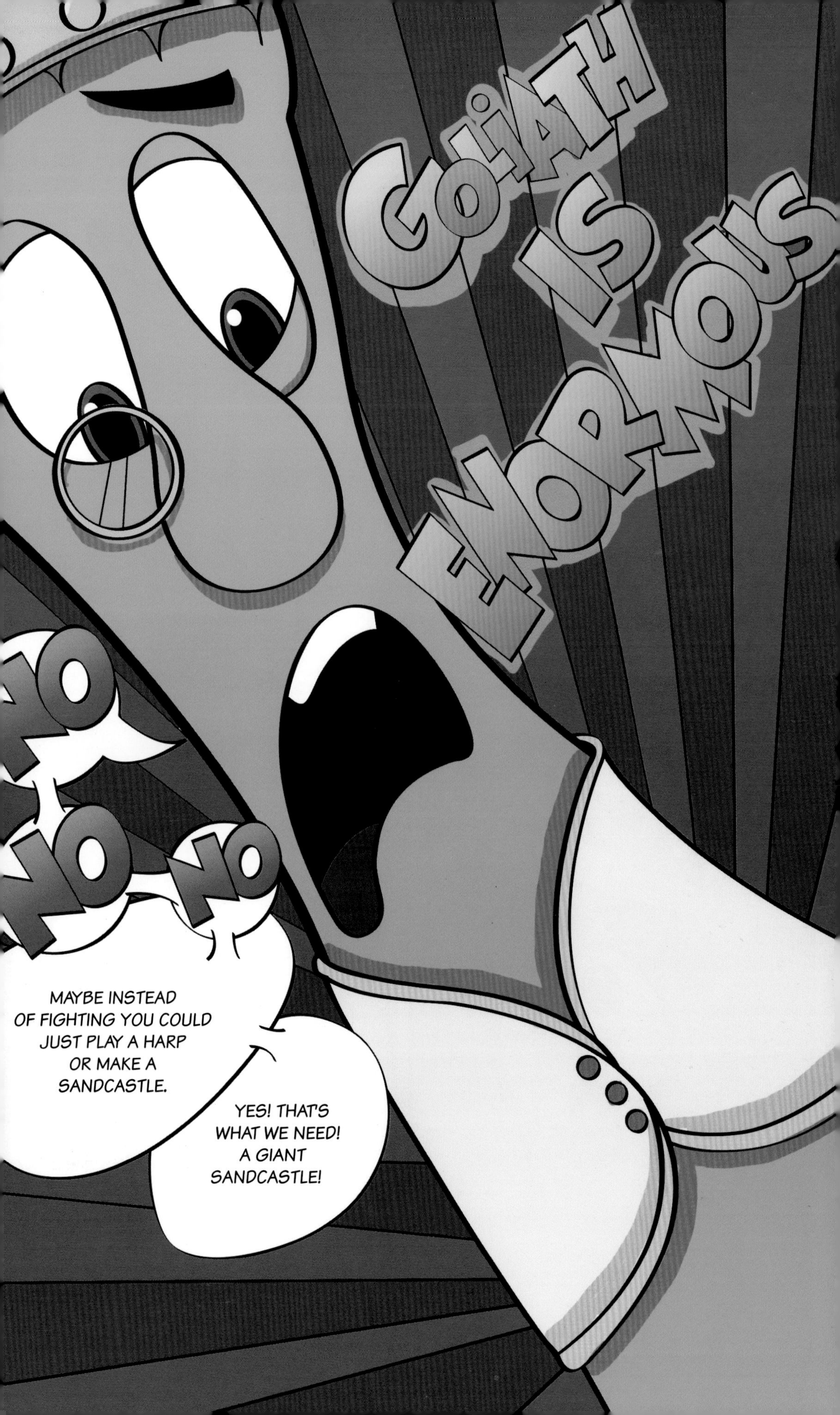
GOLIATH IS ENORMOUS
NO NO NO
MAYBE INSTEAD OF FIGHTING YOU COULD JUST PLAY A HARP OR MAKE A SANDCASTLE.
YES! THAT'S WHAT WE NEED! A GIANT SANDCASTLE!

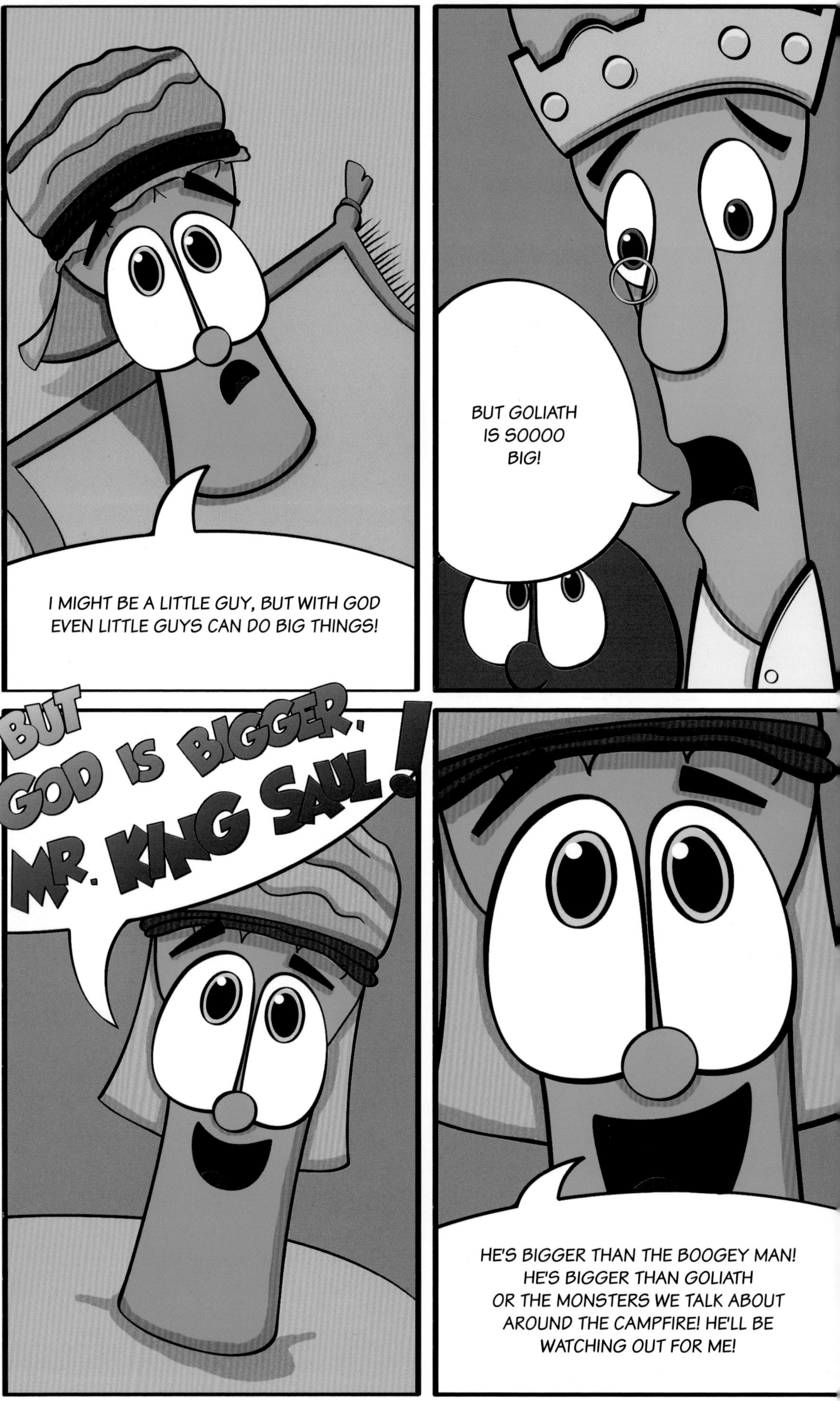
I MIGHT BE A LITTLE GUY, BUT WITH GOD EVEN LITTLE GUYS CAN DO BIG THINGS!
BUT GOLIATH IS SOOOO BIG!
BUT GOD IS BIGGER, MR. KING SAUL!
HE'S BIGGER THAN THE BOOGEY MAN! HE'S BIGGER THAN GOLIATH OR THE MONSTERS WE TALK ABOUT AROUND THE CAMPFIRE! HE'LL BE WATCHING OUT FOR ME!

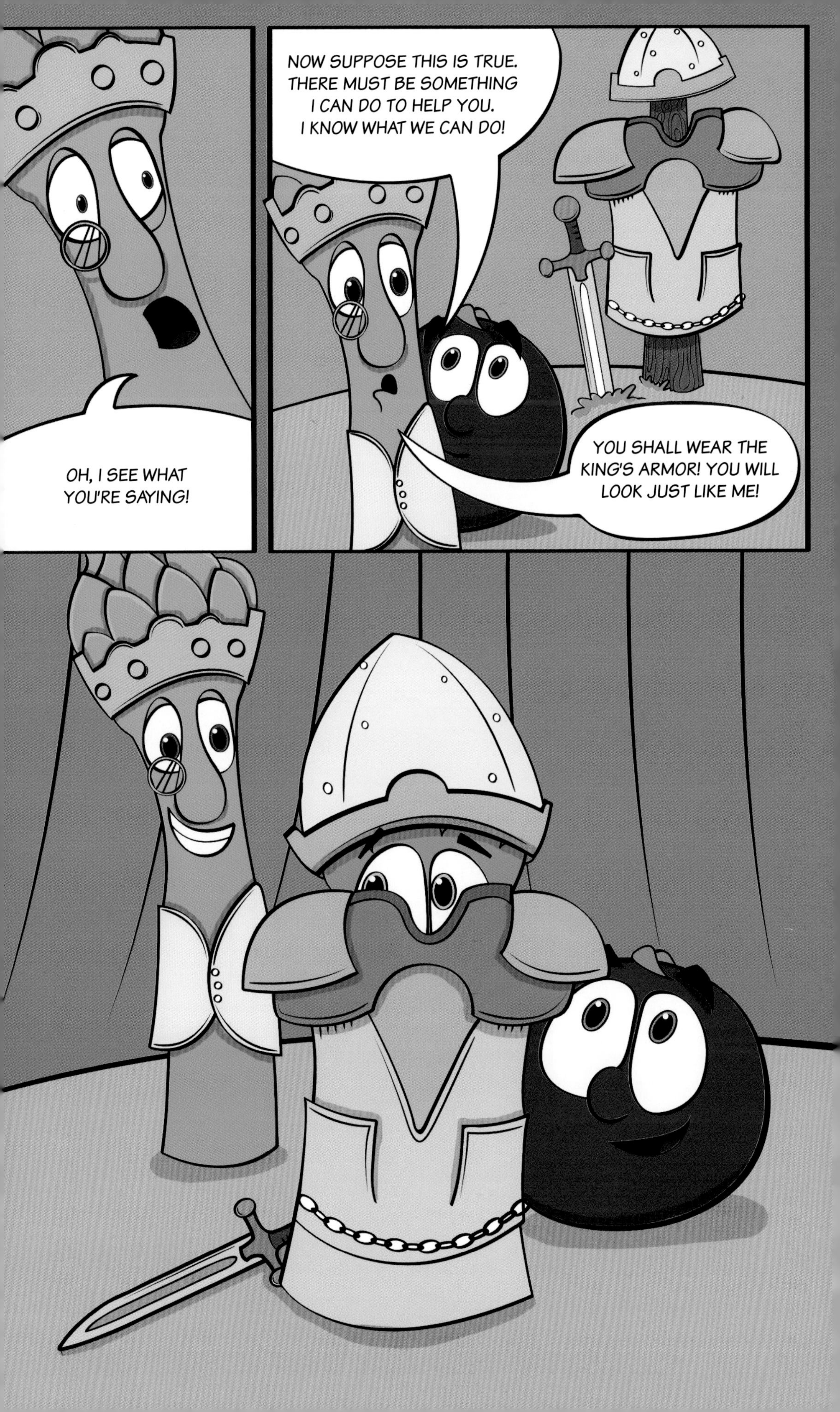
OH, I SEE WHAT YOU'RE SAYING!
NOW SUPPOSE THIS IS TRUE. THERE MUST BE SOMETHING I CAN DO TO HELP YOU. I KNOW WHAT WE CAN DO!
YOU SHALL WEAR THE KING'S ARMOR! YOU WILL LOOK JUST LIKE ME!

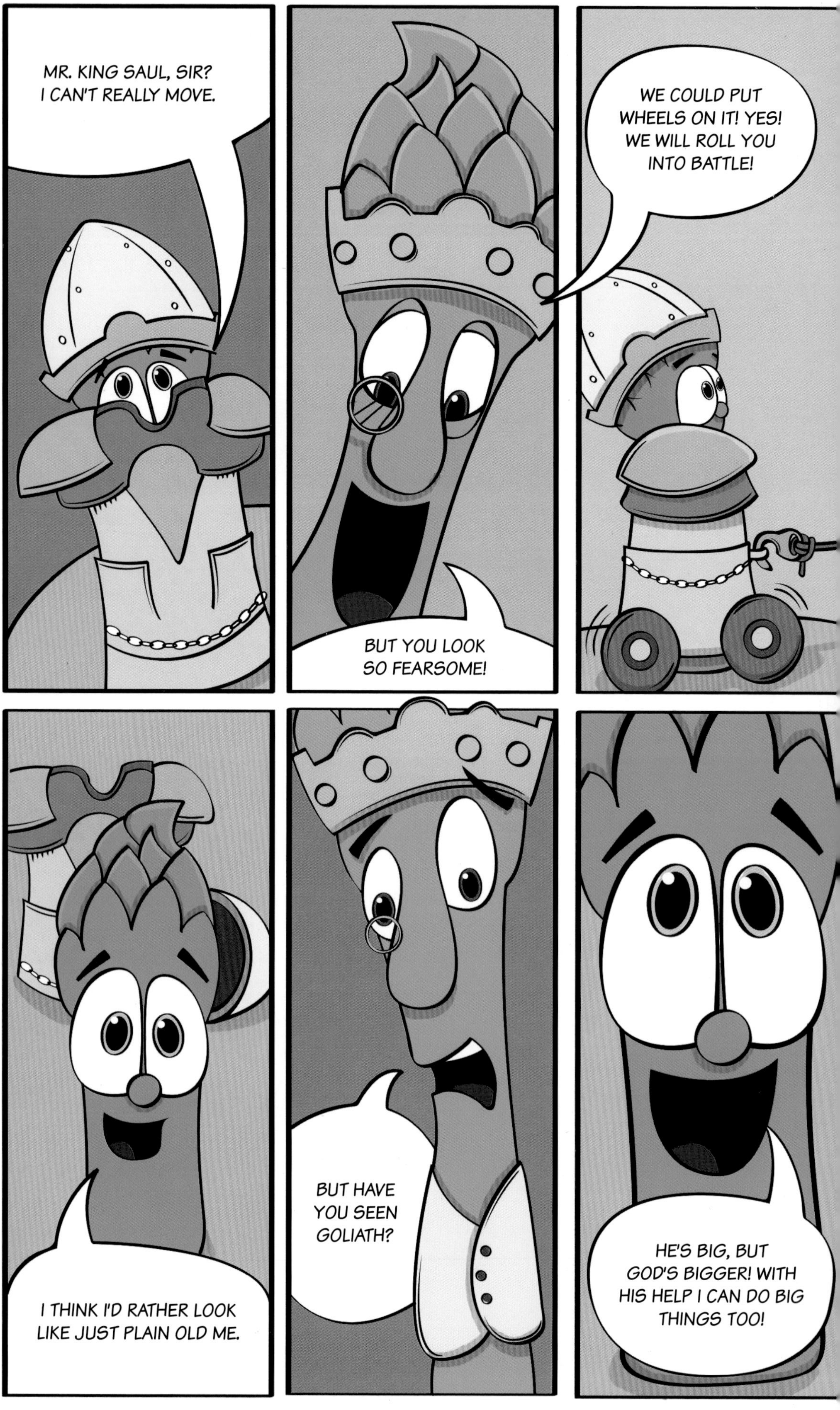
MR. KING SAUL, SIR? I CAN'T REALLY MOVE.
BUT YOU LOOK SO FEARSOME!
WE COULD PUT WHEELS ON IT! YES! WE WILL ROLL YOU INTO BATTLE!
I THINK I'D RATHER LOOK LIKE JUST PLAIN OLD ME.
BUT HAVE YOU SEEN GOLIATH?
HE'S BIG, BUT GOD'S BIGGER! WITH HIS HELP I CAN DO BIG THINGS TOO!

S A SHEPHERD, DAVE'S MAIN JOB WAS PROTECTING HIS SHEEP.
E PROTECTED THEM WITH HIS STAFF AND DEFENDED THEM
ROM LIONS WITH A SLING.

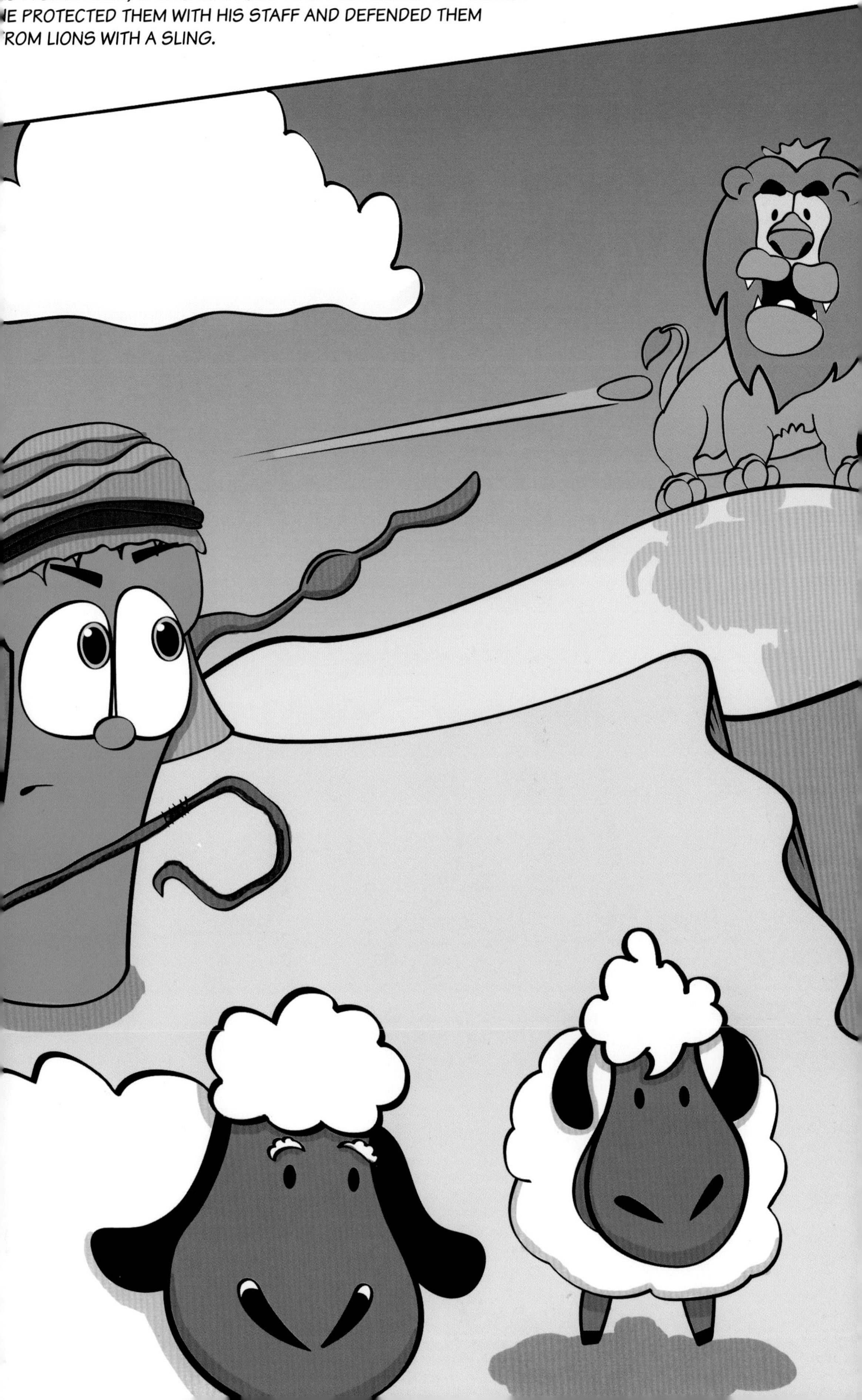

DAVE WENT TO THE STREAM AND FOUND FIVE SMOOTH STONES BEFORE GOING BACK TO THE BATTLEFIELD.

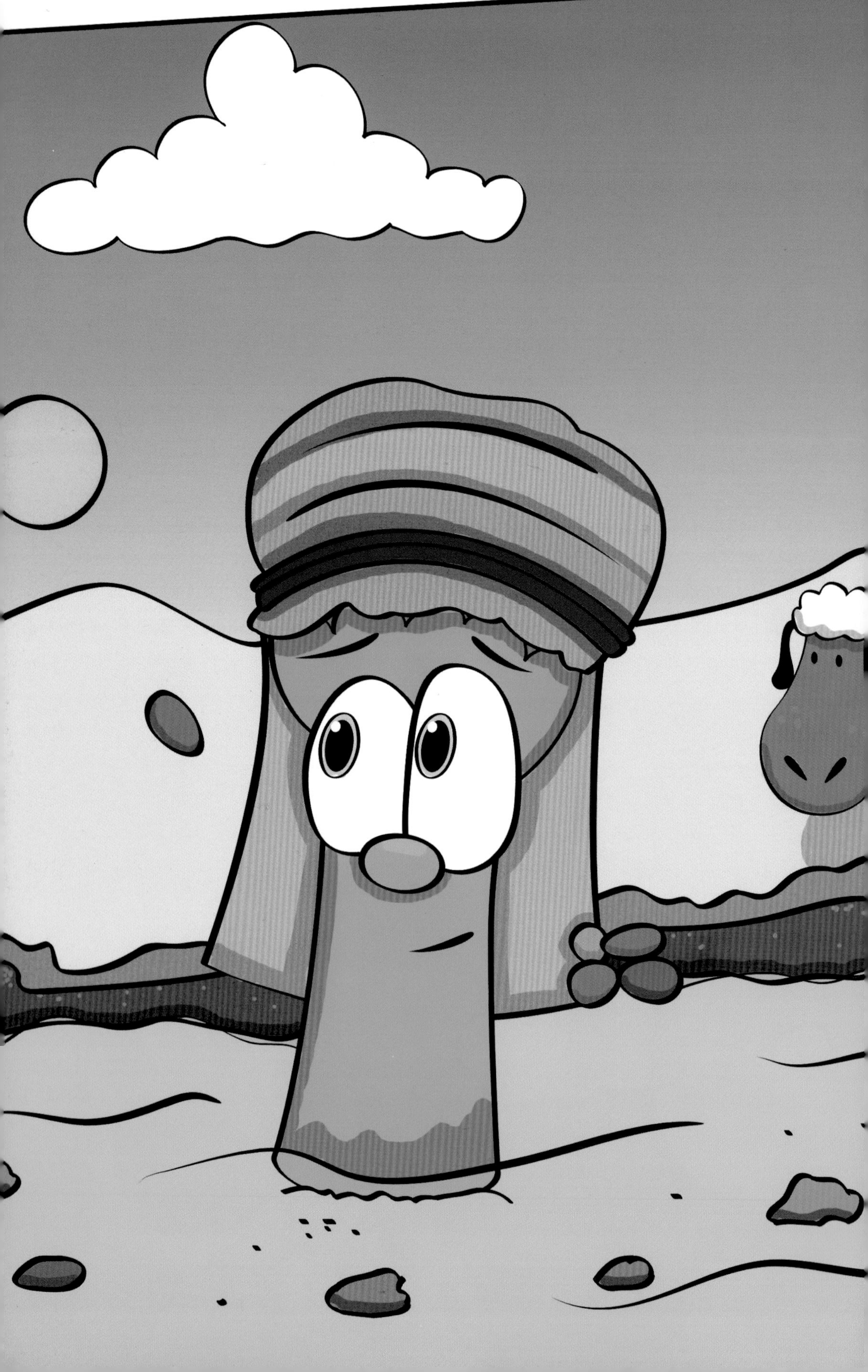

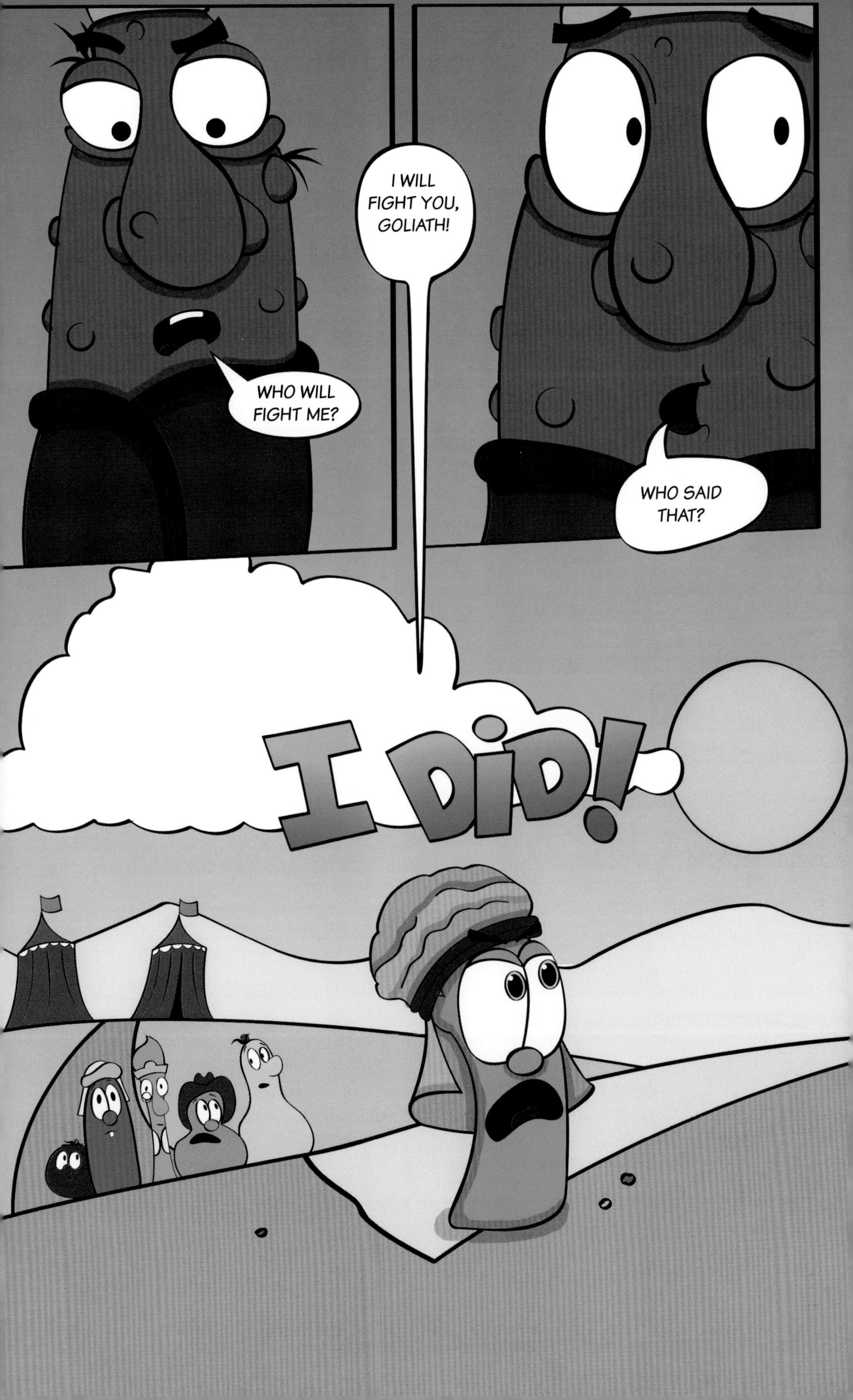
WHO WILL FIGHT ME?
I WILL FIGHT YOU, GOLIATH!
WHO SAID THAT?
I DID!

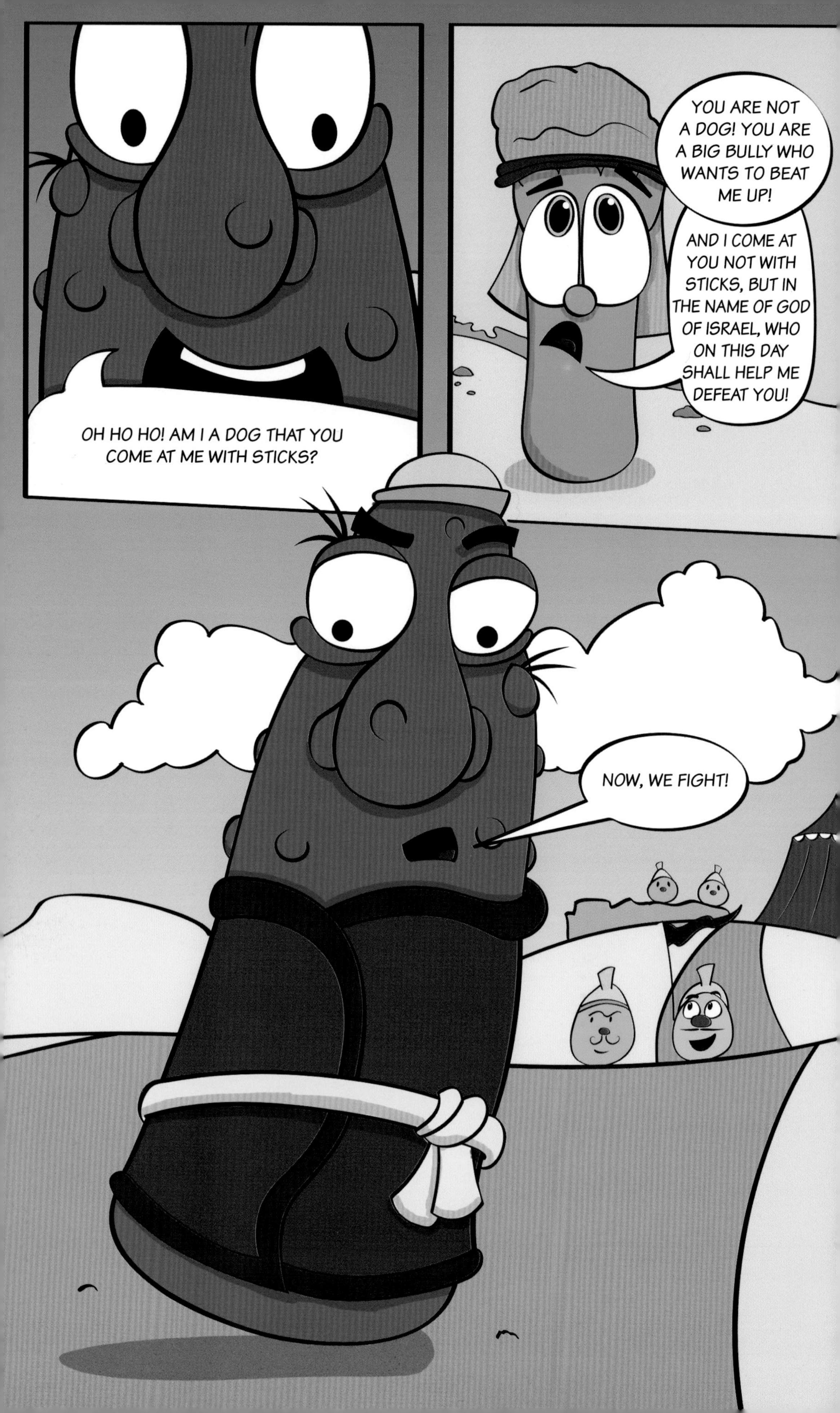
OH HO HO! AM I A DOG THAT YOU COME AT ME WITH STICKS?
YOU ARE NOT A DOG! YOU ARE A BIG BULLY WHO WANTS TO BEAT ME UP!
AND I COME AT YOU NOT WITH STICKS, BUT IN THE NAME OF GOD OF ISRAEL, WHO ON THIS DAY SHALL HELP ME DEFEAT YOU!
NOW, WE FIGHT!

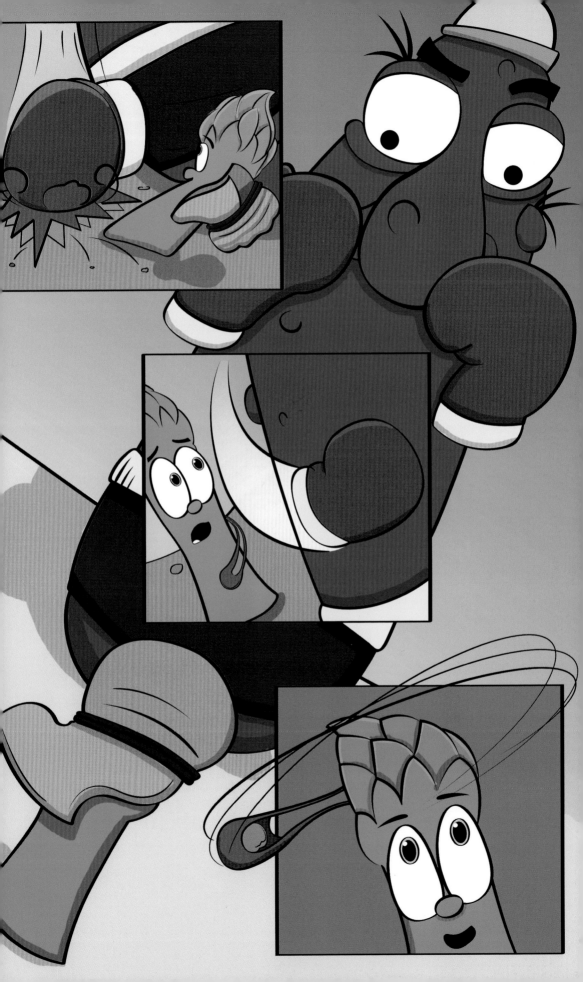

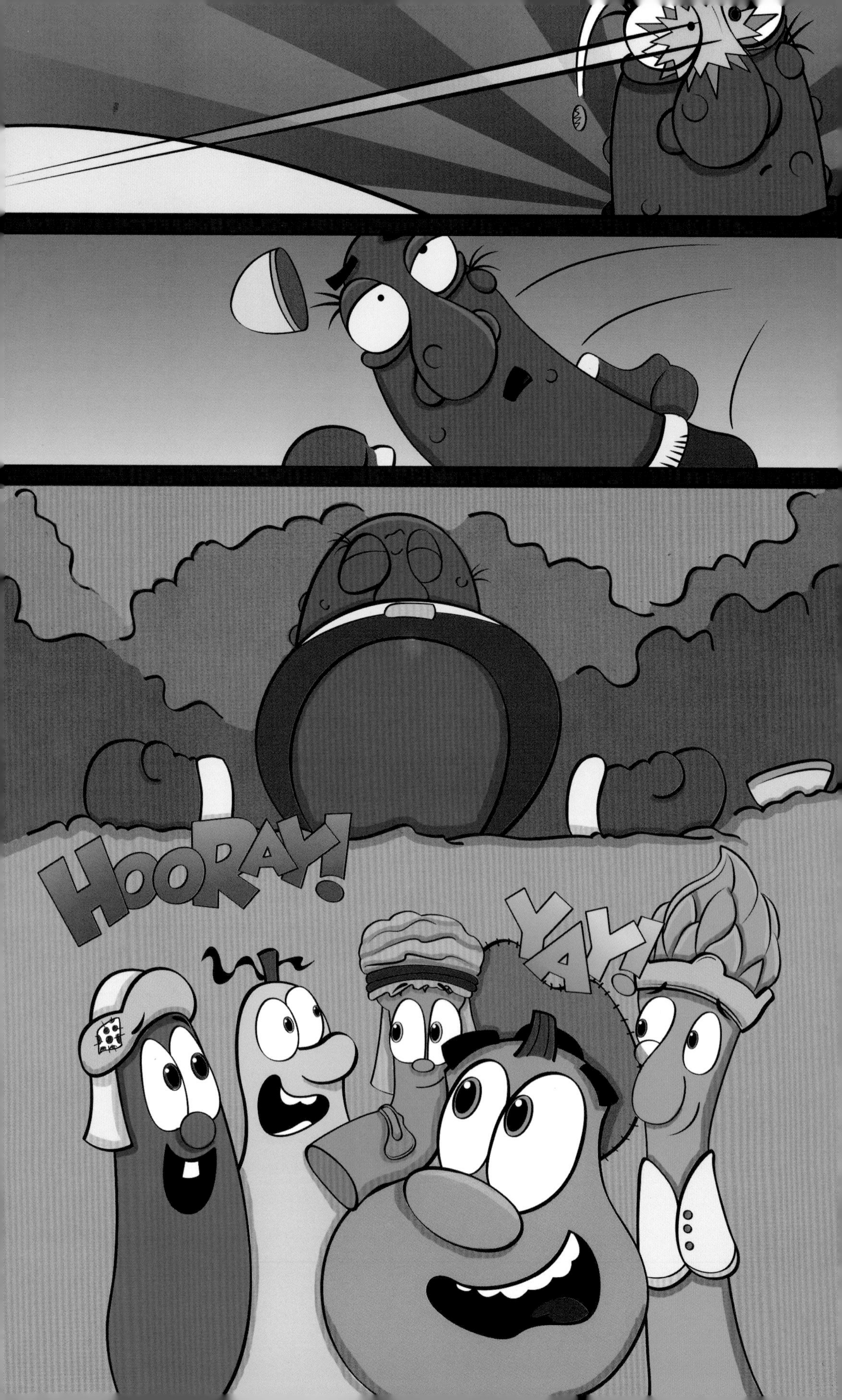
HOORAY!
YAY!

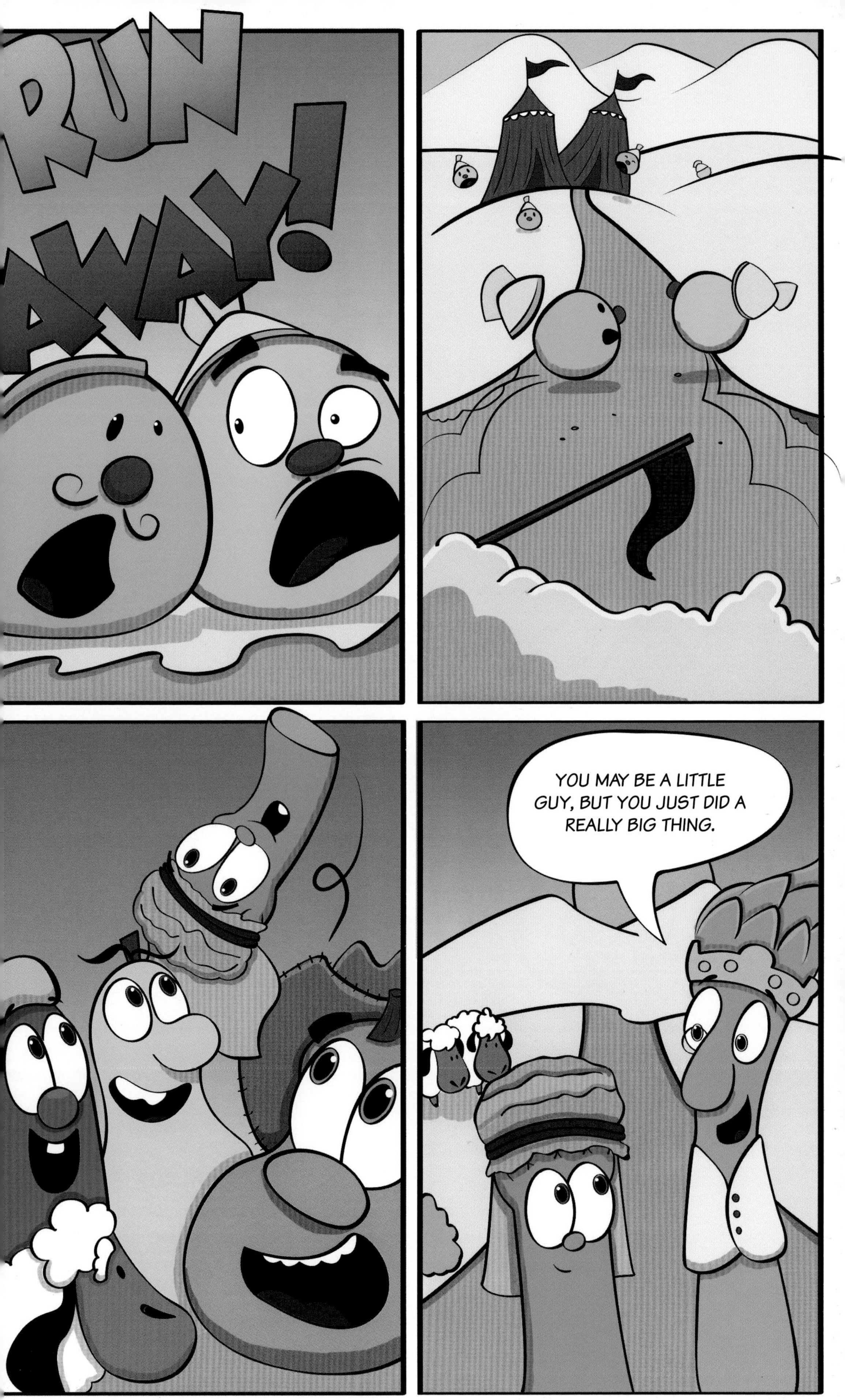
RUN AWAY!
YOU MAY BE A LITTLE GUY, BUT YOU JUST DID A REALLY BIG THING.

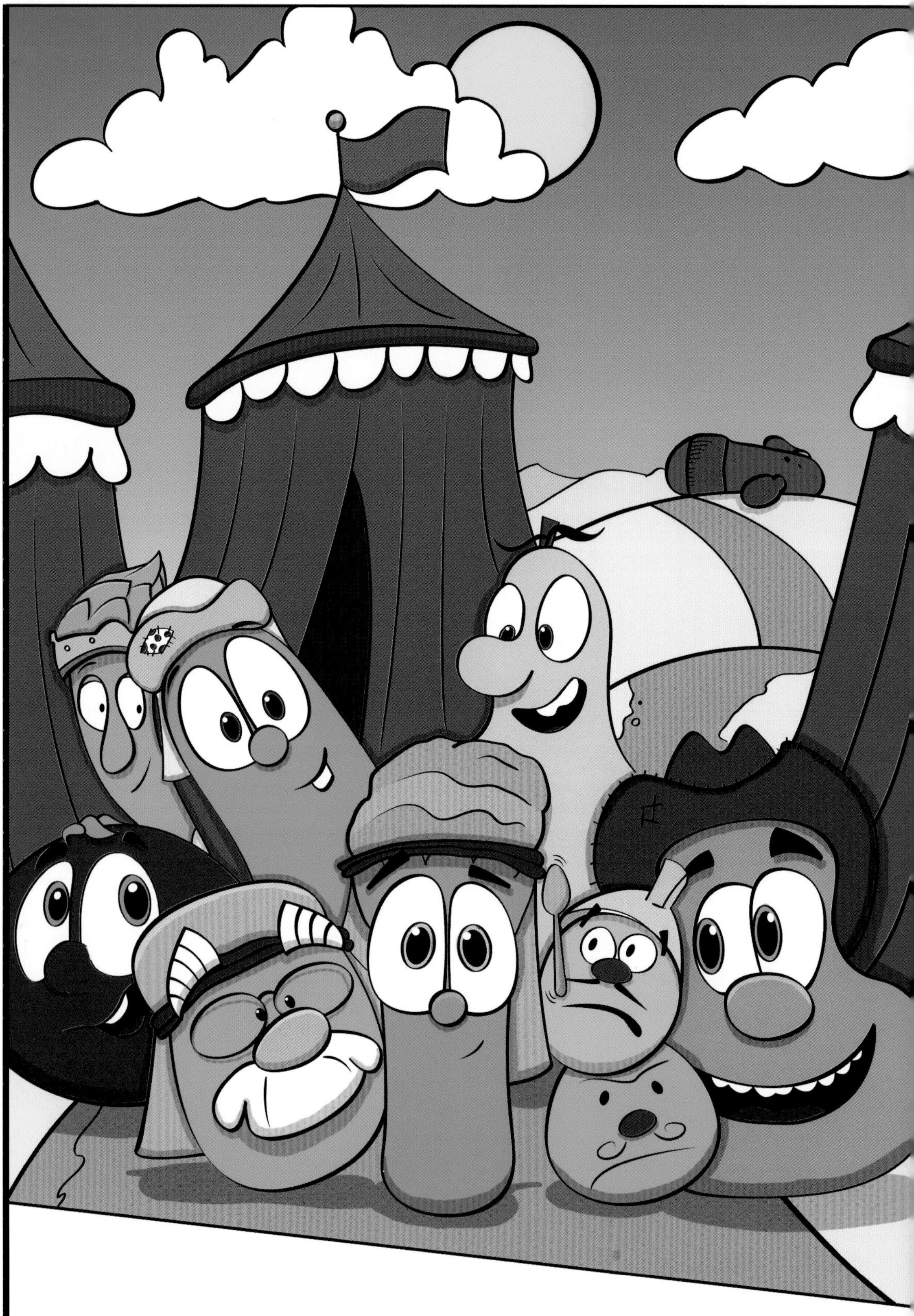

With God all things
are possible.

—MATTHEW 19:26

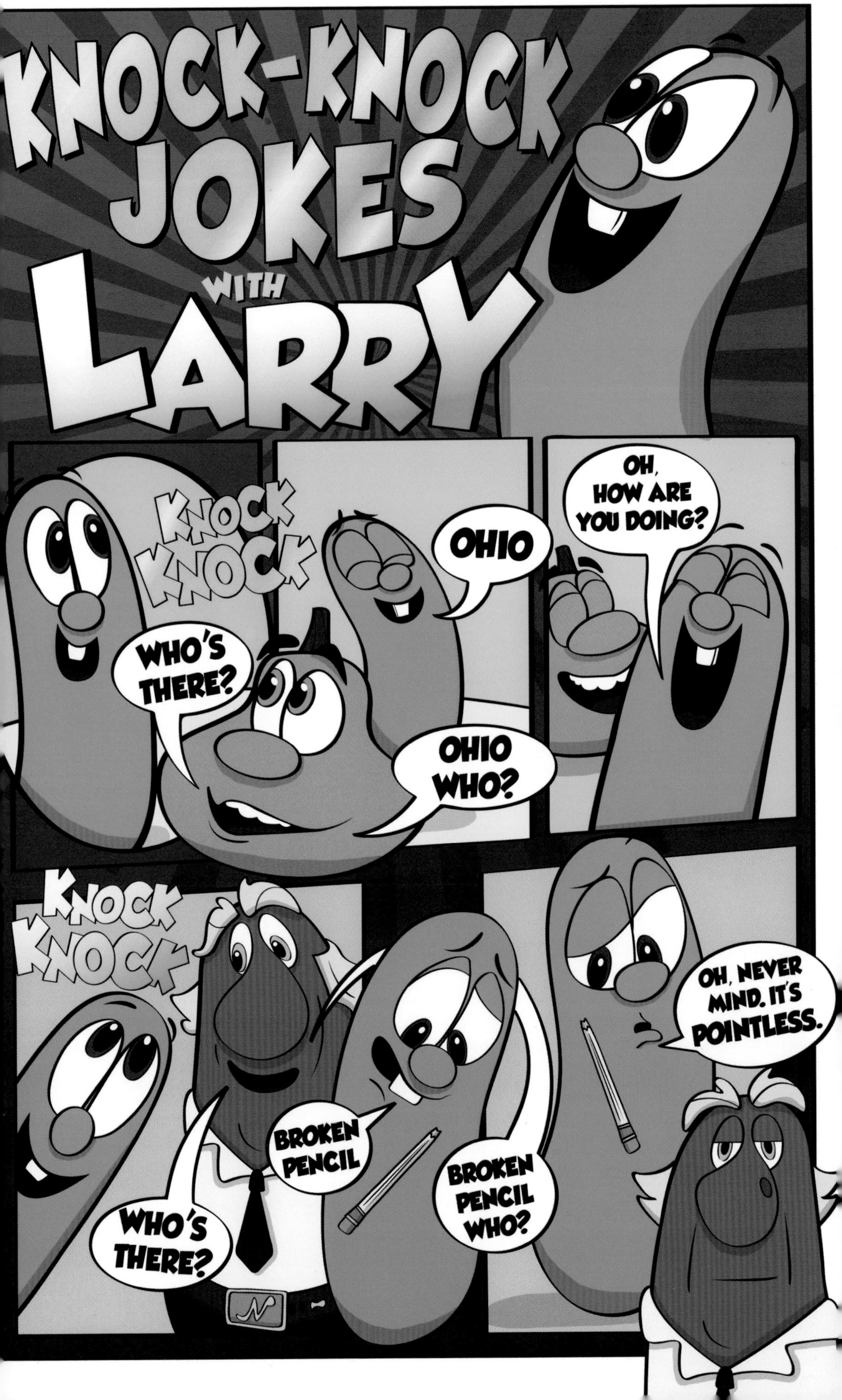
KNOCK-KNOCK JOKES WITH LARRY
KNOCK KNOCK
WHO'S THERE?
OHIO
OHIO WHO?
OH, HOW ARE YOU DOING?
KNOCK KNOCK
WHO'S THERE?
BROKEN PENCIL
BROKEN PENCIL WHO?
OH, NEVER MIND. IT'S POINTLESS.

VeggieTales

Noah's Ark

This is a story about family, faith and a flood starring one of the Bible's greatest heroes (Noah) and his reluctant son (Shem), who learn through an amazing adventure that ***God always keeps His promises.***

The story takes place in, "who knows when B.C." when God tells Noah, a simple orange farmer, that a huge flood is coming their way. God has chosen to rescue Noah and his family - all they need to do is build a giant boat for themselves and 2 of every animal on earth. Come along for a full dose of fun, adventure and faith as Noah and his family embark on the journey of a lifetime in VeggieTales epic telling of the Noah's Ark story.

THE CAST

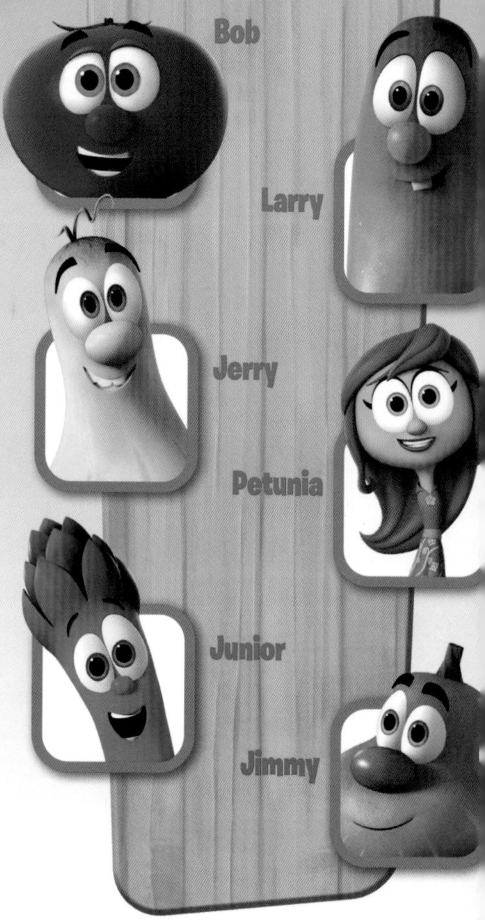

Bob
Larry
Jerry
Petunia
Junior
Jimmy

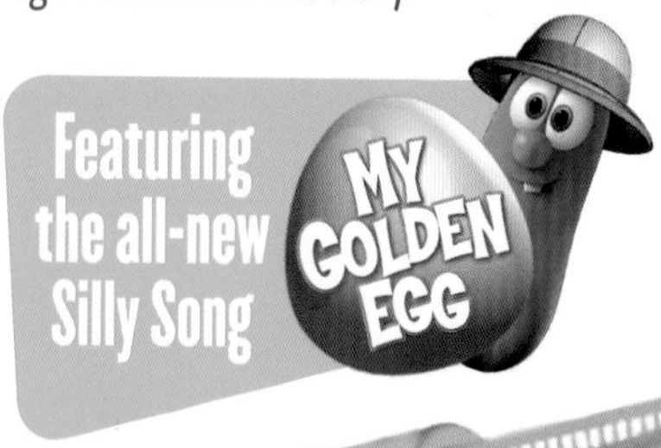

Featuring the all-new Silly Song
MY GOLDEN EGG

Includes 7 original new songs!

Noah's Ark DVD coming to a store near you Spring 2015!

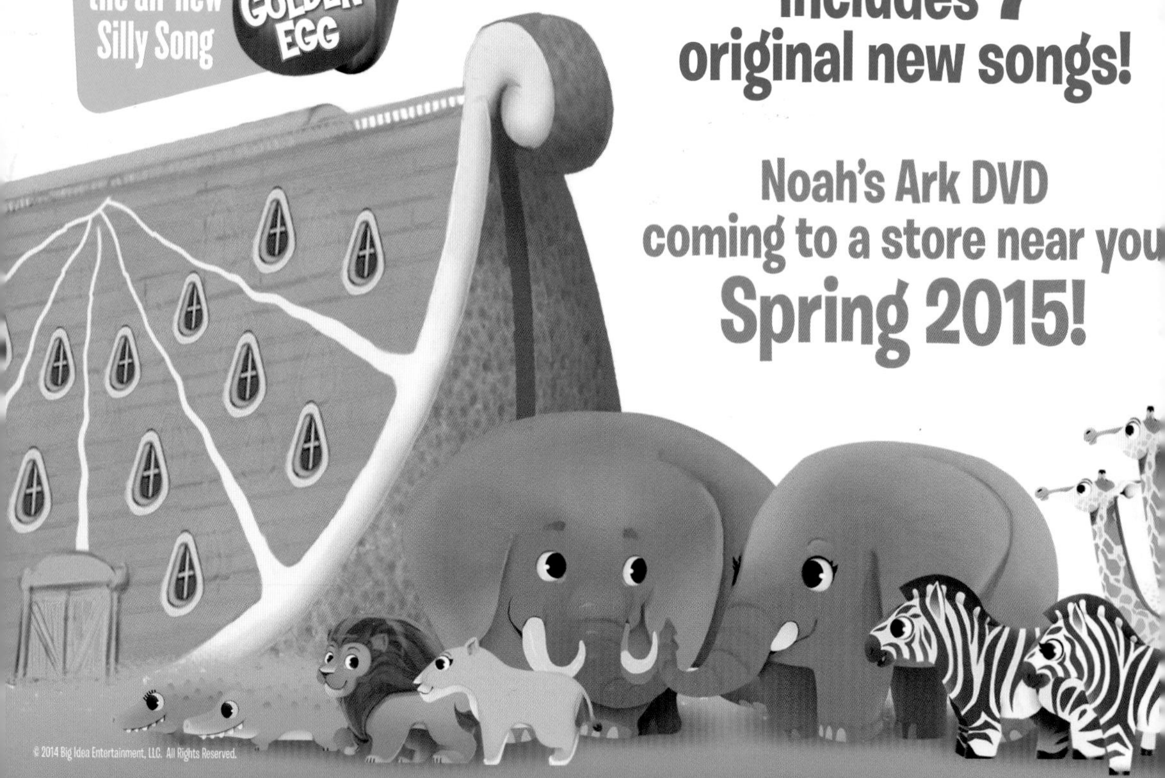

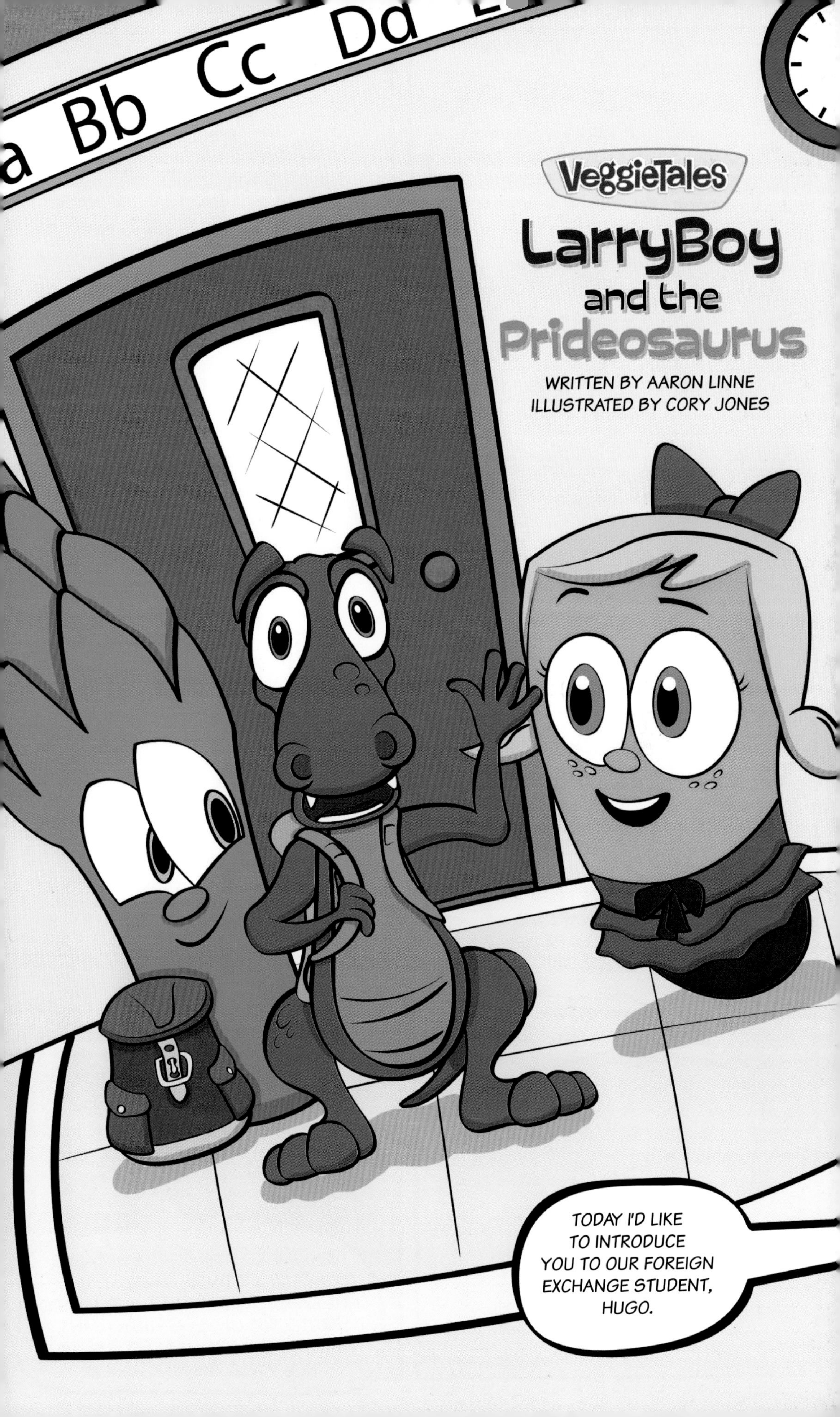
a Bb Cc Dd
VeggieTales
LarryBoy and the Prideosaurus
WRITTEN BY AARON LINNE
ILLUSTRATED BY CORY JONES
TODAY I'D LIKE TO INTRODUCE YOU TO OUR FOREIGN EXCHANGE STUDENT, HUGO.

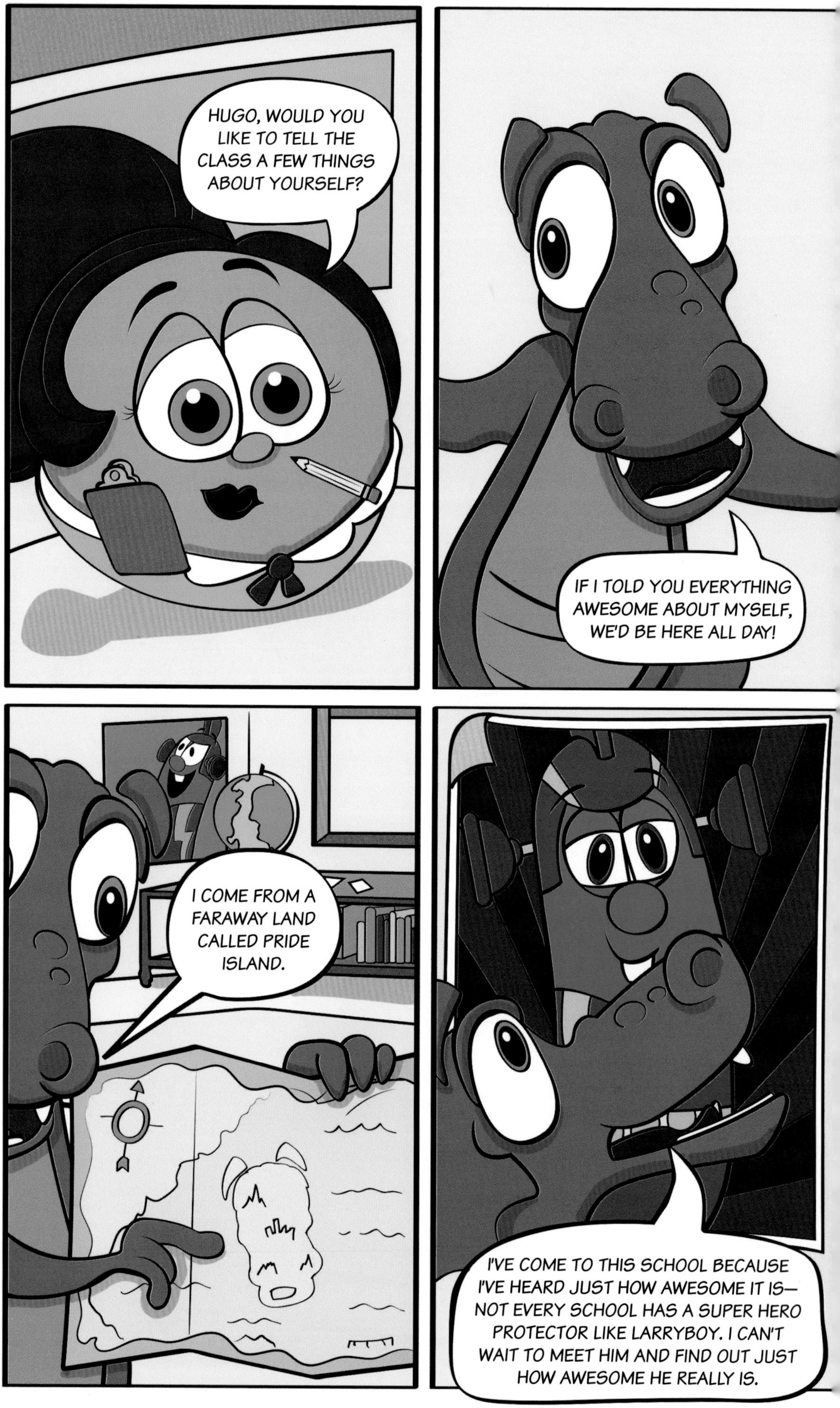
HUGO, WOULD YOU LIKE TO TELL THE CLASS A FEW THINGS ABOUT YOURSELF?
IF I TOLD YOU EVERYTHING AWESOME ABOUT MYSELF, WE'D BE HERE ALL DAY!
I COME FROM A FARAWAY LAND CALLED PRIDE ISLAND.
I'VE COME TO THIS SCHOOL BECAUSE I'VE HEARD JUST HOW AWESOME IT IS— NOT EVERY SCHOOL HAS A SUPER HERO PROTECTOR LIKE LARRYBOY. I CAN'T WAIT TO MEET HIM AND FIND OUT JUST HOW AWESOME HE REALLY IS.

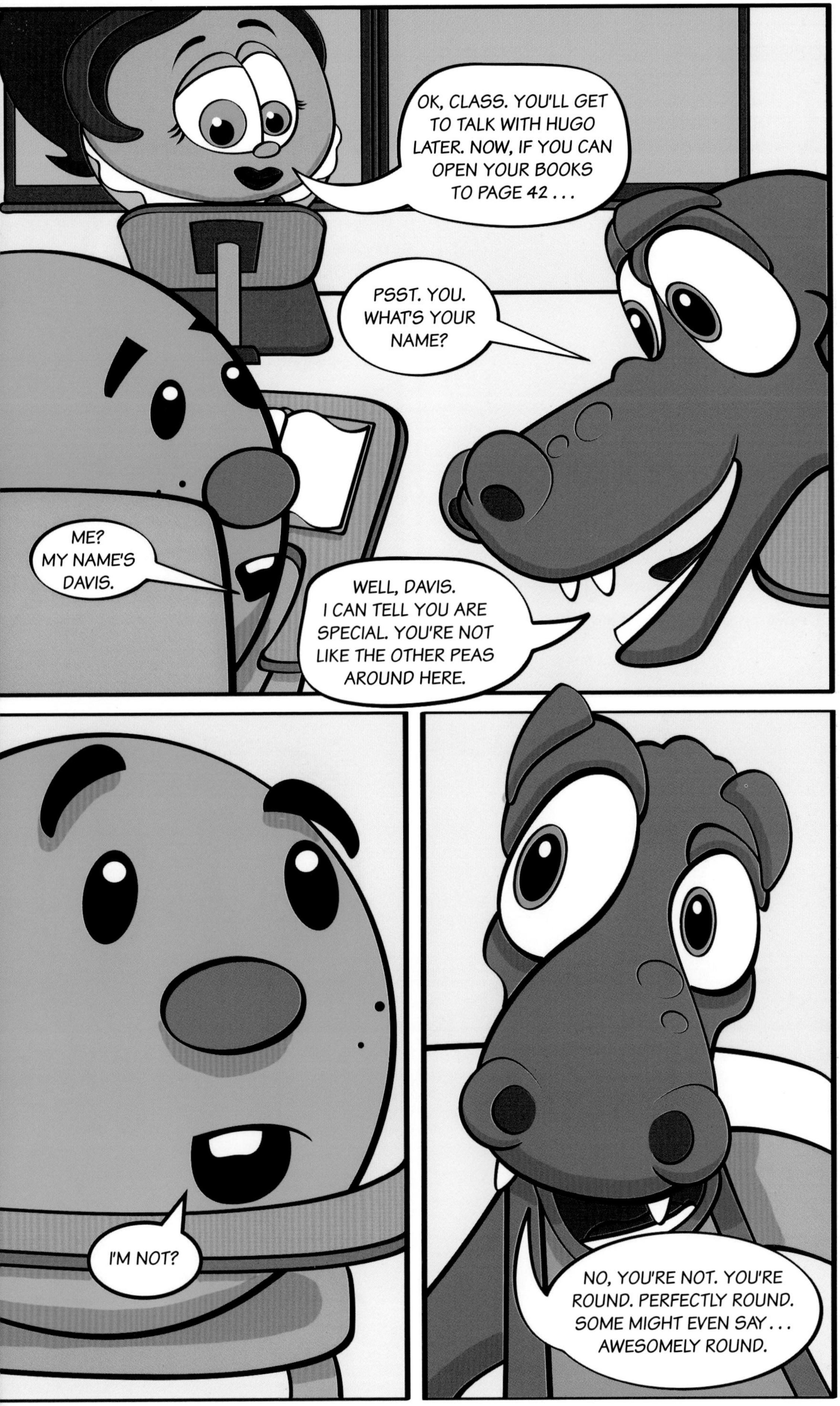
OK, CLASS. YOU'LL GET TO TALK WITH HUGO LATER. NOW, IF YOU CAN OPEN YOUR BOOKS TO PAGE 42 . . .
PSST. YOU. WHAT'S YOUR NAME?
ME? MY NAME'S DAVIS.
WELL, DAVIS. I CAN TELL YOU ARE SPECIAL. YOU'RE NOT LIKE THE OTHER PEAS AROUND HERE.
I'M NOT?
NO, YOU'RE NOT. YOU'RE ROUND. PERFECTLY ROUND. SOME MIGHT EVEN SAY . . . AWESOMELY ROUND.

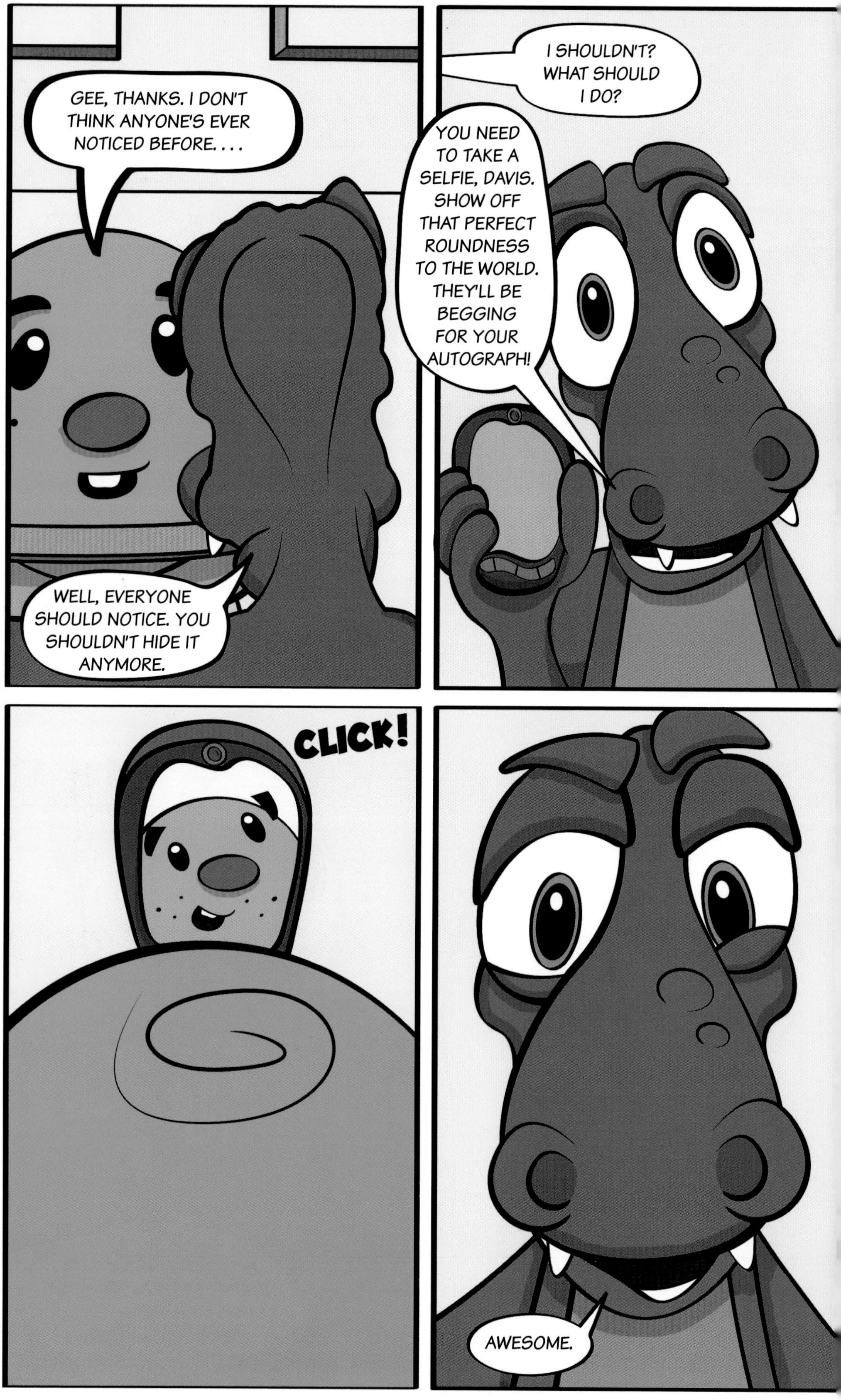
GEE, THANKS. I DON'T THINK ANYONE'S EVER NOTICED BEFORE. . . .
WELL, EVERYONE SHOULD NOTICE. YOU SHOULDN'T HIDE IT ANYMORE.
I SHOULDN'T? WHAT SHOULD I DO?
YOU NEED TO TAKE A SELFIE, DAVIS. SHOW OFF THAT PERFECT ROUNDNESS TO THE WORLD. THEY'LL BE BEGGING FOR YOUR AUTOGRAPH!
CLICK!
AWESOME.

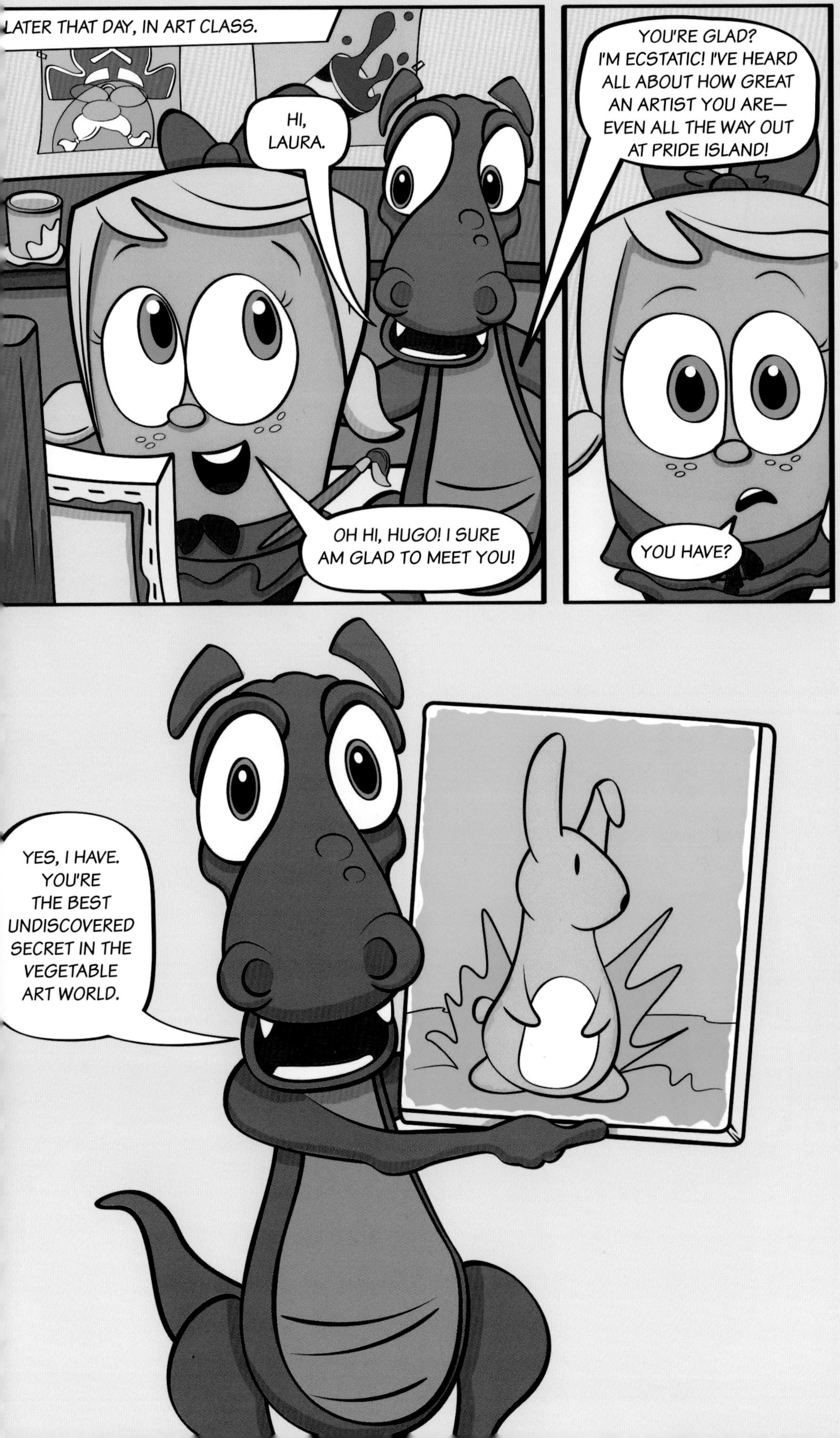
LATER THAT DAY, IN ART CLASS.
HI, LAURA.
OH HI, HUGO! I SURE AM GLAD TO MEET YOU!
YOU'RE GLAD? I'M ECSTATIC! I'VE HEARD ALL ABOUT HOW GREAT AN ARTIST YOU ARE— EVEN ALL THE WAY OUT AT PRIDE ISLAND!
YOU HAVE?
YES, I HAVE. YOU'RE THE BEST UNDISCOVERED SECRET IN THE VEGETABLE ART WORLD.

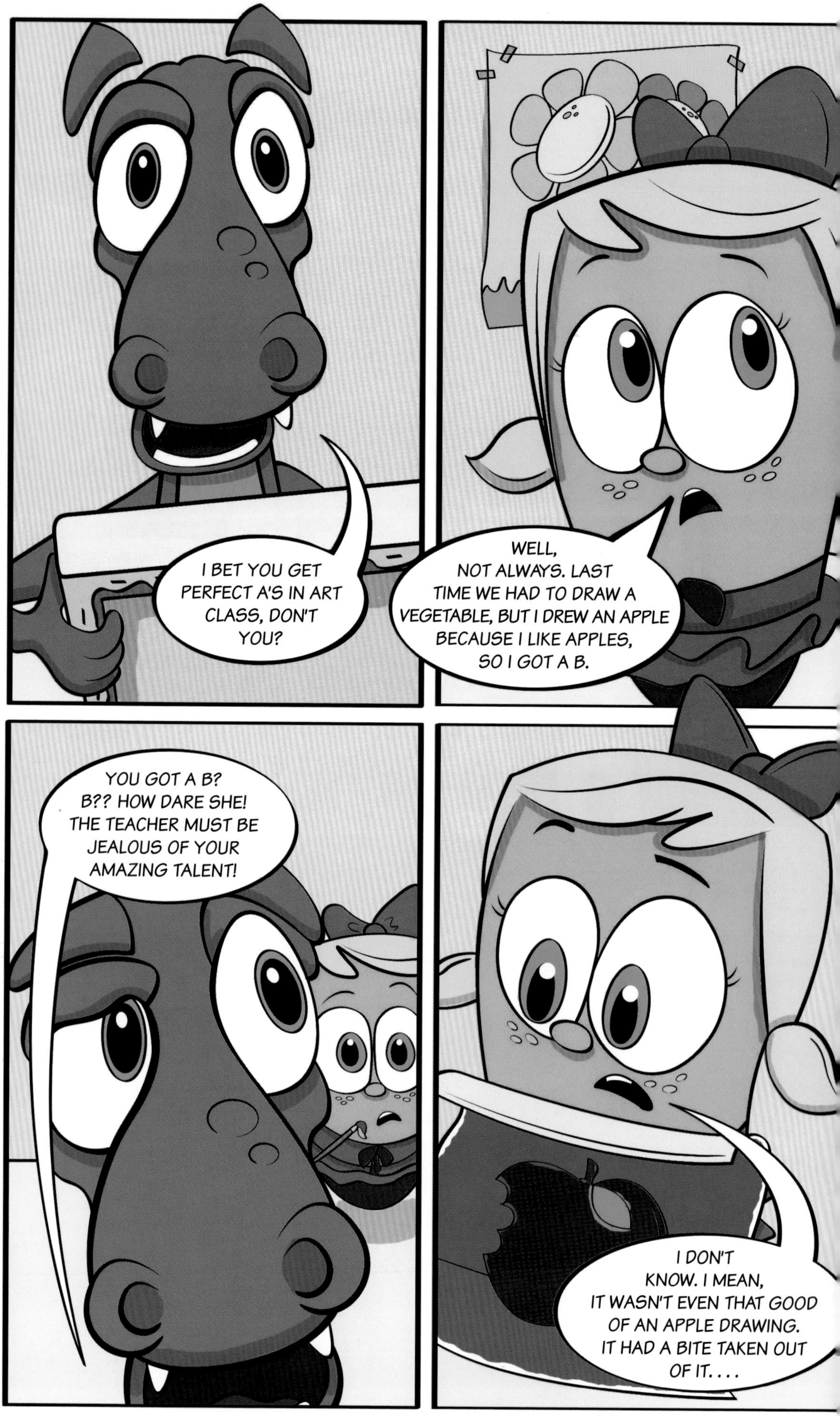
I BET YOU GET PERFECT A'S IN ART CLASS, DON'T YOU?
WELL, NOT ALWAYS. LAST TIME WE HAD TO DRAW A VEGETABLE, BUT I DREW AN APPLE BECAUSE I LIKE APPLES, SO I GOT A B.
YOU GOT A B? B?? HOW DARE SHE! THE TEACHER MUST BE JEALOUS OF YOUR AMAZING TALENT!
I DON'T KNOW. I MEAN, IT WASN'T EVEN THAT GOOD OF AN APPLE DRAWING. IT HAD A BITE TAKEN OUT OF IT. . . .

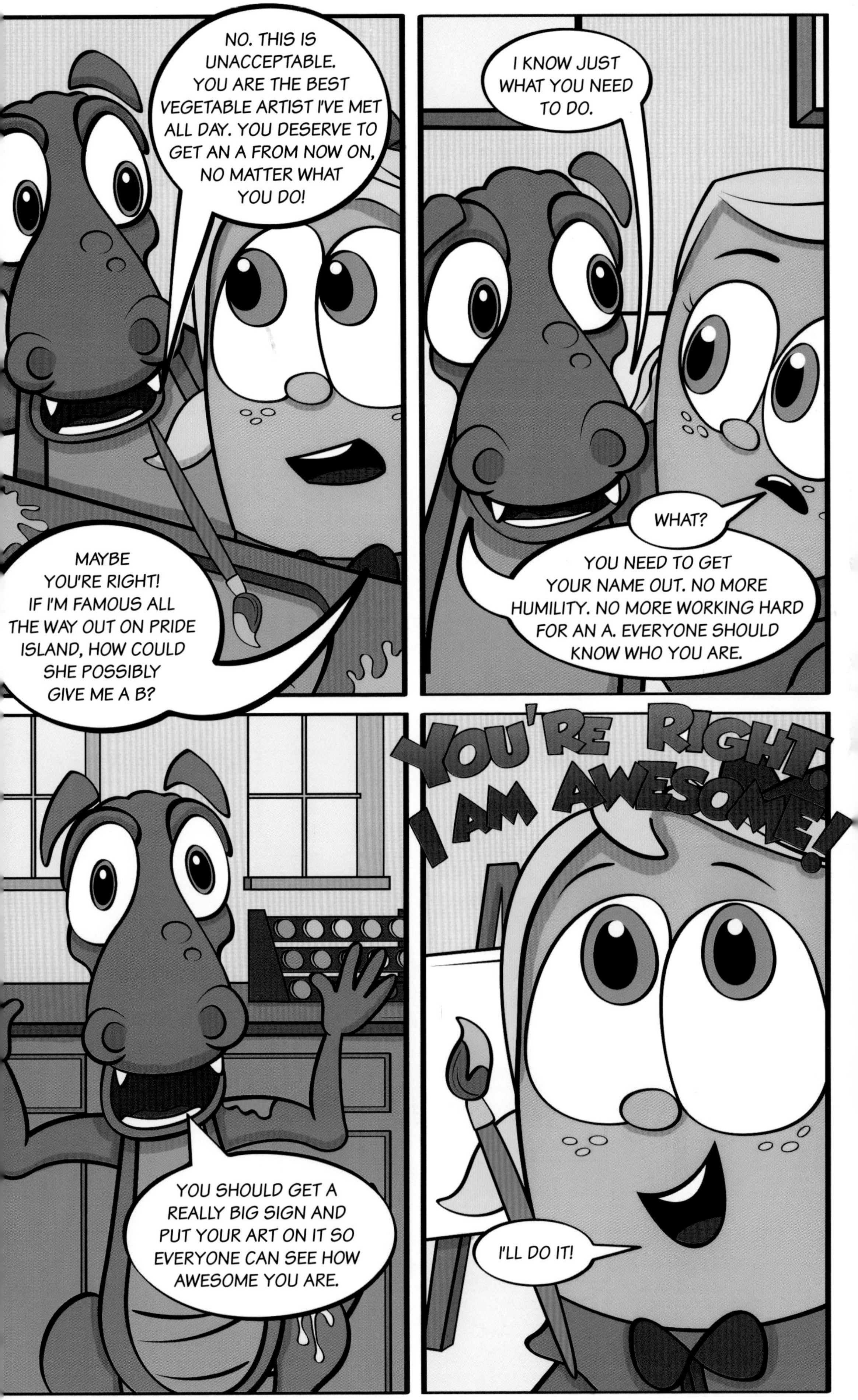
NO. THIS IS UNACCEPTABLE. YOU ARE THE BEST VEGETABLE ARTIST I'VE MET ALL DAY. YOU DESERVE TO GET AN A FROM NOW ON, NO MATTER WHAT YOU DO!
MAYBE YOU'RE RIGHT! IF I'M FAMOUS ALL THE WAY OUT ON PRIDE ISLAND, HOW COULD SHE POSSIBLY GIVE ME A B?
I KNOW JUST WHAT YOU NEED TO DO.
WHAT?
YOU NEED TO GET YOUR NAME OUT. NO MORE HUMILITY. NO MORE WORKING HARD FOR AN A. EVERYONE SHOULD KNOW WHO YOU ARE.
YOU SHOULD GET A REALLY BIG SIGN AND PUT YOUR ART ON IT SO EVERYONE CAN SEE HOW AWESOME YOU ARE.
YOU'RE RIGHT! I AM AWESOME!
I'LL DO IT!

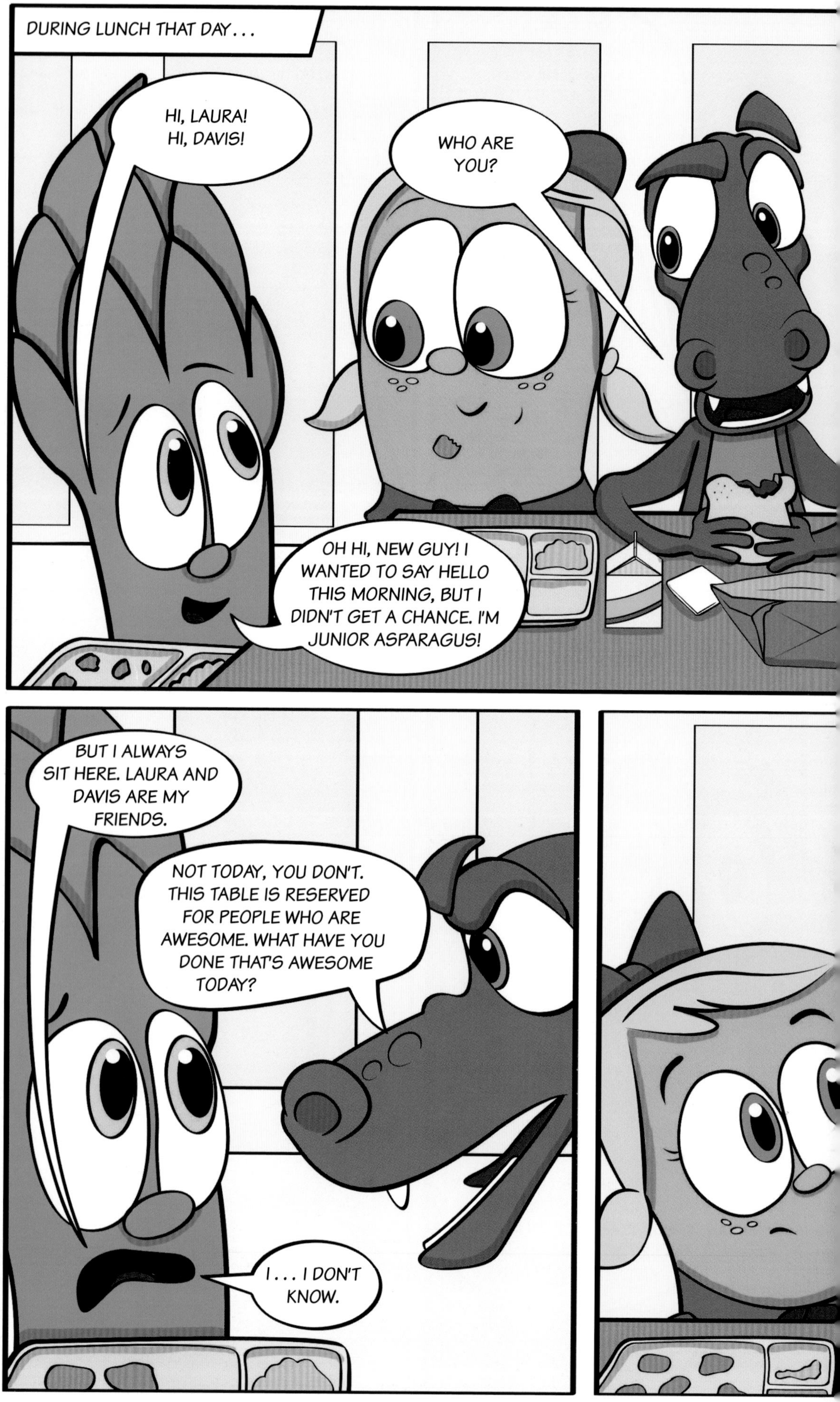
DURING LUNCH THAT DAY . . .
HI, LAURA! HI, DAVIS!
WHO ARE YOU?
OH HI, NEW GUY! I WANTED TO SAY HELLO THIS MORNING, BUT I DIDN'T GET A CHANCE. I'M JUNIOR ASPARAGUS!
BUT I ALWAYS SIT HERE. LAURA AND DAVIS ARE MY FRIENDS.
NOT TODAY, YOU DON'T. THIS TABLE IS RESERVED FOR PEOPLE WHO ARE AWESOME. WHAT HAVE YOU DONE THAT'S AWESOME TODAY?
I . . . I DON'T KNOW.

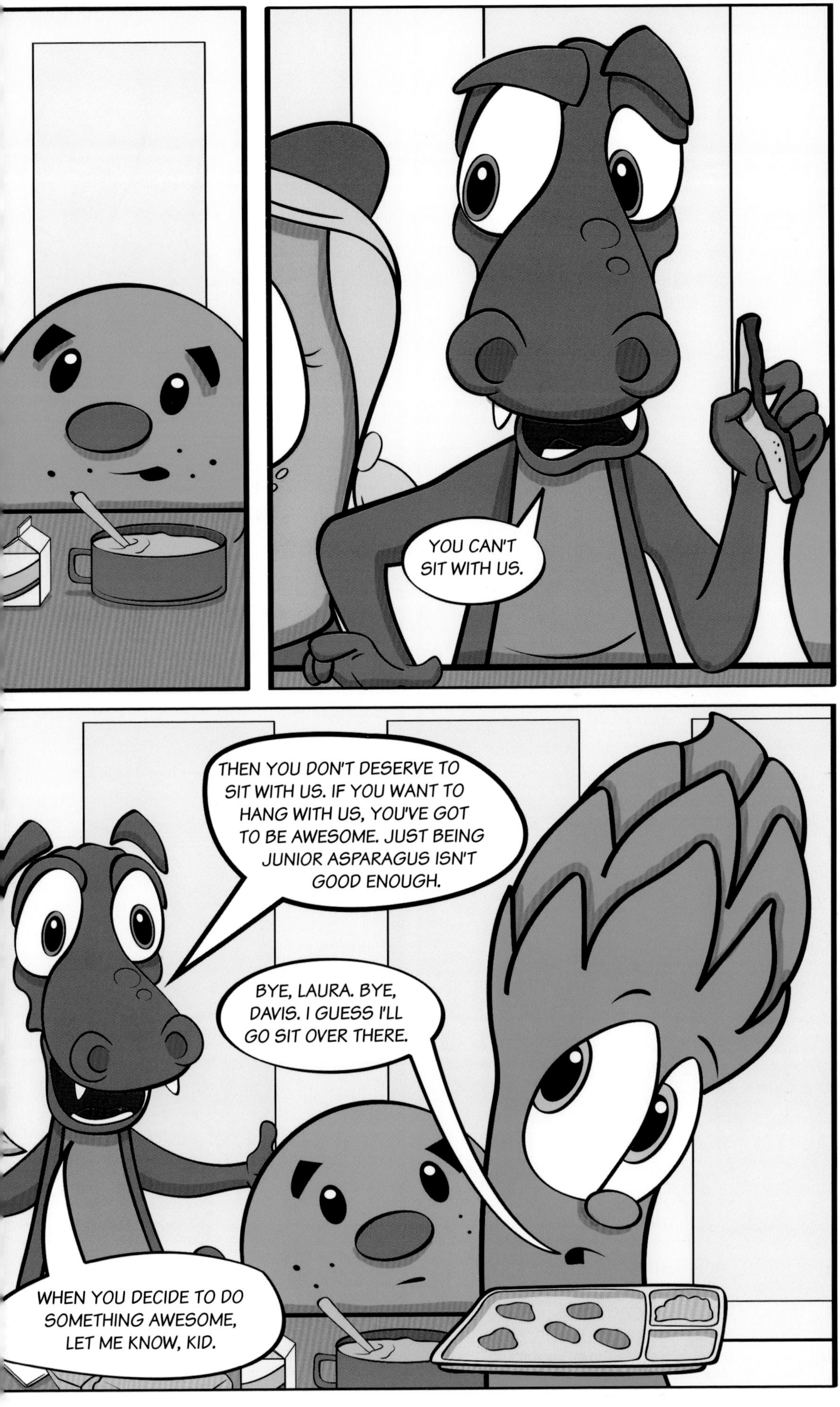
YOU CAN'T SIT WITH US.
THEN YOU DON'T DESERVE TO SIT WITH US. IF YOU WANT TO HANG WITH US, YOU'VE GOT TO BE AWESOME. JUST BEING JUNIOR ASPARAGUS ISN'T GOOD ENOUGH.
BYE, LAURA. BYE, DAVIS. I GUESS I'LL GO SIT OVER THERE.
WHEN YOU DECIDE TO DO SOMETHING AWESOME, LET ME KNOW, KID.

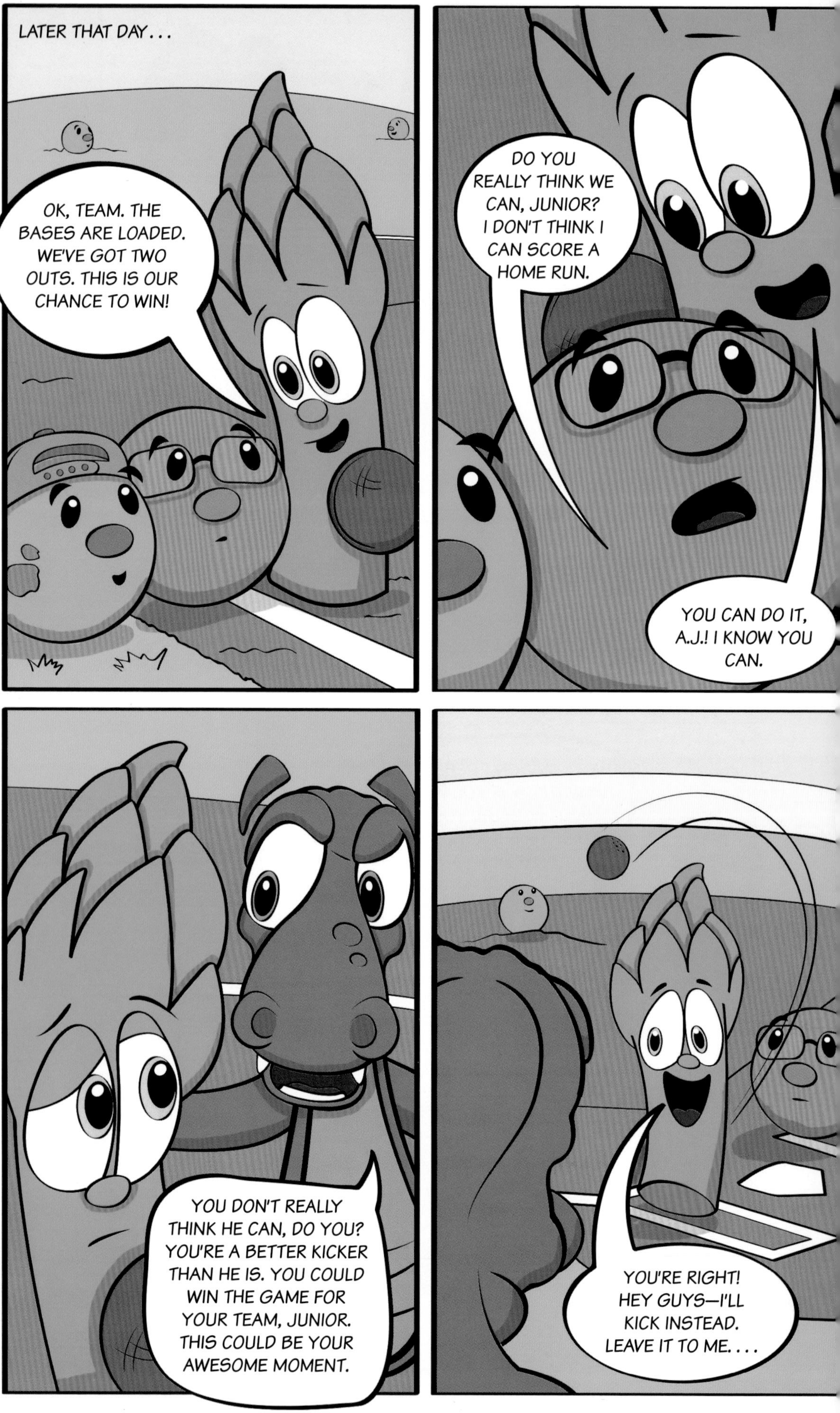
LATER THAT DAY . . .
OK, TEAM. THE BASES ARE LOADED. WE'VE GOT TWO OUTS. THIS IS OUR CHANCE TO WIN!
DO YOU REALLY THINK WE CAN, JUNIOR? I DON'T THINK I CAN SCORE A HOME RUN.
YOU CAN DO IT, A.J.! I KNOW YOU CAN.
YOU DON'T REALLY THINK HE CAN, DO YOU? YOU'RE A BETTER KICKER THAN HE IS. YOU COULD WIN THE GAME FOR YOUR TEAM, JUNIOR. THIS COULD BE YOUR AWESOME MOMENT.
YOU'RE RIGHT! HEY GUYS—I'LL KICK INSTEAD. LEAVE IT TO ME. . . .

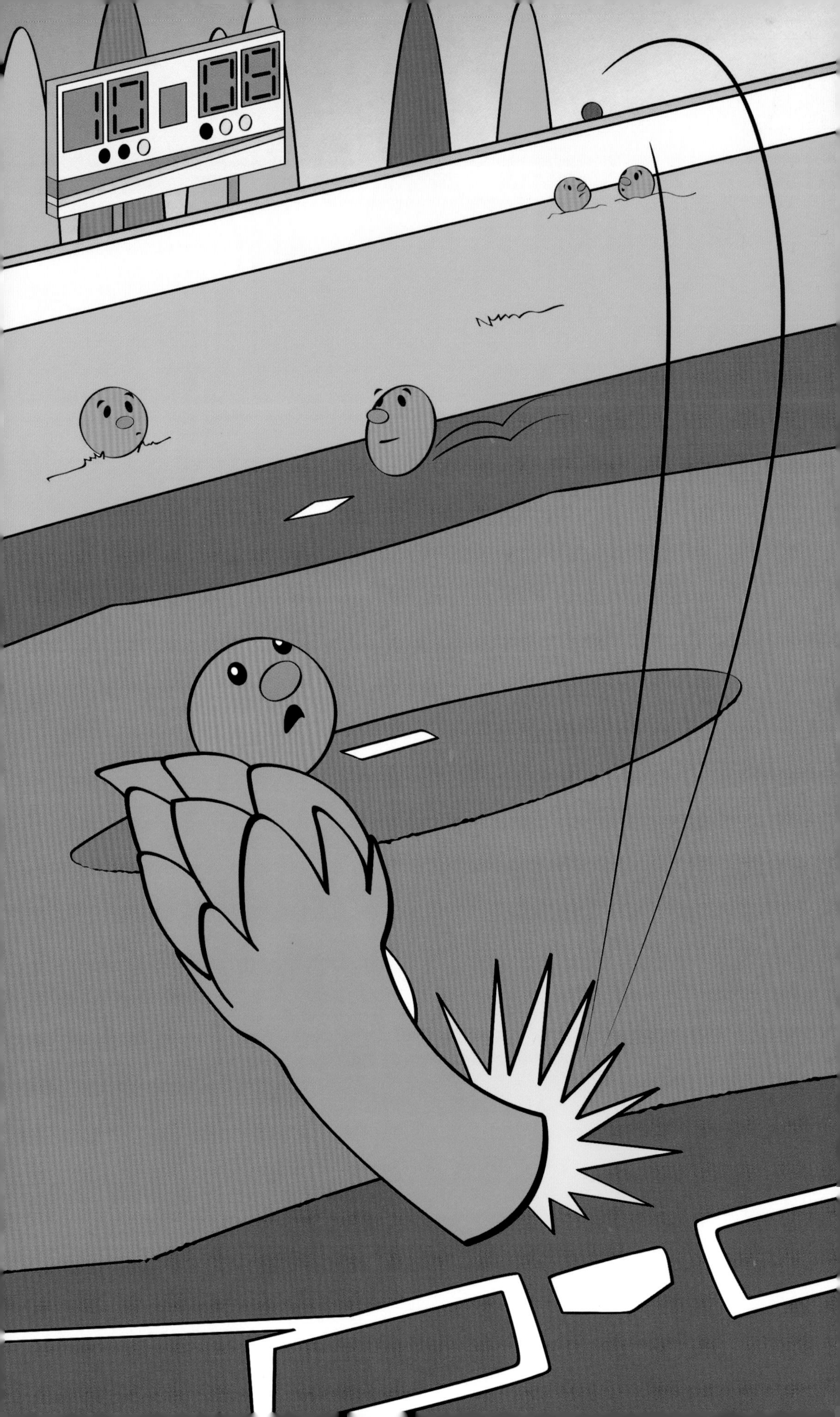

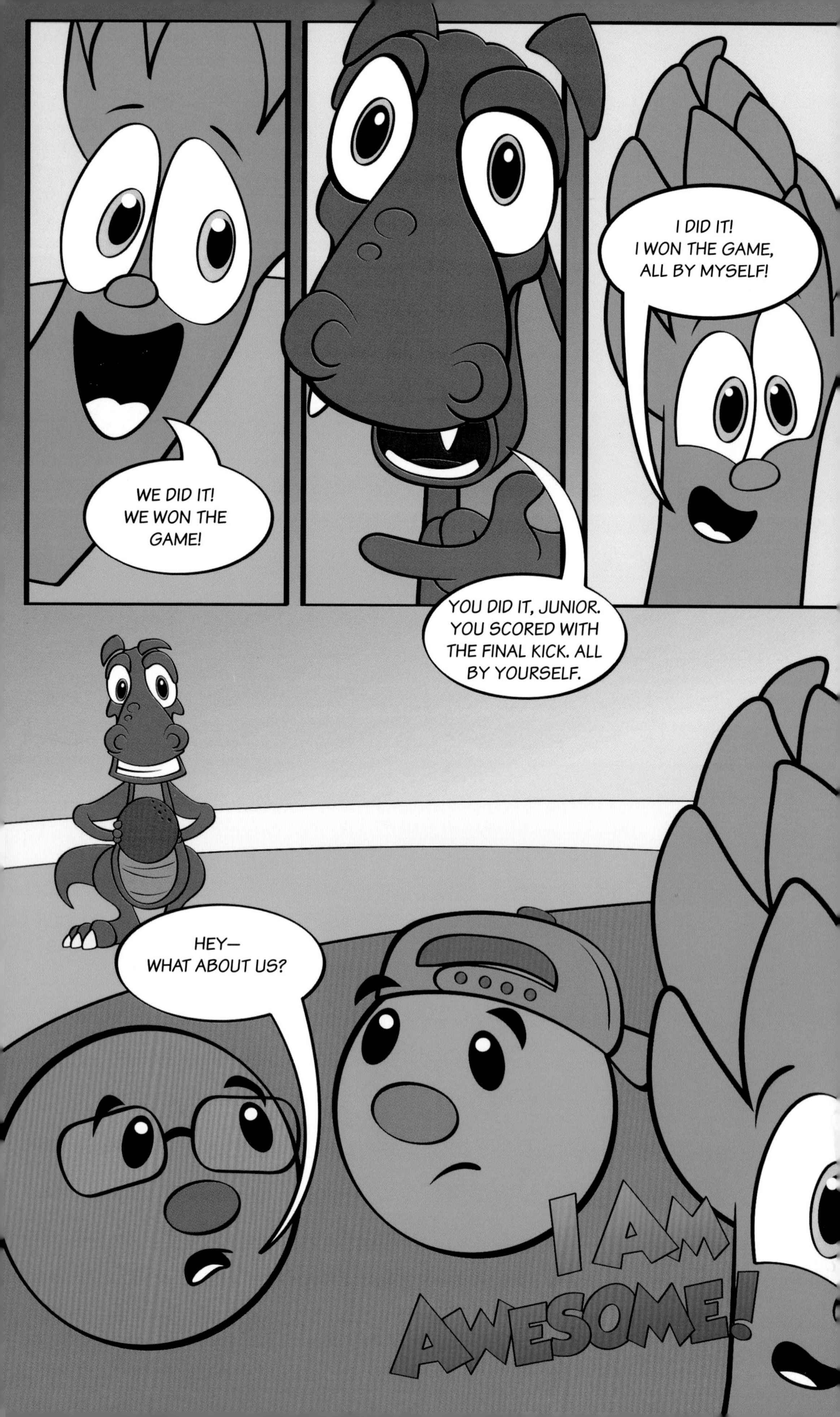
WE DID IT!
WE WON THE GAME!
YOU DID IT, JUNIOR. YOU SCORED WITH THE FINAL KICK. ALL BY YOURSELF.
I DID IT!
I WON THE GAME, ALL BY MYSELF!
HEY—
WHAT ABOUT US?
I AM AWESOME!

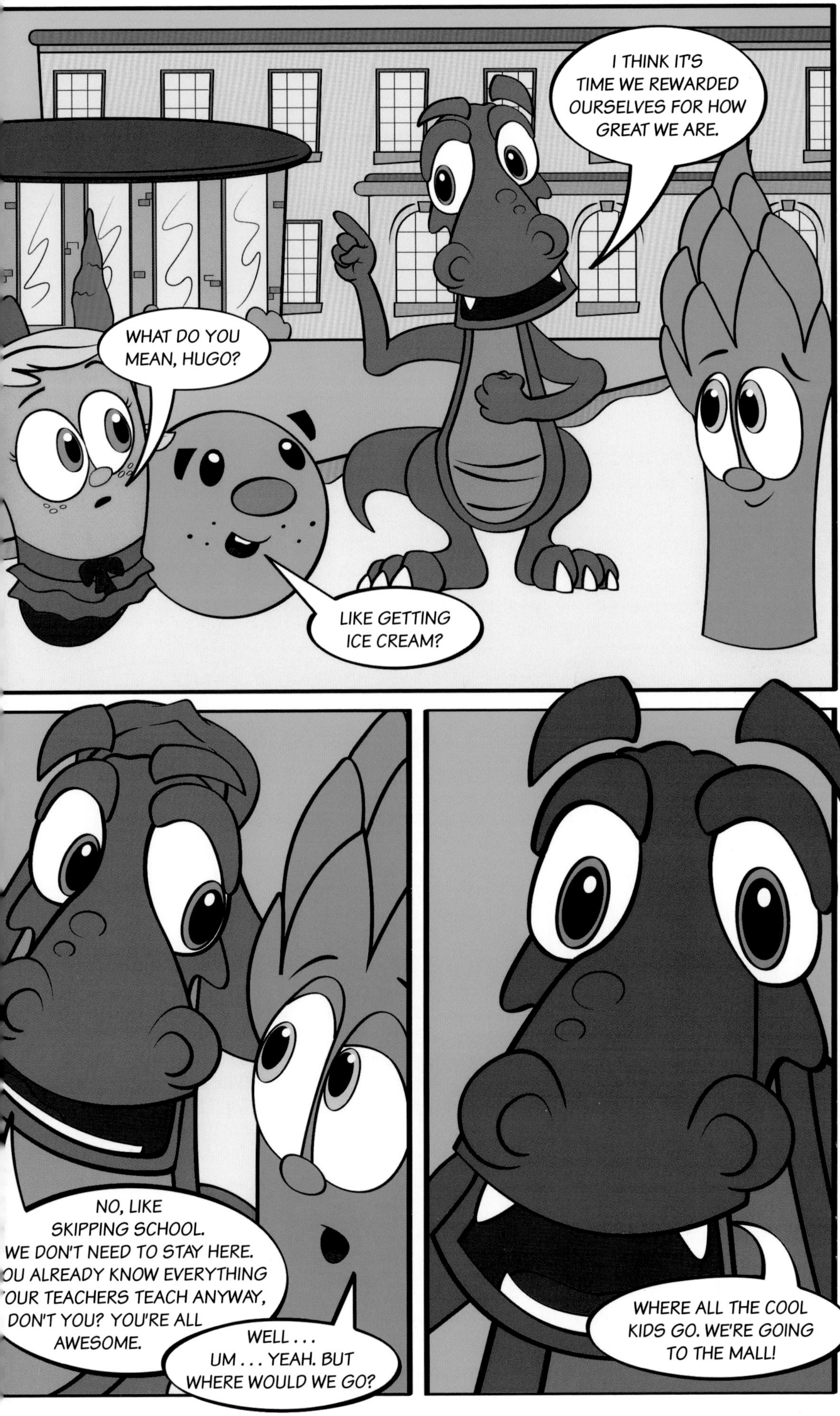
I THINK IT'S TIME WE REWARDED OURSELVES FOR HOW GREAT WE ARE.
WHAT DO YOU MEAN, HUGO?
LIKE GETTING ICE CREAM?
NO, LIKE SKIPPING SCHOOL. WE DON'T NEED TO STAY HERE. OU ALREADY KNOW EVERYTHING OUR TEACHERS TEACH ANYWAY, DON'T YOU? YOU'RE ALL AWESOME.
WELL . . . UM . . . YEAH. BUT WHERE WOULD WE GO?
WHERE ALL THE COOL KIDS GO. WE'RE GOING TO THE MALL!

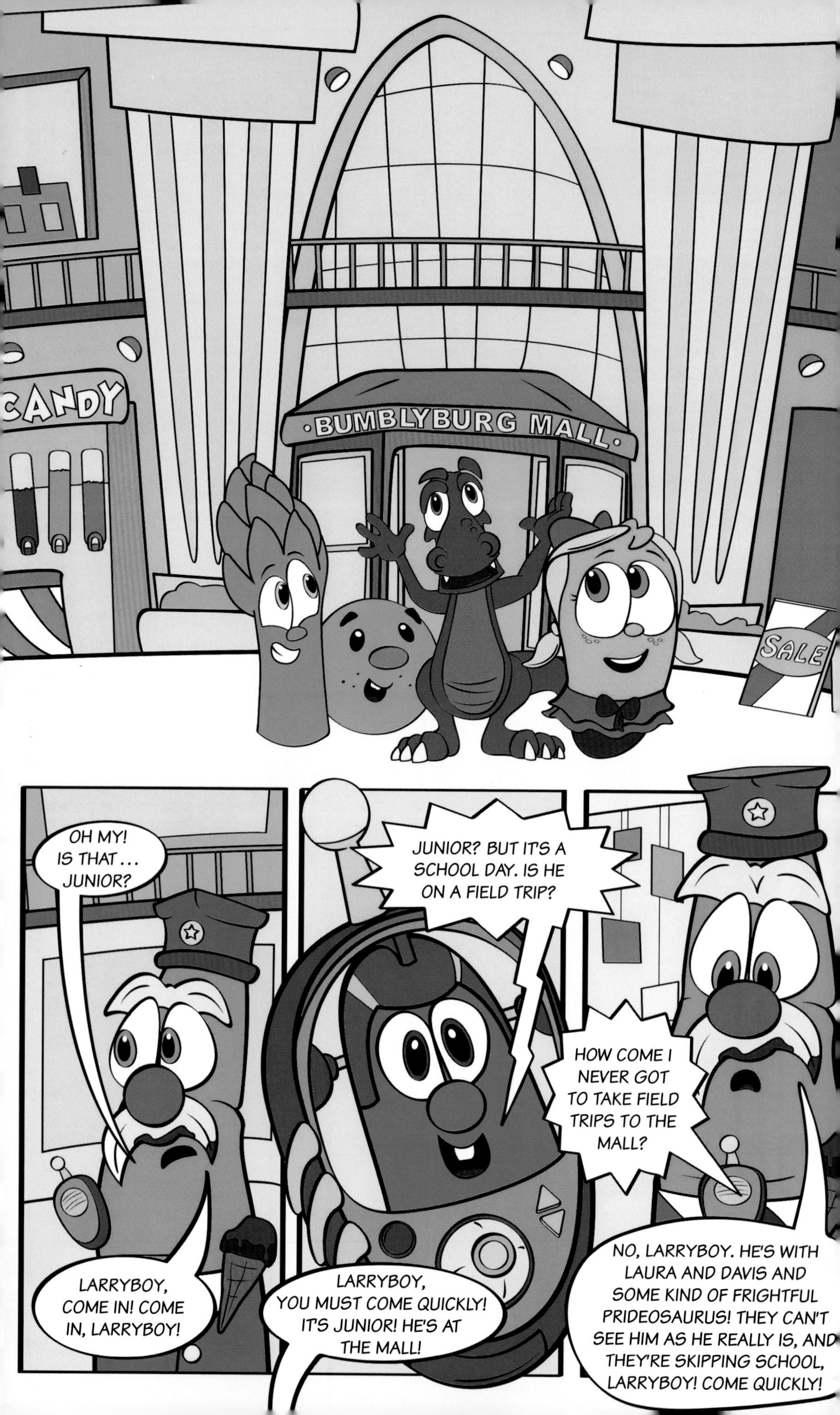
CANDY
BUMBLYBURG MALL
SALE
OH MY! IS THAT... JUNIOR?
LARRYBOY, COME IN! COME IN, LARRYBOY!
JUNIOR? BUT IT'S A SCHOOL DAY. IS HE ON A FIELD TRIP?
LARRYBOY, YOU MUST COME QUICKLY! IT'S JUNIOR! HE'S AT THE MALL!
HOW COME I NEVER GOT TO TAKE FIELD TRIPS TO THE MALL?
NO, LARRYBOY. HE'S WITH LAURA AND DAVIS AND SOME KIND OF FRIGHTFUL PRIDEOSAURUS! THEY CAN'T SEE HIM AS HE REALLY IS, AND THEY'RE SKIPPING SCHOOL, LARRYBOY! COME QUICKLY!

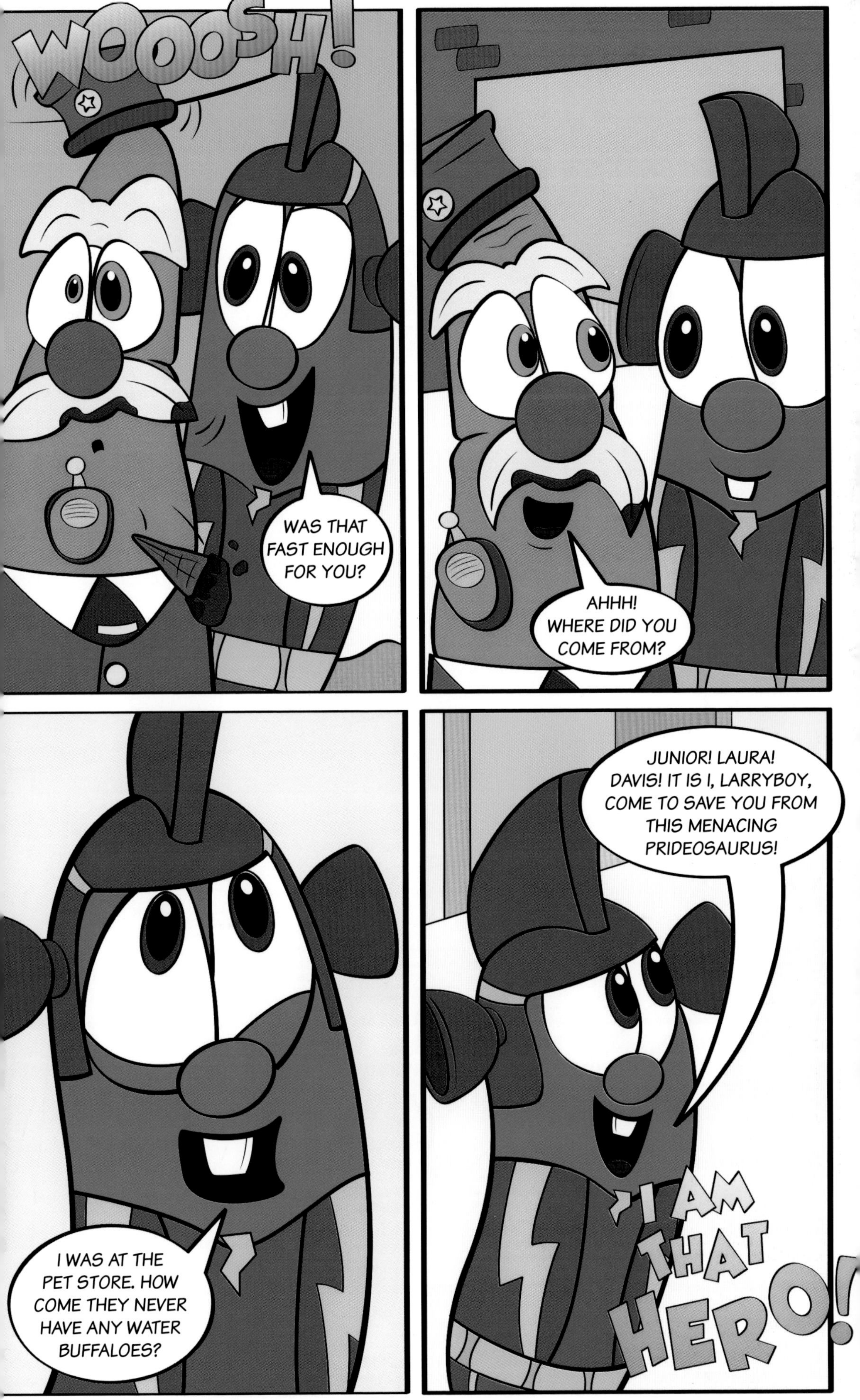
WOOOSH!
WAS THAT FAST ENOUGH FOR YOU?
AHHH! WHERE DID YOU COME FROM?
I WAS AT THE PET STORE. HOW COME THEY NEVER HAVE ANY WATER BUFFALOES?
JUNIOR! LAURA! DAVIS! IT IS I, LARRYBOY, COME TO SAVE YOU FROM THIS MENACING PRIDEOSAURUS!
I AM THAT HERO!

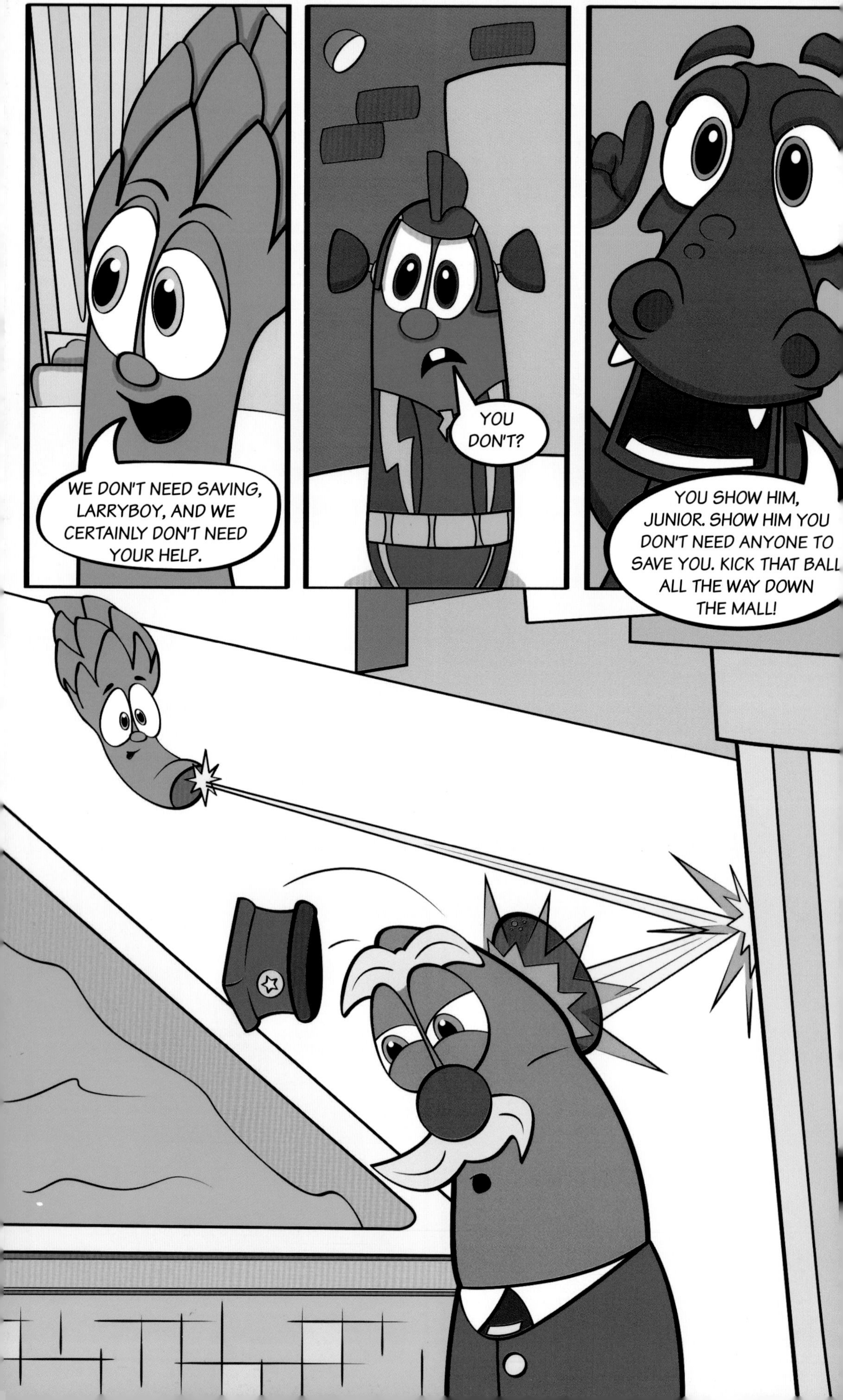
WE DON'T NEED SAVING, LARRYBOY, AND WE CERTAINLY DON'T NEED YOUR HELP.
YOU DON'T?
YOU SHOW HIM, JUNIOR. SHOW HIM YOU DON'T NEED ANYONE TO SAVE YOU. KICK THAT BALL ALL THE WAY DOWN THE MALL!

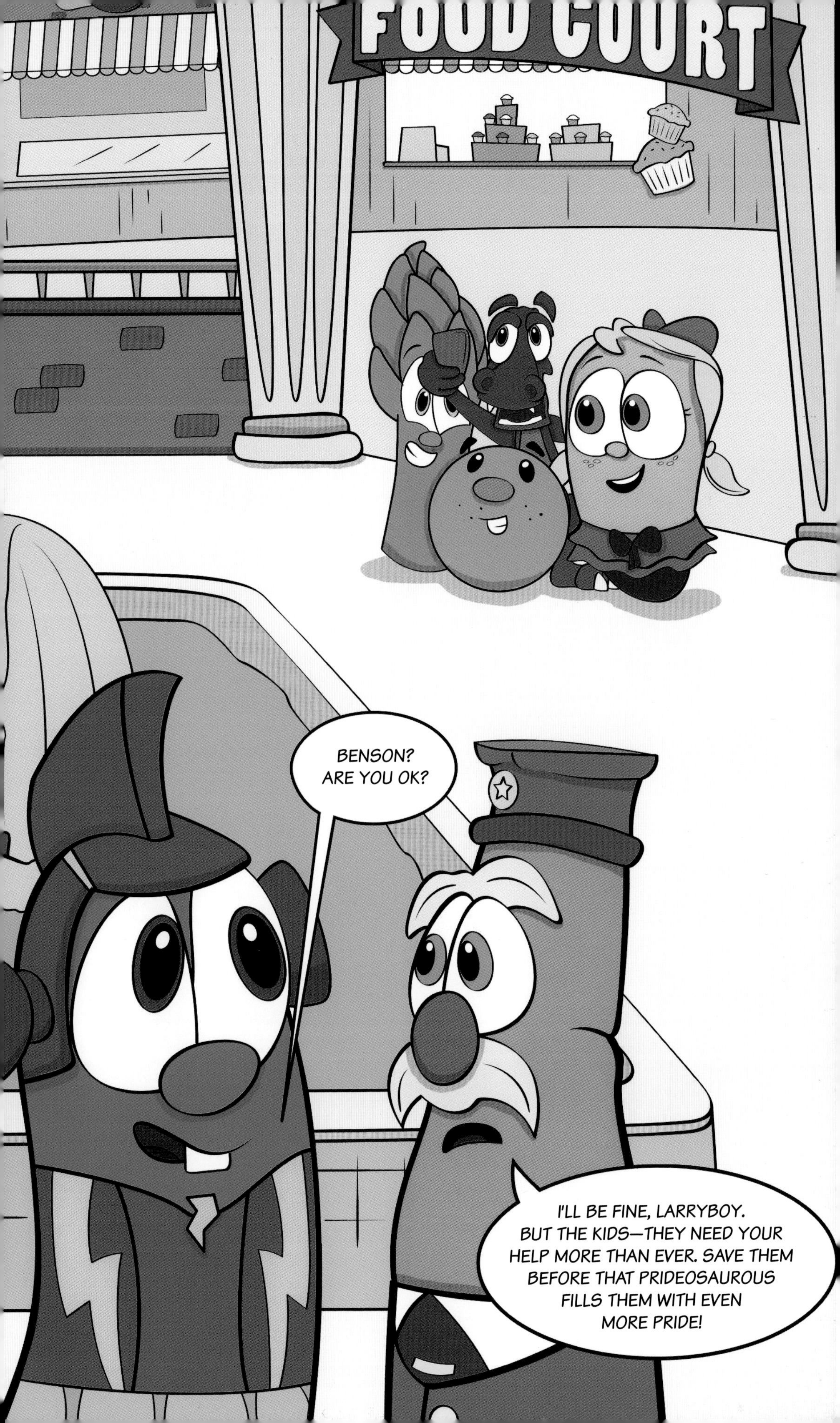
FOOD COURT
BENSON? ARE YOU OK?
I'LL BE FINE, LARRYBOY. BUT THE KIDS—THEY NEED YOUR HELP MORE THAN EVER. SAVE THEM BEFORE THAT PRIDEOSAUROUS FILLS THEM WITH EVEN MORE PRIDE!

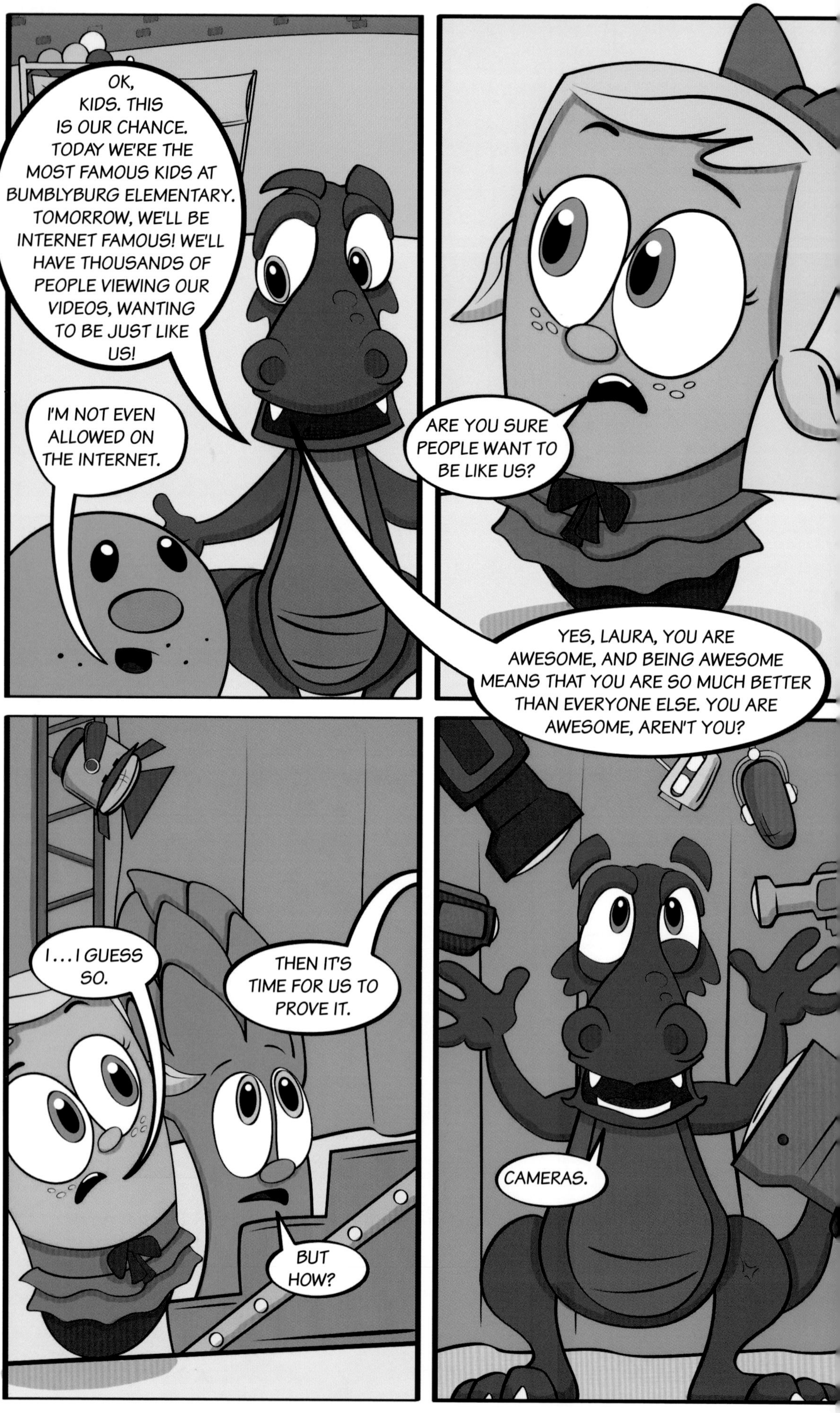
OK, KIDS. THIS IS OUR CHANCE. TODAY WE'RE THE MOST FAMOUS KIDS AT BUMBLYBURG ELEMENTARY. TOMORROW, WE'LL BE INTERNET FAMOUS! WE'LL HAVE THOUSANDS OF PEOPLE VIEWING OUR VIDEOS, WANTING TO BE JUST LIKE US!
I'M NOT EVEN ALLOWED ON THE INTERNET.
ARE YOU SURE PEOPLE WANT TO BE LIKE US?
YES, LAURA, YOU ARE AWESOME, AND BEING AWESOME MEANS THAT YOU ARE SO MUCH BETTER THAN EVERYONE ELSE. YOU ARE AWESOME, AREN'T YOU?
I... I GUESS SO.
THEN IT'S TIME FOR US TO PROVE IT.
BUT HOW?
CAMERAS.

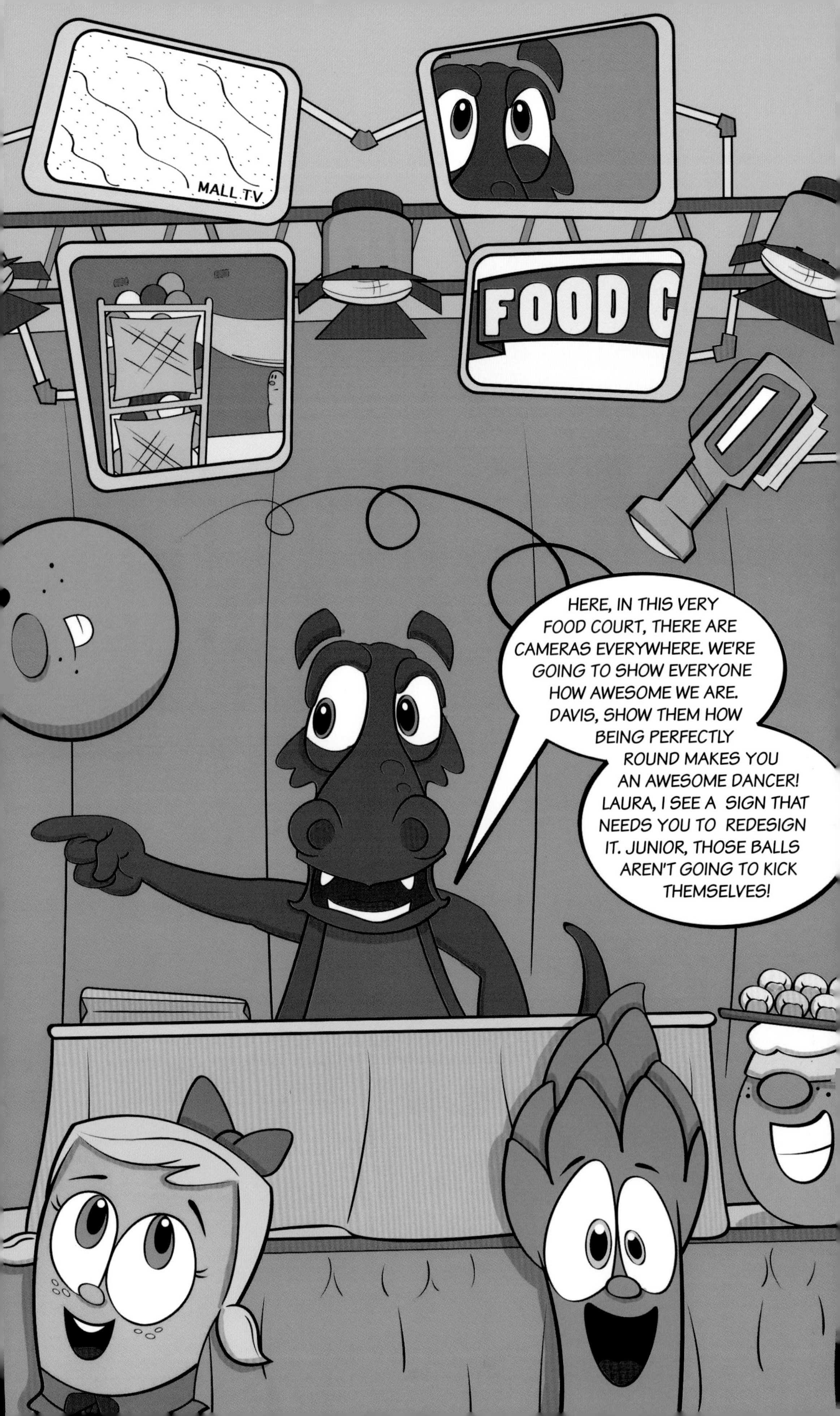
MALL TV
FOOD C
HERE, IN THIS VERY FOOD COURT, THERE ARE CAMERAS EVERYWHERE. WE'RE GOING TO SHOW EVERYONE HOW AWESOME WE ARE. DAVIS, SHOW THEM HOW BEING PERFECTLY ROUND MAKES YOU AN AWESOME DANCER! LAURA, I SEE A SIGN THAT NEEDS YOU TO REDESIGN IT. JUNIOR, THOSE BALLS AREN'T GOING TO KICK THEMSELVES!

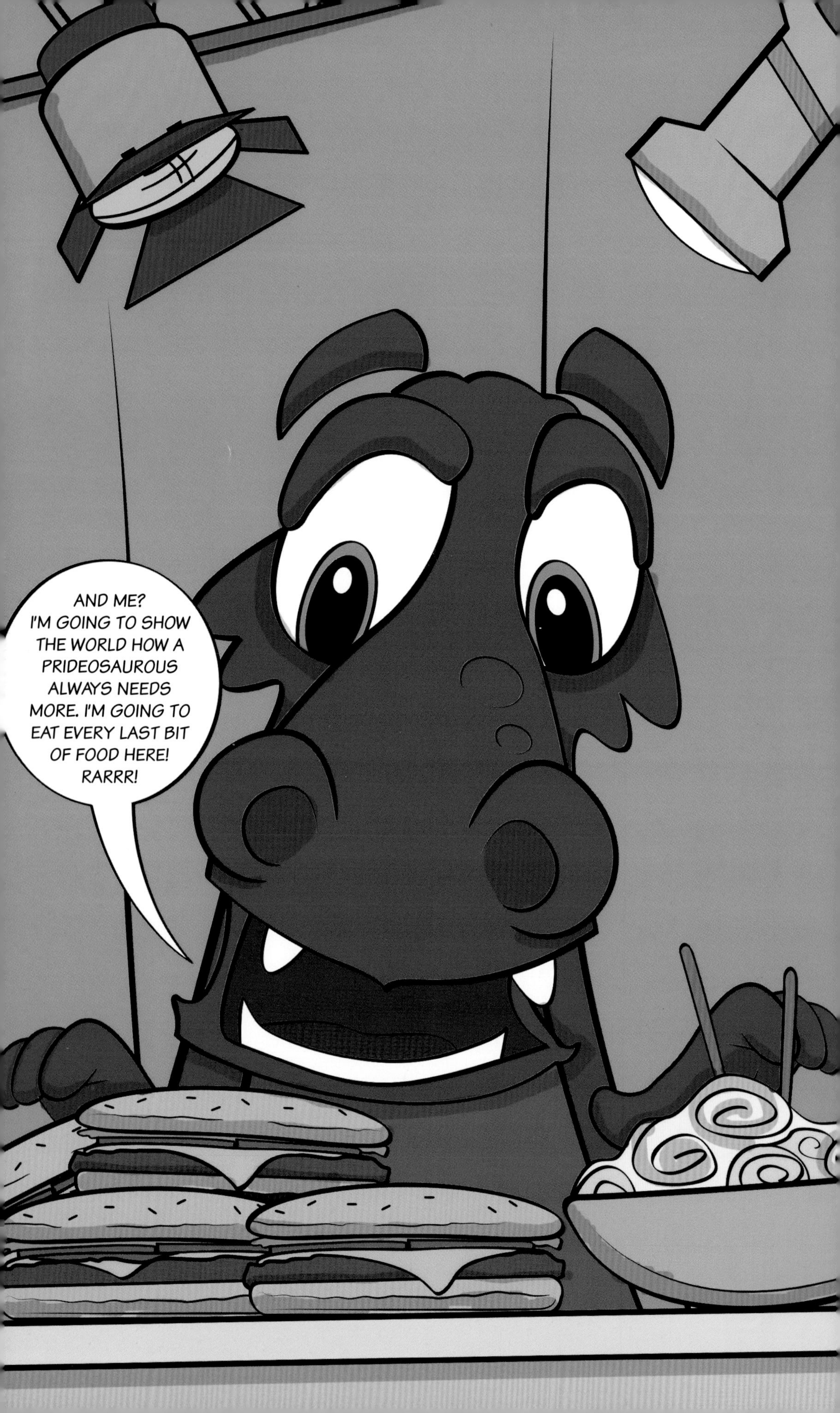
AND ME? I'M GOING TO SHOW THE WORLD HOW A PRIDEOSAUROUS ALWAYS NEEDS MORE. I'M GOING TO EAT EVERY LAST BIT OF FOOD HERE! RARRR!

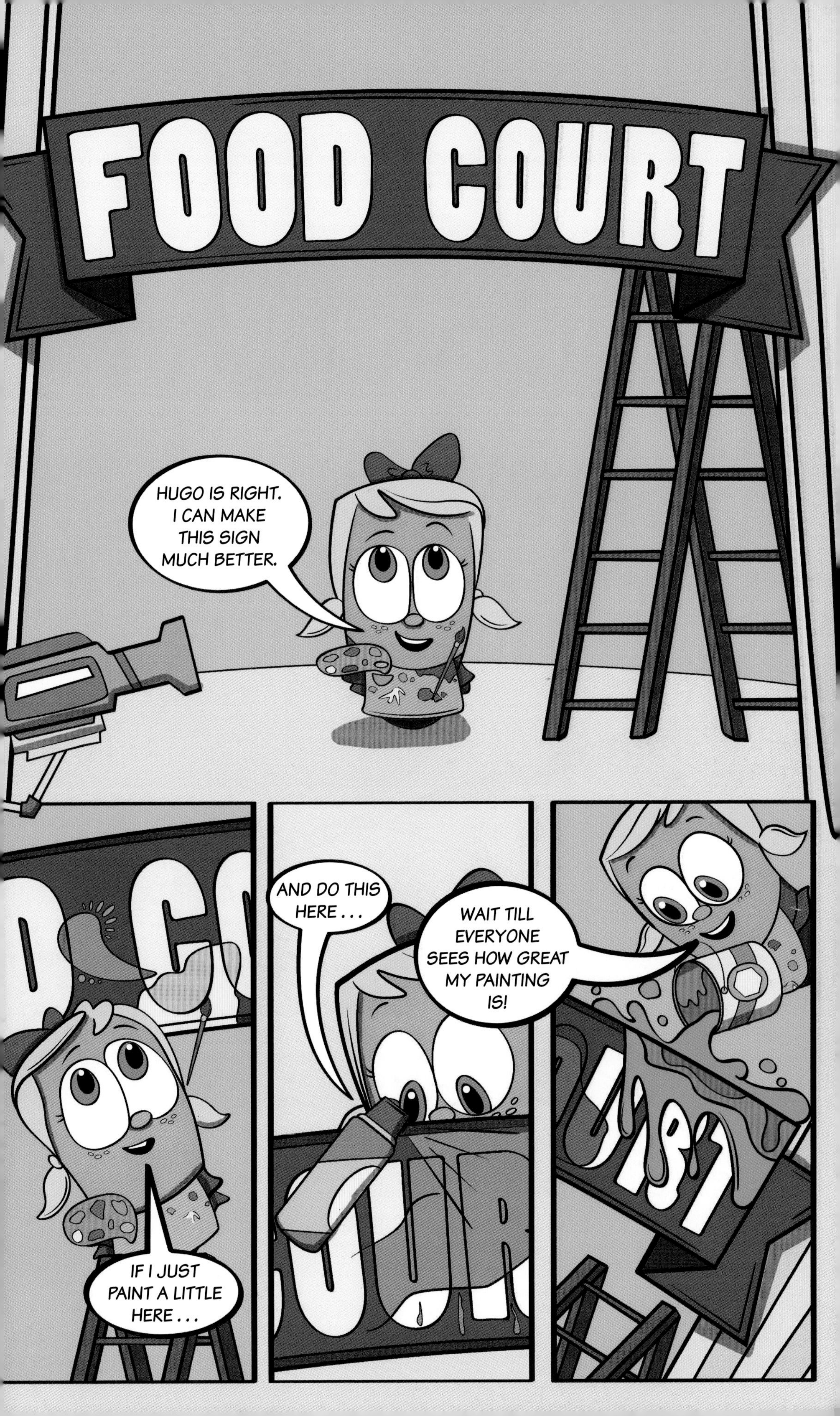
FOOD COURT
HUGO IS RIGHT. I CAN MAKE THIS SIGN MUCH BETTER.
IF I JUST PAINT A LITTLE HERE . . .
AND DO THIS HERE . . .
WAIT TILL EVERYONE SEES HOW GREAT MY PAINTING IS!

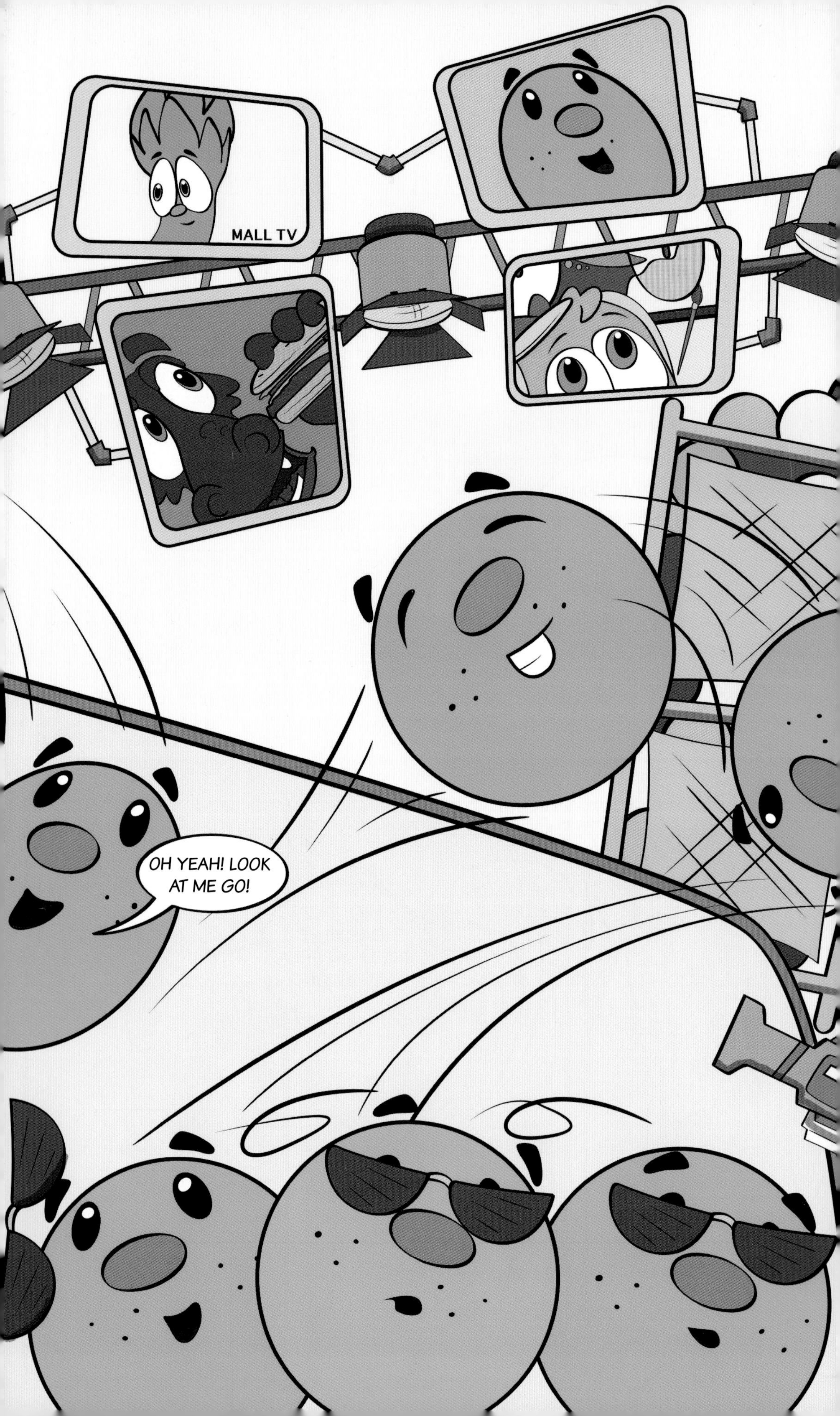
MALL TV
OH YEAH! LOOK AT ME GO!

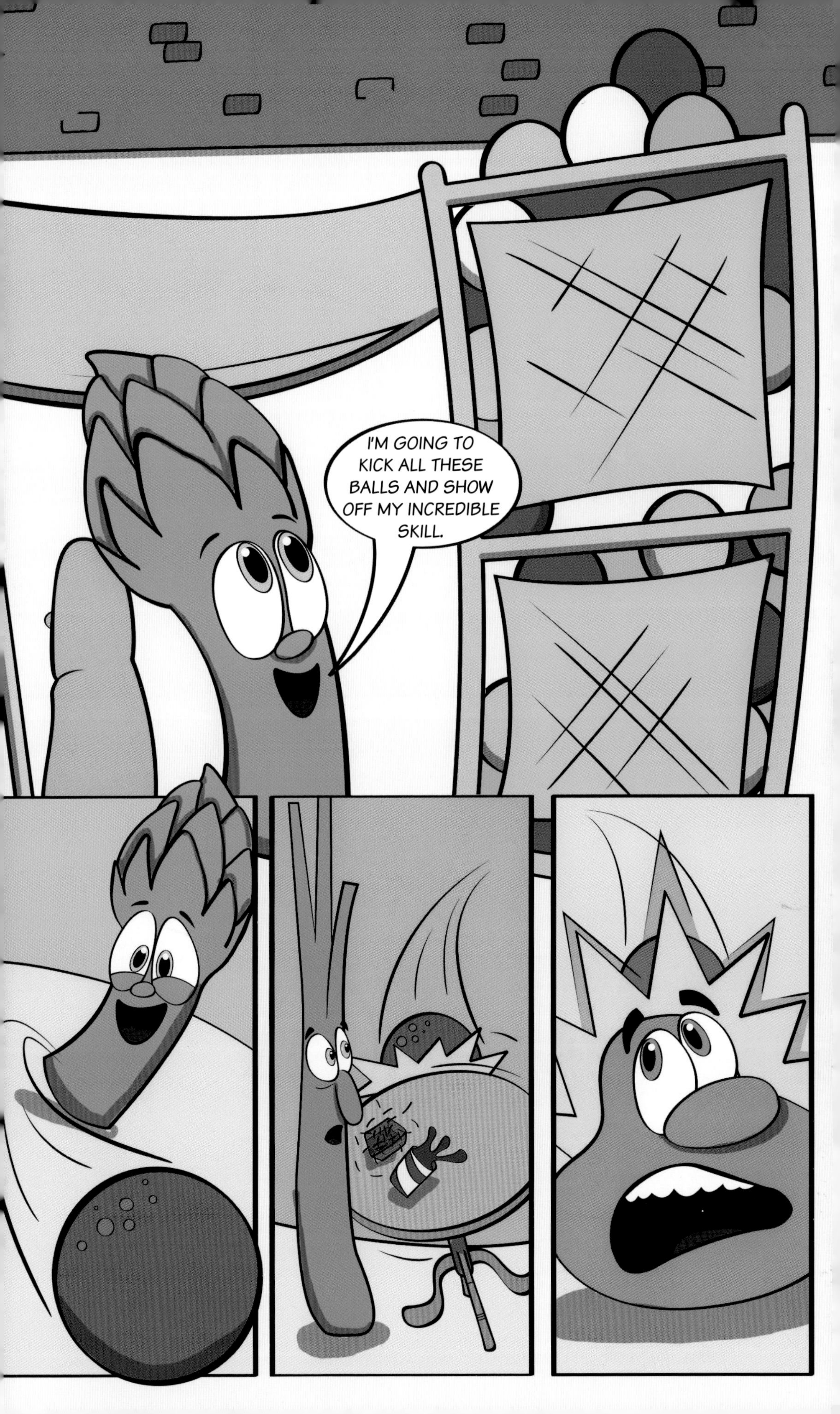
I'M GOING TO KICK ALL THESE BALLS AND SHOW OFF MY INCREDIBLE SKILL.

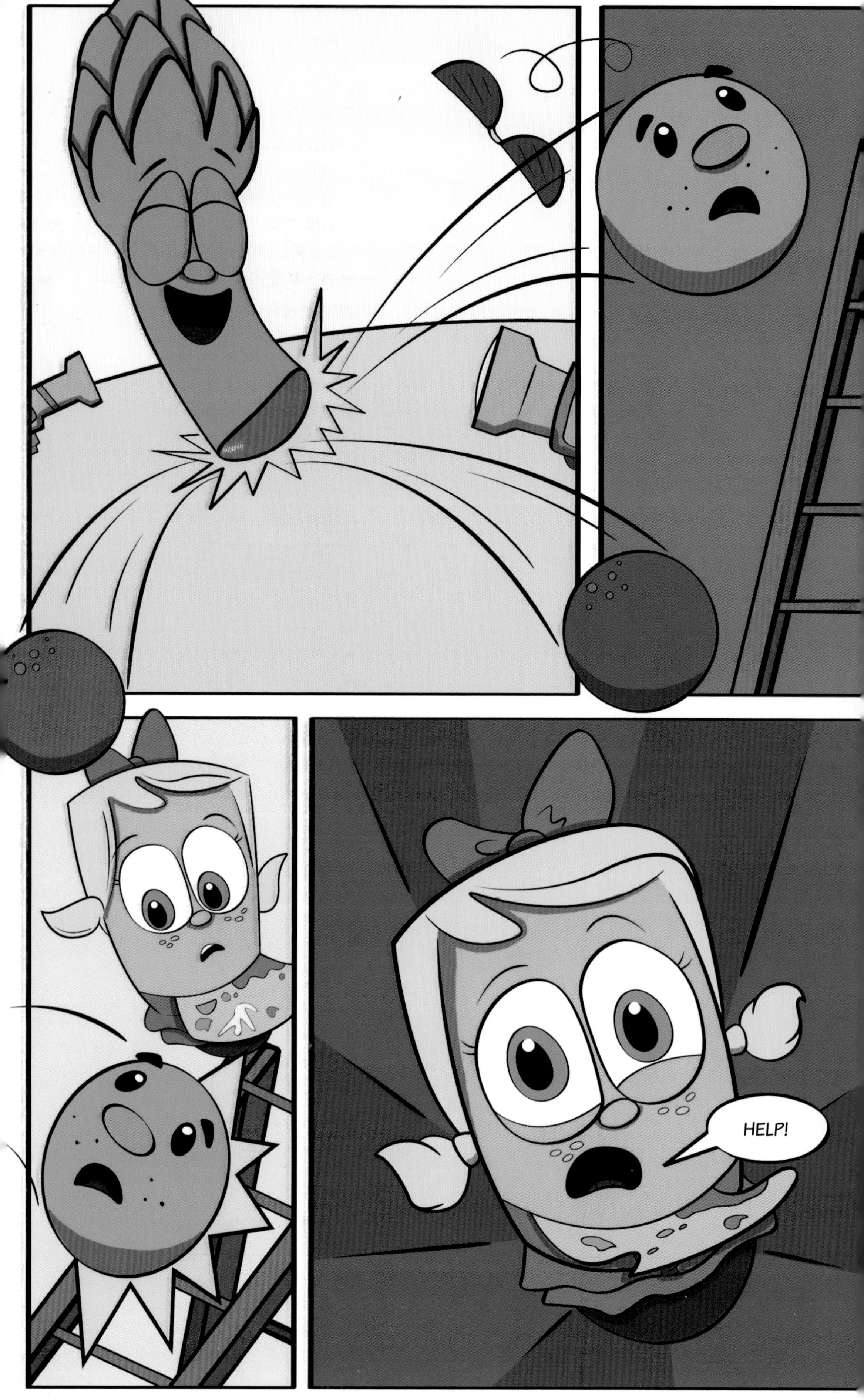
HELP!

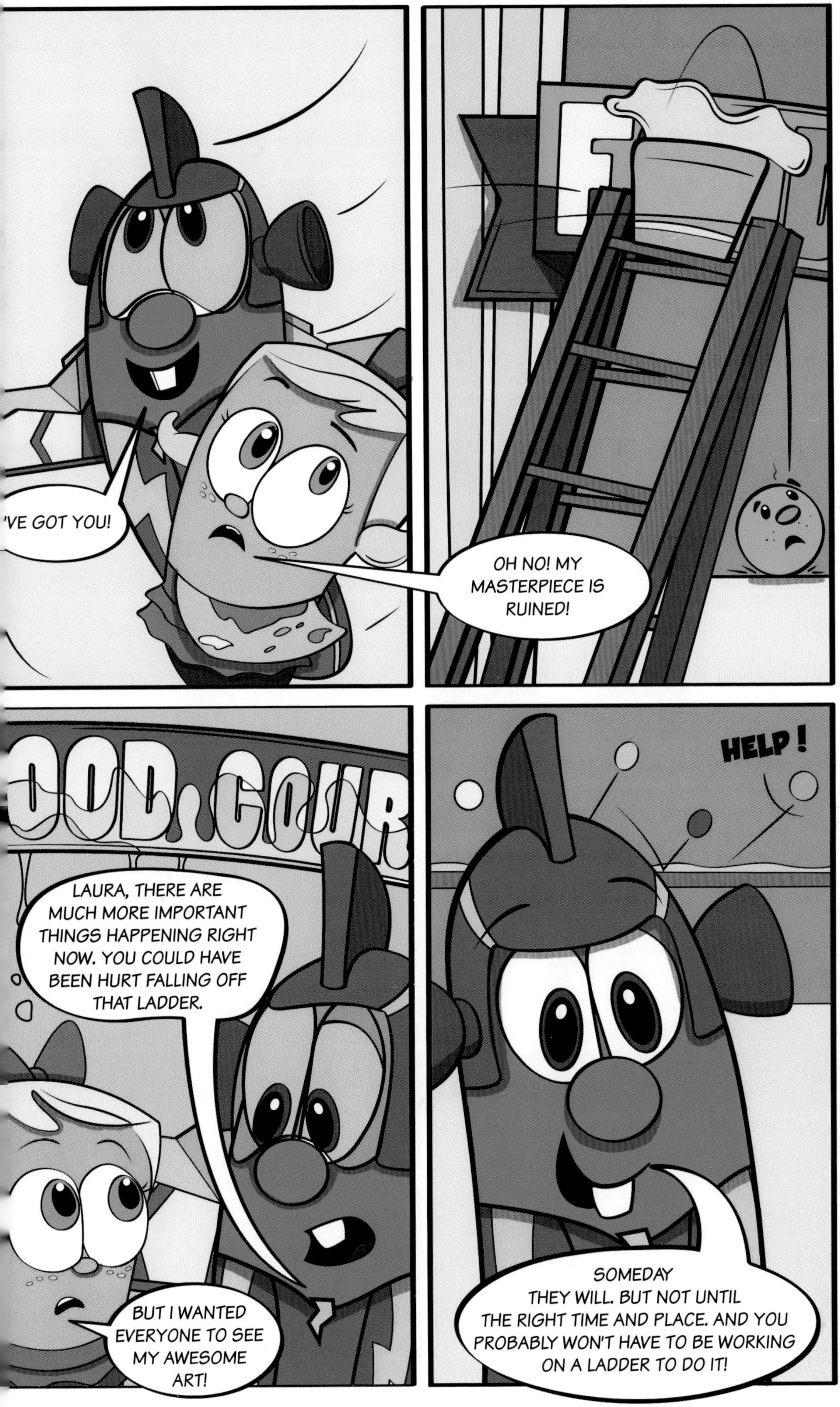
'VE GOT YOU!
OH NO! MY MASTERPIECE IS RUINED!
FOOD COUR
HELP!
LAURA, THERE ARE MUCH MORE IMPORTANT THINGS HAPPENING RIGHT NOW. YOU COULD HAVE BEEN HURT FALLING OFF THAT LADDER.
BUT I WANTED EVERYONE TO SEE MY AWESOME ART!
SOMEDAY THEY WILL. BUT NOT UNTIL THE RIGHT TIME AND PLACE. AND YOU PROBABLY WON'T HAVE TO BE WORKING ON A LADDER TO DO IT!

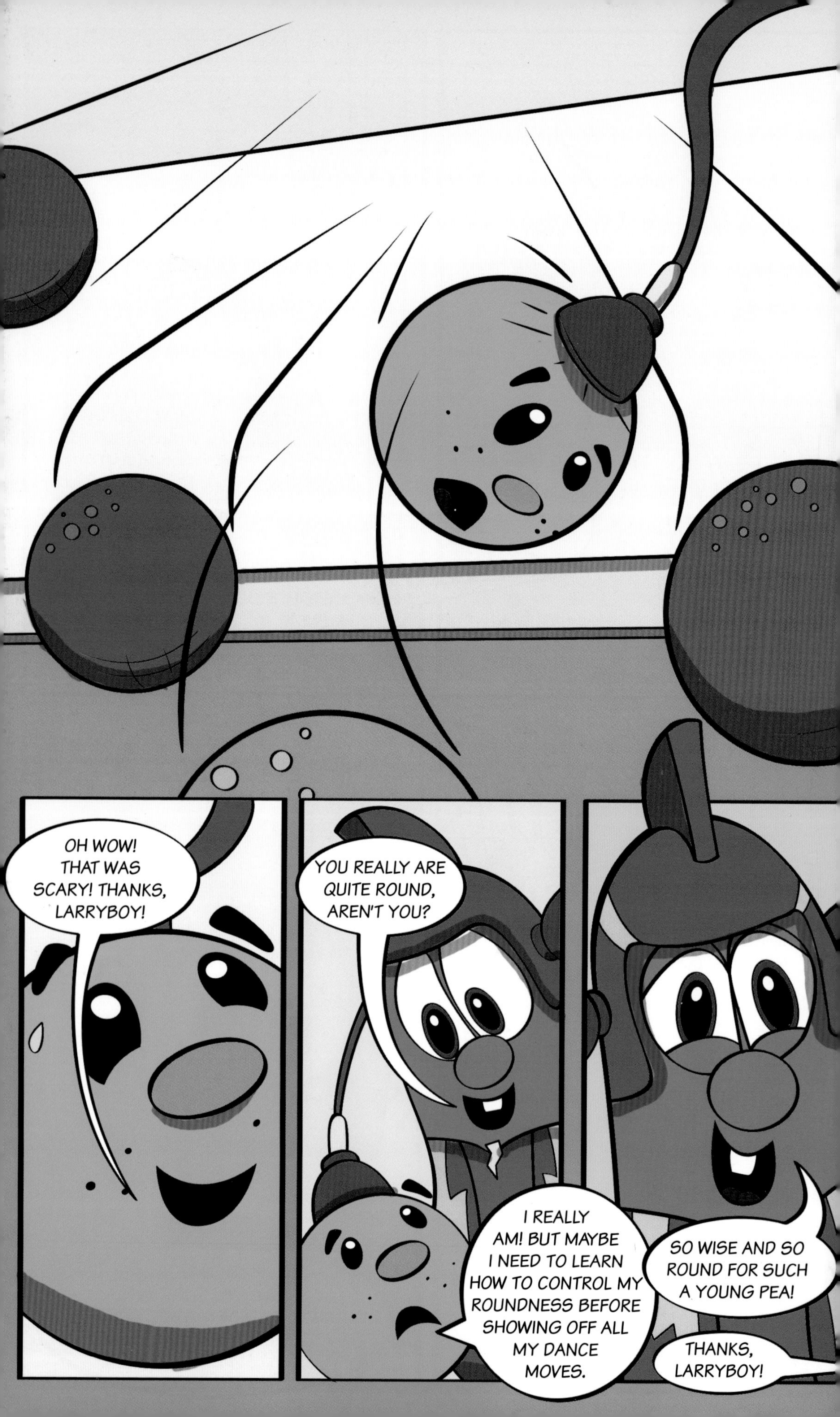
OH WOW! THAT WAS SCARY! THANKS, LARRYBOY!
YOU REALLY ARE QUITE ROUND, AREN'T YOU?
I REALLY AM! BUT MAYBE I NEED TO LEARN HOW TO CONTROL MY ROUNDNESS BEFORE SHOWING OFF ALL MY DANCE MOVES.
SO WISE AND SO ROUND FOR SUCH A YOUNG PEA!
THANKS, LARRYBOY!

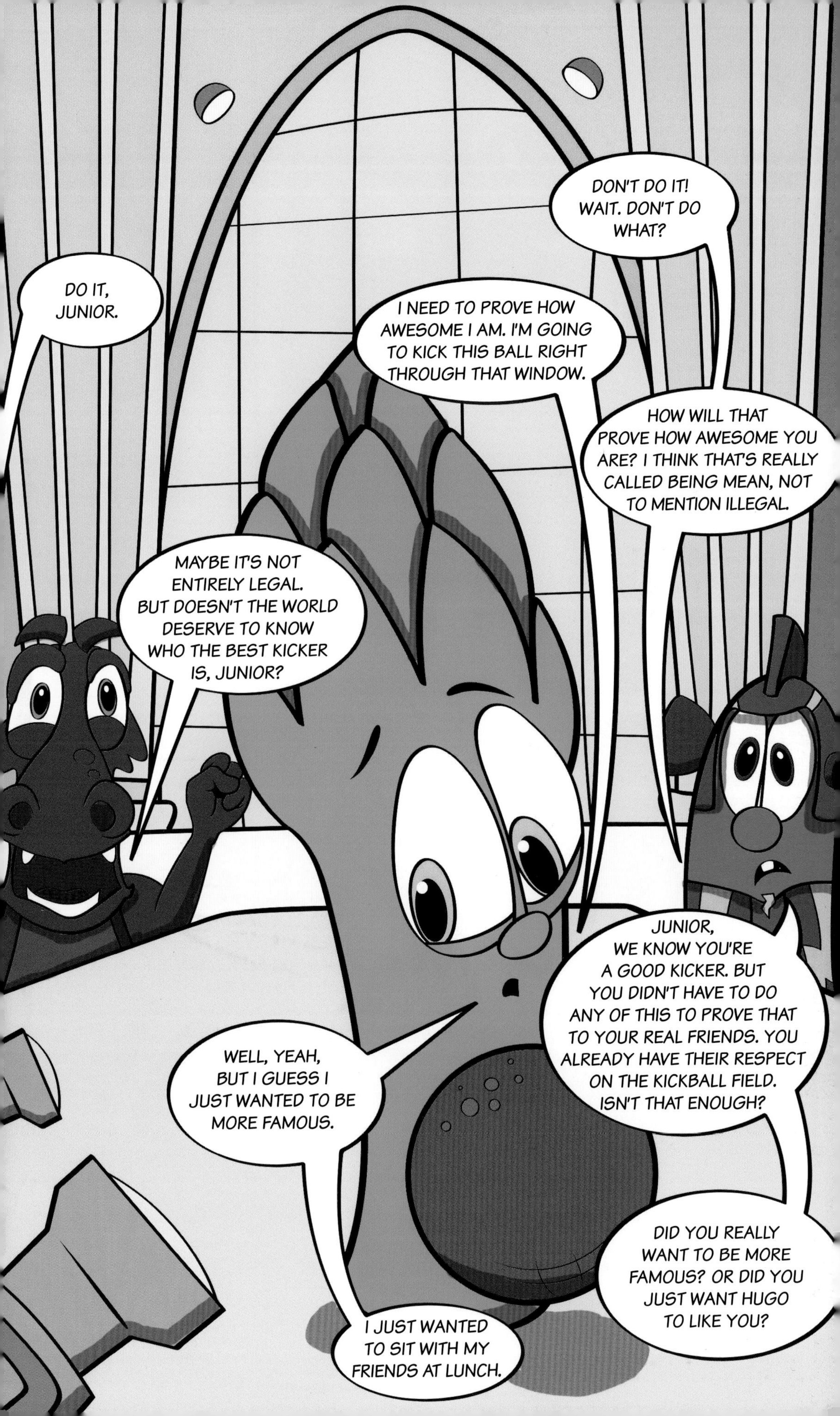
DO IT, JUNIOR.
DON'T DO IT! WAIT. DON'T DO WHAT?
I NEED TO PROVE HOW AWESOME I AM. I'M GOING TO KICK THIS BALL RIGHT THROUGH THAT WINDOW.
HOW WILL THAT PROVE HOW AWESOME YOU ARE? I THINK THAT'S REALLY CALLED BEING MEAN, NOT TO MENTION ILLEGAL.
MAYBE IT'S NOT ENTIRELY LEGAL. BUT DOESN'T THE WORLD DESERVE TO KNOW WHO THE BEST KICKER IS, JUNIOR?
JUNIOR, WE KNOW YOU'RE A GOOD KICKER. BUT YOU DIDN'T HAVE TO DO ANY OF THIS TO PROVE THAT TO YOUR REAL FRIENDS. YOU ALREADY HAVE THEIR RESPECT ON THE KICKBALL FIELD. ISN'T THAT ENOUGH?
WELL, YEAH, BUT I GUESS I JUST WANTED TO BE MORE FAMOUS.
DID YOU REALLY WANT TO BE MORE FAMOUS? OR DID YOU JUST WANT HUGO TO LIKE YOU?
I JUST WANTED TO SIT WITH MY FRIENDS AT LUNCH.

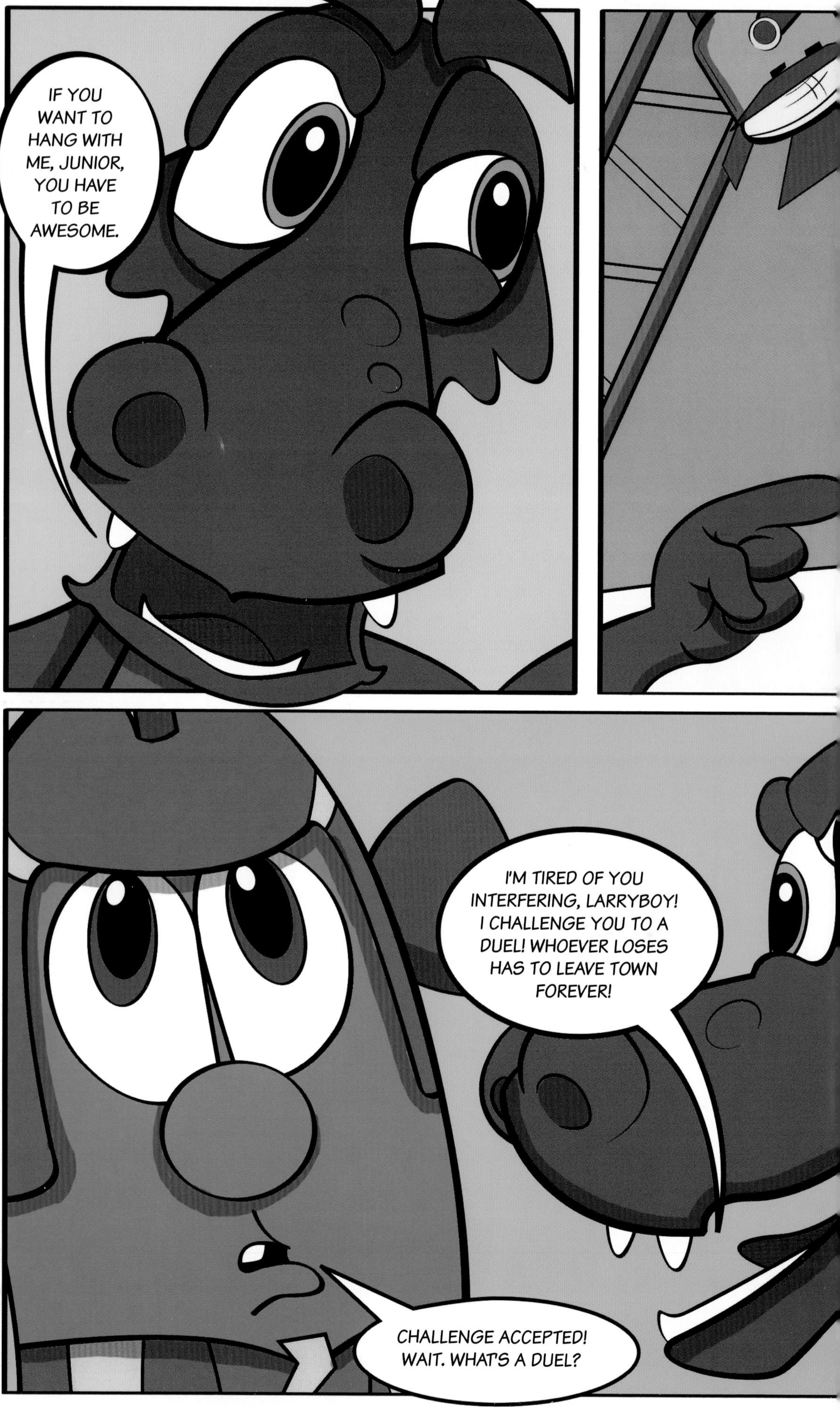
IF YOU WANT TO HANG WITH ME, JUNIOR, YOU HAVE TO BE AWESOME.
I'M TIRED OF YOU INTERFERING, LARRYBOY! I CHALLENGE YOU TO A DUEL! WHOEVER LOSES HAS TO LEAVE TOWN FOREVER!
CHALLENGE ACCEPTED! WAIT. WHAT'S A DUEL?

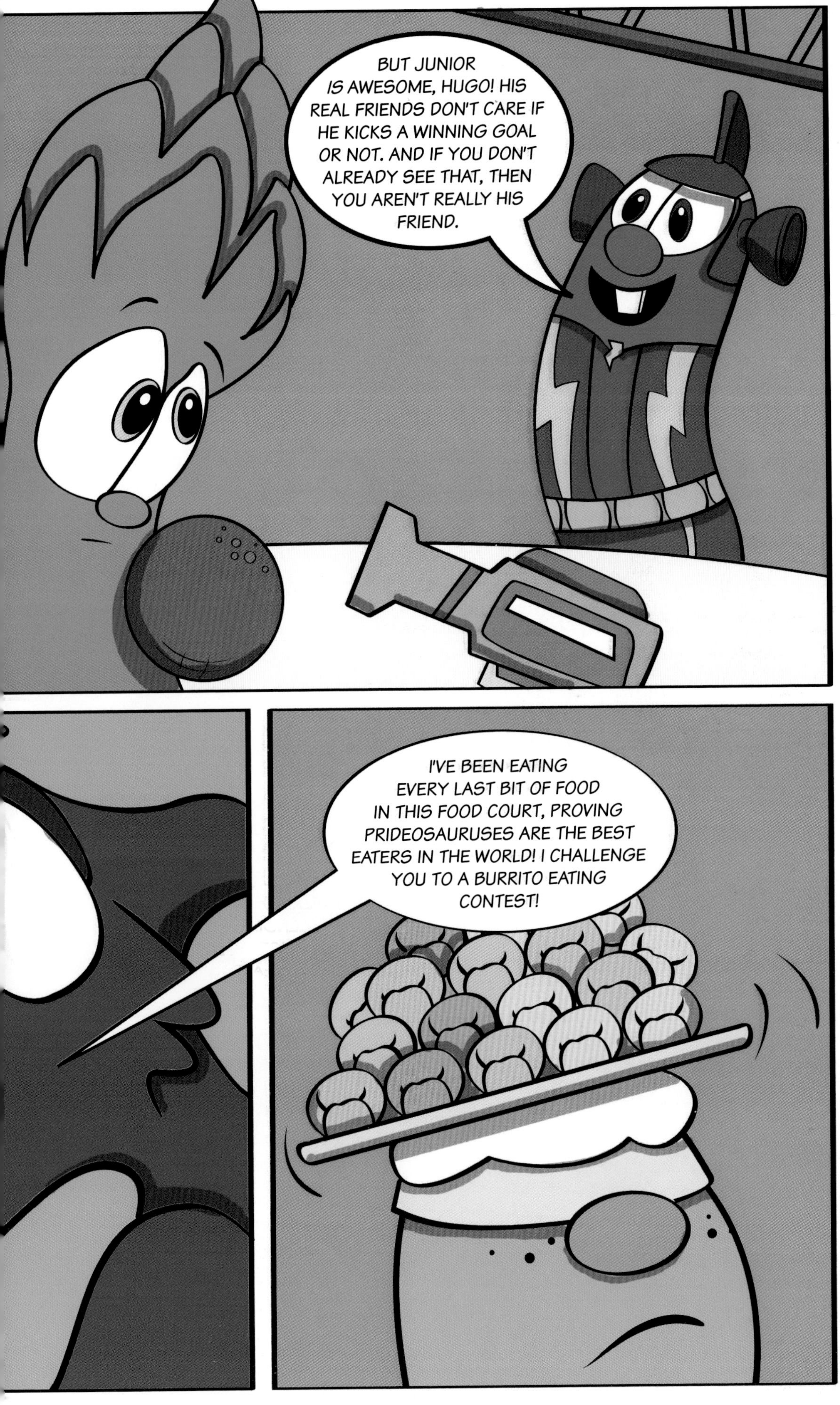
BUT JUNIOR IS AWESOME, HUGO! HIS REAL FRIENDS DON'T CARE IF HE KICKS A WINNING GOAL OR NOT. AND IF YOU DON'T ALREADY SEE THAT, THEN YOU AREN'T REALLY HIS FRIEND.
I'VE BEEN EATING EVERY LAST BIT OF FOOD IN THIS FOOD COURT, PROVING PRIDEOSAURUSES ARE THE BEST EATERS IN THE WORLD! I CHALLENGE YOU TO A BURRITO EATING CONTEST!

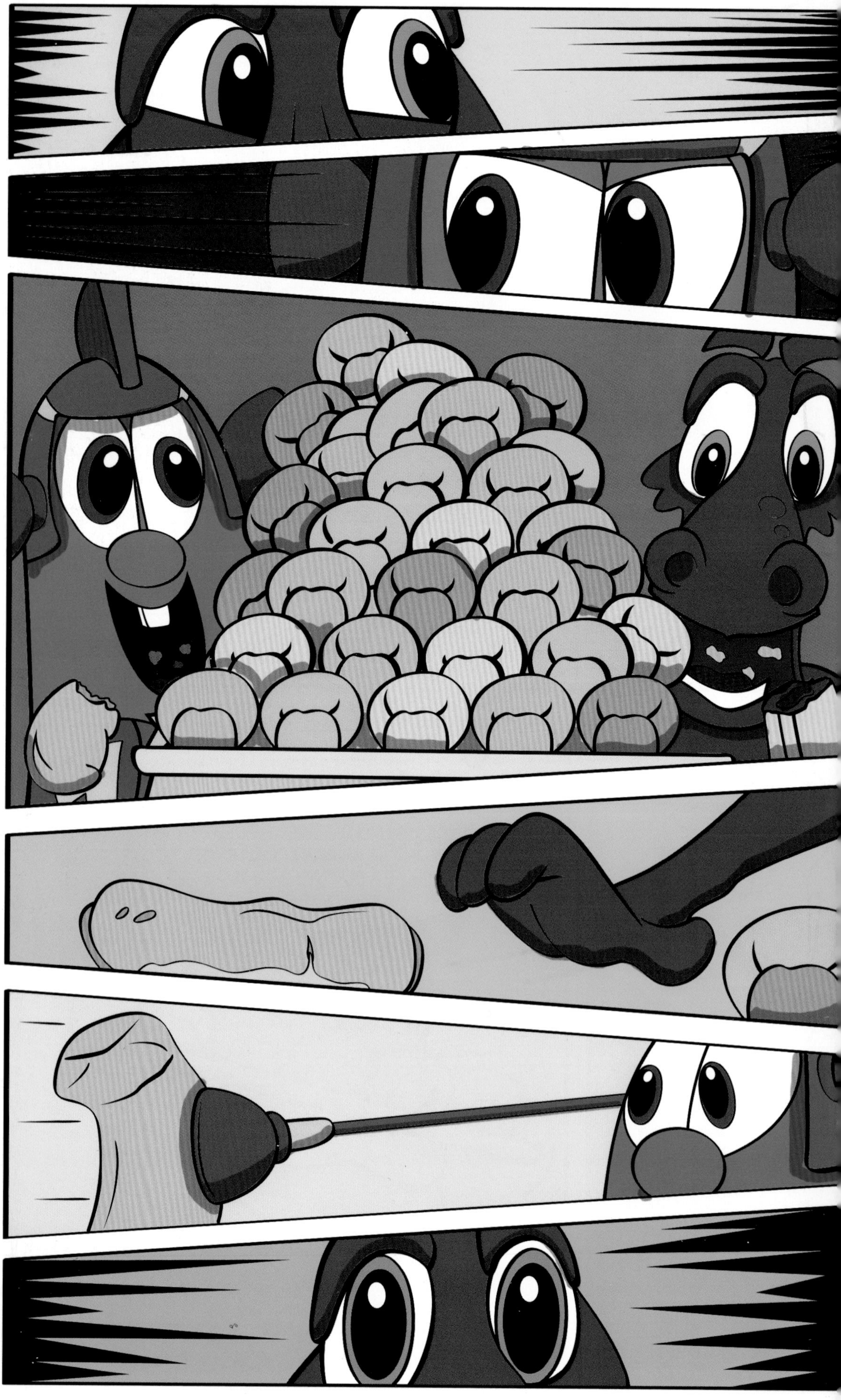

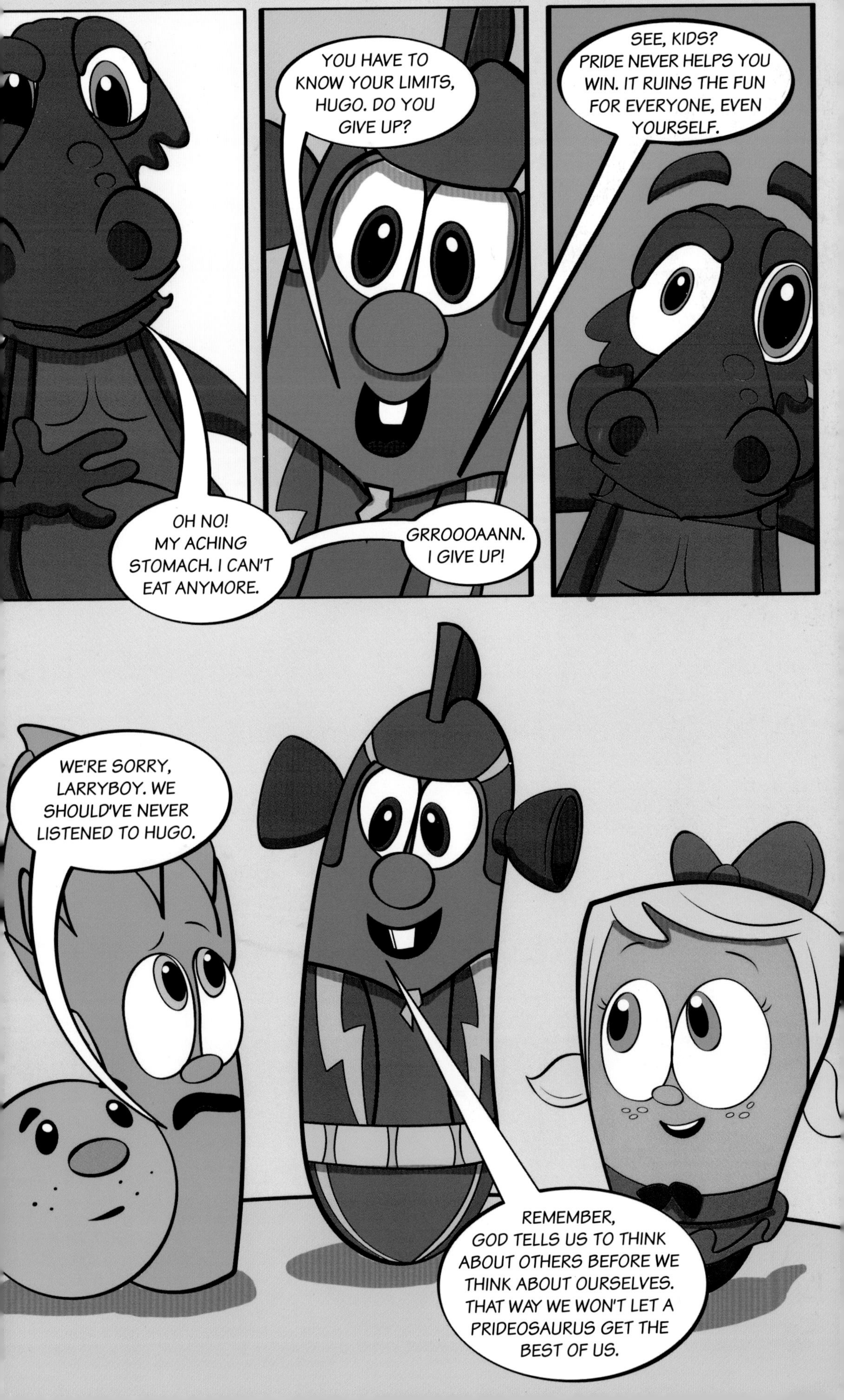
YOU HAVE TO KNOW YOUR LIMITS, HUGO. DO YOU GIVE UP?
OH NO! MY ACHING STOMACH. I CAN'T EAT ANYMORE.
GRROOOAANN. I GIVE UP!
SEE, KIDS? PRIDE NEVER HELPS YOU WIN. IT RUINS THE FUN FOR EVERYONE, EVEN YOURSELF.
WE'RE SORRY, LARRYBOY. WE SHOULD'VE NEVER LISTENED TO HUGO.
REMEMBER, GOD TELLS US TO THINK ABOUT OTHERS BEFORE WE THINK ABOUT OURSELVES. THAT WAY WE WON'T LET A PRIDEOSAURUS GET THE BEST OF US.

DO NOTHING OUT OF RIVALRY OR CONCEIT, BUT IN HUMILITY

...consider others as more important than yourselves.

—PHILIPPIANS 2:3

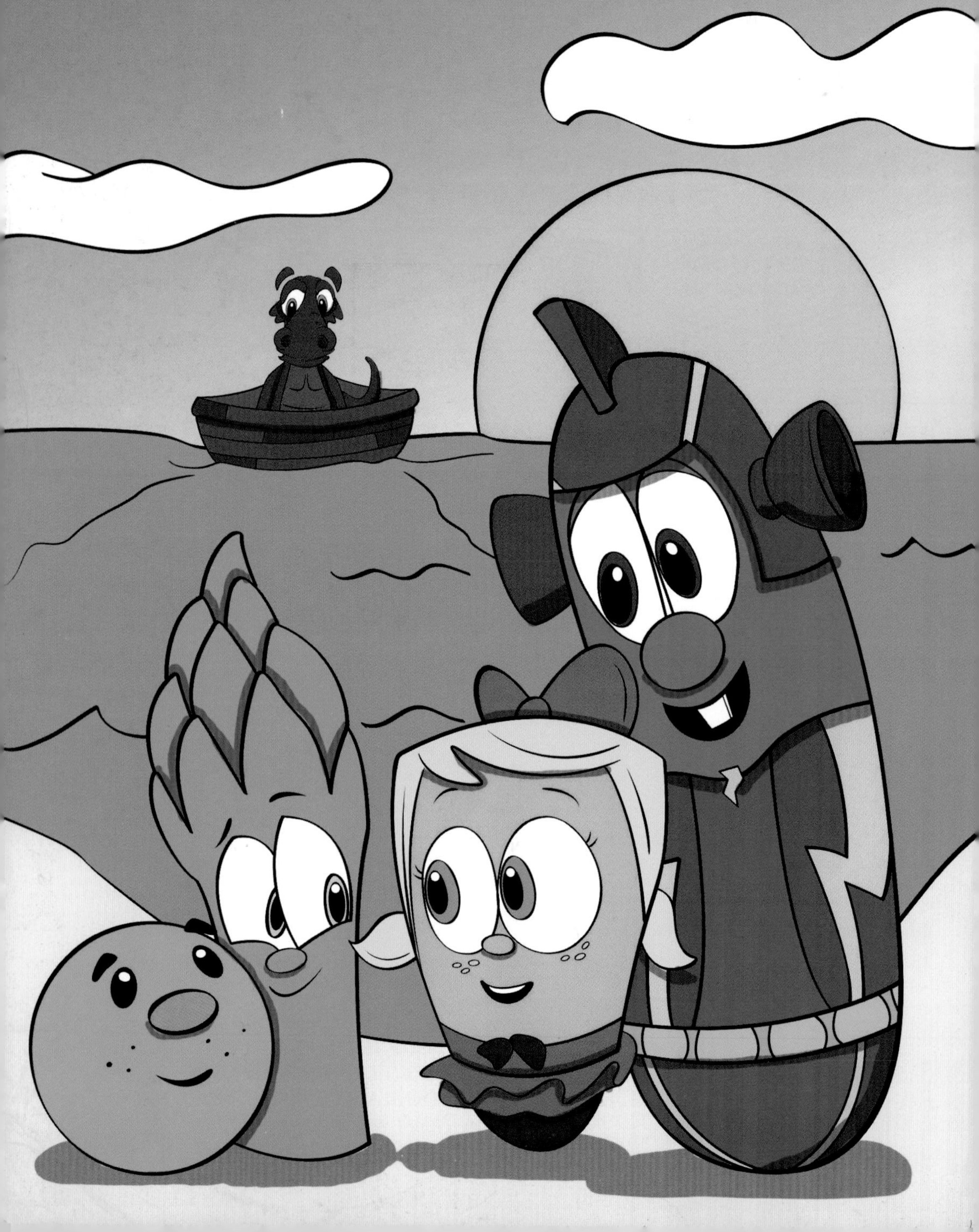